TO
CONQUER
ᴬ SCOT

THE
TIME-TRAVELER'S
HIGHLAND LOVE
SERIES

TAMARA GILL

Entangled Publishing, LLC
2614 South Timberline Road
Suite 109
Fort Collins, CO 80525
Visit our website at www.entangledpublishing.com.

Select Historical is an imprint of Entangled Publishing, LLC.

Edited by Erin Molta
Cover design by Erin Dameron-Hill
Cover art from Deposit Photos and Period Images

Manufactured in the United States of America

First Edition September 2017

TO
CONQUER
A SCOT

THE
TIME-TRAVELER'S
HIGHLAND LOVE
SERIES

Prologue

1601 Highlands, Scotland

He should have locked her up when he had the chance. His sisters were the bane of his life. Aedan MacLeod, Laird of Druiminn Castle, stormed toward the small cottage his youngest sister Gwen used while treating the sick and infirm.

Not even the calming view of the ocean could tamper his temper. The fact he'd heard whispers from the servants that Gwen was "up to something" as they'd put it, had given him enough cause to chase her down today and demand an explanation and a promise that she was not.

"Gwen!" he called out as he neared, hearing the muffled reply from inside. He burst through the door, startling the elderly woman who was hobbling out. Aedan waited for her to go before shutting the door and catching his sister's gaze. "I've heard whispers."

"Whispers?" She smiled and his annoyance increased. "What sort of whispers?"

"You're forbidden to use magic, Gwendolyn. We've had

this conversation before and it's certainly not one I want to repeat."

"Och, I am in trouble when ye use my full name. Tell me what you've heard this time. I'm sure it's nothing to concern yer wee mind."

"The servants are talking about ye. Stating how ye're all secretive again, sneaking away to this cottage at all times of day and night. Picking lots of herbs and such."

"Herbs ye say." Gwen laughed, walking over to a nearby cupboard and getting down a bowl. "And this equates to magic?"

"I know what ye are capable of, lass. Dinna think for one moment I'm not aware of what could happen to you, or this family, should it be known. You know as well as I, ye'd be dead and there'd be nothing I could do for ye."

She waved away his concerns and started to pummel lavender flowers with a mortar and pestle. She continued with her tasks, ignoring him. "Well," he prompted.

"Brother, I've been using magic since I was a babe and no harm has been done. It's the same now. Ye worry too much."

"I know you're up to something, and I demand to know what it is. Braxton mentioned it to me yesterday after he came back from visiting ye here."

"Braxton told ye, did he? That'll teach me to trust him."

He watched as she took her frustration out on the plants that hung from a wooden rack above her work table. He dismissed the flicker of guilt that he'd possibly caused trouble for his fellow clansman and glowered at Gwen instead. She pulled the leaves off with enough force that the rack rocked above their heads.

"He was concerned. Ye know the lad loves ye, and like me, he doesn't like you putting yourself at risk. So tell me what I want to know. Why are ye being so secretive all of a sudden? What are ye planning?"

She shook her head, her red curls bouncing over her shoulders. "Nothing at all. I assure ye. I'm behaving myself, as the laird's sister should. Do not worry, Aedan. Everything will turn out for the best."

"Yes, but what is this 'best' ye speak of? That concerns me."

She didn't reply, merely shrugged. Aedan fisted his hands. Obstinate, pigheaded wench. "Ye better not be trying to meddle in who I choose for a wife. 'Tis none of yer business, and I willna take nicely to ye using magic to sway women to warm me bed."

She slammed down the pestle and glared back at him. "I assure ye, I would never interfere in your grand plans for a wife. I know you'll marry someone who has an opinion, a mind, and the willingness to share their thoughts when required."

"Your sarcasm isn't appreciated." He walked toward the door of her cottage and placed his hands on his hips. Better there than her neck. "Ye know what I want in a wife and I'll find her myself. So if ye don't mind, and if ye don't want me to lock ye in the castle dungeons, you'll behave and keep out of my business. I may not know what ye be planning, but I know you're up to something and no doubt it'll involve me. I've put up with a lot of ye tricks over the years, but with the clans coming for the games, it's time ye grew up. I'll no longer stand for it."

His sister curtsied and he ground his teeth. He might as well be talking to a stone wall. "Dinna push me on this, Gwen."

"Of course not, brother. When have I ever not listened to ye?"

He sighed and cursed as he left before he was tempted to strangle the idiocy out of her. Why couldn't his parents have had sons? Brothers, right at this moment, seemed like a blissful thought indeed.

Chapter One

Abigail Cross walked from her hotel and breathed deep the fresh, somewhat chilly Highland air. The sun was shining, finally, which was a nice change from the past week where drizzle and endless fog had shrouded Druiminn, the small Scottish town where she was staying. It had seemed a lot larger on the travel brochure.

She pulled her coat up around her neck, her choice of jeans and a woolen sweater had been a sensible decision. Probably her best yet, since this vacation had been anything but fun. Never again would she jump on a plane and fly halfway across the world. Salem, Oregon, and the plain boring life she led there, suddenly seemed fun-filled and exciting.

Not to mention a little less wet…and that was saying something, since Salem was anything but dry.

Abby shook away the thought that her vacation was a waste of time. She was in Scotland, for heaven's sake. The place of myths and legends. Where the filming of fabulous historical movies were shot, sporting men in kilts…and little else. Her own ancestors hailed from this part of the world. Not that she knew of any still living in Scotland, after her great, great—so many greats she no longer knew—grandfather had emigrated to America.

The weather, the expense—one she really couldn't afford, that would take years to pay off, no longer signified, for today she was determined to enjoy the magnificence of the Highlands. Not let the darkening clouds to the south scare her back inside the hotel she'd come to know intimately. Castle Druiminn was her destination. A step back in time, a castle and home to the MacLeod Clan, where treachery, missionaries, and mayhem should've been the family's motto.

She walked up the main street of the town and entered the bakery. The air in the warm store was filled with the aroma of cooking bread and spices. She bought some chocolate frosted croissants before continuing on her way to the castle.

It was a bit of a walk, and Abby took her time enjoying the view of heather, and rolling hills, and craggy rock faces, as she continued toward the castle. On the opposite side of the road, the beautiful Isle of Skye glistened in the sun. The sense of belonging to this land coursed through her. Scotland was in her blood, her ancestors had survived living in the lowlands for years, had raised children, fought the English, disease, and a harsh environment she couldn't even begin to imagine.

It was a humbling thought and for once, the tinge of red that streaked through her dark hair didn't annoy her, but filled her with pride.

Scotland was magnificent.

She gazed down on the information map she'd acquired the week before, noting that the castle was only a five minute walk through woodlands and ocean view lanes. She was relatively sheltered from the elements up to the point where she walked over a rise and the sea breeze buffeted her. She blinked rapidly as her eyes watered from the icy gale.

She really should've bought the more expensive jacket, instead of scrimping, but her poor credit card really couldn't take too many more beatings.

The path followed the line of the beach, and she came to a sign that stated the Square Walled Garden was up a little lane, but a small, quaint cottage caught her attention. The building was made of stone, a similar color to that of the buildings in town, but looked like a one-room structure with a chimney. Grass grew on the roof, making the house blend into the environment like some modern "green" home. A small garden grew in front with a whitewashed picket fence surrounding it.

For its age, it seemed relatively sturdy and in reasonable condition. She stood staring at it and wondered at its history. Who'd lived here? Who had built it and why? Was it haunted?

She chuckled and said hello to other tourists heading toward the castle which was her next stop.

Walking up to the door, she read the sign that explained the cottage's past. It was part of the Druiminn Castle estate and believed to be the Apothecary's or healer's building. She peeked around the door and was met by darkness and the smell of dampness.

"Hello? Anybody here?" Abby stood at the threshold for a moment, but hearing no reply, she pushed the door open and entered. Inside was a plain square room, with an unlit fireplace and a window beside the door. The floor was covered in flagstones, years of dirt and dust making up its mortar.

Abby walked around and wondered what the building had seen over the years. How it must have been set up to help those in need. How many babies had been birthed here, children healed, and people stitched up?

Looking out the window, she sighed. Rain fell, the dark clouds to the south had arrived earlier than she'd hoped. Well, at least in the cottage she was dry, if not warm.

She sat on the window ledge. There was nothing else for her to do but wait out the storm and hope it passed quickly. It was an overly ambitious thought. The weather had been miserable ever since her arrival. Why would it change now?

Her hand slipped against something cold, and she looked down to find a small vial. It was bottle-like shaped with a neck and looked to be made of clay.

Abby picked it up, studied it a moment before placing it back down. Nausea spiked in her stomach and she clutched her abdomen, trying to calm her breathing. She gasped and stood, dizziness threatening. The room spun, voices, faces—she couldn't comprehend. *What is happening to me?*

Fear froze her to the spot. She tried to fight her way to the door, but the room turned at an increasing rate, making it impossible to leave. Something bad was happening. Something she couldn't control.

She screamed and then hit the floor with an *oomph* before blackness enfolded her.

Chapter Two

"Abigail, are ye well?"

Abby opened her eyes, the stone floor beneath her back seeping coldness into her bones. She sat up and looked about. The memory of what had happened to her was as clear as the woman sitting before her. Smiling at her like some long lost friend.

"Who are you?" She sat up and scooted away from the girl—woman, she corrected herself—as the stranger stood and Abby was able to get a better look at her. She was tall, and well into her twenties.

"I'm Gwen MacLeod. I summoned ye."

"What?" Abby rubbed her hand and looked about the room. The empty, lifeless building she'd walked into was now full to the brim with bottles with different colored ointments. Herbs hung from the ceiling, some freshly picked and others dried. A roaring fire burned in the grate and a pot hung over it, cooking some sort of food that smelled nicer than anything she'd tasted since landing in Scotland.

"What do you mean by 'summoned'?"

"Please, don't stress yourself. I promise I can send you home. Eventually, mind ye. Just let me explain."

Abby narrowed her eyes. The woman's Scottish dialect was strong, and yet she spoke clear enough that Abby could understand what she'd said. "Are you going to hurt me?" There was no way in hell she was hanging around here if this summoner wanted her in the pot of stew now bubbling in the grate.

"I would never hurt ye, I promise. I'm a healer, a forward-thinking woman who likes to study other spiritual beliefs. But that declaration must stay between us, if ye don't mind. Only my family knows of my gifts, and I would like it to stay that way."

Abby stepped toward the fire, spotting a large iron pole beside it. If only she could reach it without being obvious, she may have some way of getting out of here. Although, where she'd go was another question altogether, if she was in fact no longer in the twenty-first century.

"Very interesting, but I fail to understand why you've summoned me here. And where is here, exactly? What have you done?"

The woman's cheeks flushed in what Abby assumed to be embarrassment. Well good. She should be embarrassed. Dragging people out of their lives, supposably, for who knew if this woman was speaking the truth, was unacceptable. Not to mention dangerous.

"Ye are in Scotland in the year of our Lord, 1601. At my home, Druiminn Castle. This cottage is where I tend to our people, and heal them."

Abby took another step. "1601." She rubbed her temple, a headache forming behind her eyes. "I can't be in seventeenth century Scotland. Everyone died of disease or was slaughtered in battle, male or female. I've seen *Braveheart*. I've learned all I need to know about this time and I don't want to stay here.

You have to send me home. Now." Abby craned her neck to look out the window, but couldn't spot anyone to give her a sense of what was real or make-believe.

The woman stared at her a moment before laughing. "I knew ye would be perfect. I've been watching ye for some time, although I had to wait for ye to be in Scotland before I could bring ye back." She clapped her hands together and thunder rumbled outside.

Abby slid her hand around the pole and held it up in front of her as she walked to the window. The view made the hair on the back of her neck stand up. Where there was once a garden before the cottage, now there was nothing but a few herbs and a rugged path.

The well-defined gravel walkway she'd used to get to the cottage was gone, in fact, trampled grass was the only indication that people walked this way at all.

This isn't good. "I demand you send me home. Now. This very instant. You've gone too far and I don't know what you think I'm going to be perfect for, but I'm not having any of it. So, unless you want me to do something I might regret later, you'll do as I ask, *right now*."

Gwen's shoulders sagged, and she held out her hands to stall her. "Please, I really don't mean ye any harm. Just let me explain."

"You have exactly ten seconds to explain, and then you can send me home." Abby glared to emphasize her point. The woman seemed to get it.

"Ever since I was born I've had the ability to see things, not of my own time unfortunately, but places, events, well into the future. All my life I've known of ye, as you've grown, so have I, even though we were born centuries apart. I feel like I know ye verra well."

"That's all very nice for you, but what do you want from me? I don't belong in this time. I'll probably be slaughtered the moment I walk out that door by some English army who hates everything Scottish. Or some Highlander lord with a penchant for killing innocent women with axes." Gwen laughed and Abby waved the pole.

"My brother the laird must marry and produce a child as deemed by our father's dying wish. My brother will proclaim any day now his intention to marry. You, Abigail Cross, are perfect for him and must marry the laird as soon as ye may."

Abby dropped the pole and then scrambled to pick it up. "What, that's crazy! I'm not marrying some barbaric, filthy Scottish laird. There may be some hot historical romance novels out there sporting lairds with delightful packages under their kilts, but it's fiction. Your brother probably never bathes, has bad breath, kills on a whim, and demands obedience from everyone." Abby started to pace. The absurdity of the situation made perspiration break out everywhere. *Great, now I'll smell as well.* "Do you know what century I'm from? What year? I can't be here because you decided I would make your brother a good wife. I need to go home. Now."

Gwen paled, and Abby was glad of it. The troublemaking witch needed to back the hell off and send her home.

"I can't. Not right at this moment. Magic doesn't work that way. You've traveled through time, Abigail. To send you back straight away could leave you stranded in some other time that isn't your own. I'm sorry, but for the time being, you must stay."

"What am I going to do? I'll stick out like a sore thumb. I mean, look at me!" Abby gestured at her clothes. "I think you'll agree what I'm wearing isn't appropriate for the period." The nausea was back and Abby searched for a bucket, anything she could vomit in. Not seeing anything of use, she opened the door and ran out into the claiming dusk, right into a solid mass of muscle.

She stumbled back, this was going to hurt and she'd had

about enough of today, but suddenly two large hands wrapped around her arms, saving her dignity and pain.

Abby looked up and up and up some more and felt her mouth open on a sigh. *Holy sweet Jesus, who is this?*

He stared at her, his gaze narrowed and brow furrowed in disapproval. Abby pushed back a little, bent over, and heaved all over his boots. She distantly heard a curse, but she was beyond caring. Darkness swamped her, and with it came relief. Maybe the heathen Scottish Braveheart holding her had shoved a knife in her heart, putting her out of her misery.

Chapter Three

Aedan MacLeod looked down at the lass asleep in one of the guest chamber beds and cursed. "What the hell do ye think you're doing, Gwen? You've used magic to bring her here? Are ye daft, lass?"

His survival instinct roared to be rid of her and the magic that surrounded her, a beacon for anyone who suspected them of such. The gifts of the MacLeod clan were a blessing and a curse. Should anyone discover their powers, all would be lost, including his head. And he was rather fond of his head exactly where it was. The lass needed to go home, and soon.

"It'll be fine, Aedan. Ye worry too much. No one will ever find out about her. As soon as she wakes, I'll explain to her why she's here, and she'll understand. I promise she'll not cause ye any trouble."

"And what is it that you've brought her here for? I'm interested to know myself." His sister's inability to meet his gaze made his stomach churn. "Gwendolyn, what has your scheming mind been thinking up?"

She sighed. "She's perfect for ye. Strong-willed,

independent, and alluring." His sister gestured at the woman. "I thought if you got to know her a little you might form an attachment and have a handfasting ceremony."

"That's no reason to risk our lives. I want the truth. Why her, and not a lass from our time?"

Gwen sighed and slumped in a chair. "I know you've been showing interest in Aline Grant, and I'll not have it. Surely, you know of the rumors that follow the lass. That she's slept with half of Scotland and no doubt, half of England, as well."

Aedan had heard the rumors. Though with a brother like Evan Grant, a hawk hovering over Aline's every move, he'd not believed them. But his sister's dislike of the girl, a disappointment, to be sure, wouldn't stop him from marrying who he needed to. "She's chaste. I'm certain of it, or I wouldn't be considering her."

His sister met his eyes and compassion flickered in their depths. He grit his teeth, not at all liking when his sister looked at him like that. "Do you not see that this Abigail lass resembles Gail? It's almost as if she's been re-born hundreds of years from now."

He held up his hand, having heard enough. There was no bringing back the woman he'd loved as a lad. A girl who'd grown into a woman who matched him in every way, until a fever in her sixteenth year had taken her life.

Looking down on the lass once more, he studied her. Aye, she was similar, in coloring and looks to Gail, but she wasn't what his clan needed. "Whoever I choose, sister, whether it is Aline Grant or a lass from an allied clan, she'll bring our family coin, a good name, and valuable men for our forthcoming battle with Clan O'Cain."

"Forget the O'Cains. What's done is done, and you're no use to any of us dead. And we're not in need of coin or what Aline could bring to our home. You are not always correct in your path through life, brother. You do not have to sacrifice your future happiness for the safety of your people."

Aedan rounded on his sister and only just remembered he wasn't allowed to kill the girl. Of all the idiotic foolery she was talking. "I'll hear no more of it. My decision is made. And if it hasn't escaped your notice, dear little sister, we have half of the Highland families bearing down on us right at this moment, for the Highland Games. They'll be bringing their daughters for me to choose from. This woman could tell everyone of our acquaintance what we're capable of. What if she wants to go home to her time? What year, pray, is she from?"

"She's from the twenty-first century. Twenty seventeen, to be precise."

"Och, you're mad, lass, and we're doomed. When she wakes up, you need to send her back immediately." Aedan ran a hand through his hair and started to pace. "We can't have her running around the castle grounds screaming about what you've done. If the clans hear of this magic, even I cannot save you, or myself, from certain death. You'll be labeled a witch, and rightfully so."

Gwen came to stand beside the bed. The woman hadn't woken. She was as still as death, the only sign she was alive was the small rise and fall of her chest. Aedan tore his gaze from the soft, inviting curves he suspected she housed under her strange garments.

"You know I cannot send her back straight away, so whether ye approve of my actions or not, she is here for a time. I will talk to her and settle her nerves. Please give me some time. Trust me. I've never let ye down before."

Aedan pointed to the woman in the bed. "You've let me down now. Fix this." He stormed from the room and headed toward the main hall where the night's meal was being served. Gwen's magic was strong, he knew that, but she'd never acted without such thought before. To bring someone through time, putting the woman and his family in danger from those who would use anything to conquer and lay claim to their home, was beyond him.

The timing couldn't be worse. With the other clan families due to arrive for the games, their daughters paraded for his perusal, he was loath to have to worry about anything other than the unwanted responsibility of who he should marry and make the future MacLeod bride.

Not that he really desired one. After Gail had passed, such a future had seemed lost. His sister, once married, could produce offspring as well as any other, his home passing to a nephew. A wife might warm his bed, but she'd never warm his heart.

Not to mention that the O'Cains had sent Aedan's other sister back, half-blind and in disgrace, clearly taunting him to engage in another war. The thought of sweet Jinny being used by his rival made the blood boil in his veins.

The day she'd arrived home, battered, blind, and a figment of who she'd once been had bombarded him with shame. He had truly believed the O'Cains had wished for peace as much as he. How wrong he'd been.

They had used her, bartered her body, while letting her become the clan's amusement and plaything.

He wouldn't stand for the insult, and once the Highland Games were over, he'd seek justice for his sibling. Never again would he outstretch his hand in peace toward the O'Cains.

Aedan sat at the dais, away from the rest of his clan, and watched his fellow clansmen eat and boast about the forthcoming revelry. He could find no interest in the night or the delectable wenches who served at the table. If the family secret was revealed, all this would be taken from them. The name MacLeod would be tarnished, forever remembered with distaste. Not to mention, the O'Cains would take advantage of their misfortune and claim his home and lands for themselves.

He couldn't allow any of his fears to come to pass.

"Trouble, laird?"

Aedan nodded in welcome to his best swordsman, and distant family member, Braxton, as he sat beside him. His clansman ripped into a turkey leg and moaned his delight.

"Aye," Aedan said. "Of the worst kind. A secret kind. A kind that could get those we love killed. Your betrothed has brought a woman from the future to be my bride."

Braxton laughed, startling the few people that sat before them to turn and stare.

Aedan glowered. "I don't see it as a laughing matter. She could ruin us all. Ye included."

His clansman tried and failed to rein in his mirth. "Apologies, but does it surprise you? So far, you've dismissed all the women paraded before ye. Why, there are bets even now that the women due to arrive with their respective families, will all leave with their respective families." His friend slapped him on the back. "Face it, old friend, your sister likes to meddle. It is nothing new, and it's one of the reasons why we both love her. Is it not?"

"Aye, I know, but damn it. I must crush the O'Cains for their treachery. A wife from an allied clan, with a bountiful amount of fighting men, is what I need." Aedan rubbed his jaw. "Not to mention, the lass she's brought back is going to stick out like a Saxon wearing a kilt in the Highlands."

The thought of the woman, the memory of her long legs in the tight trews she'd had on, her ass the perfect size for his hands, made him shift in his seat. Aedan would wager all the gold in his coffers that her skin was softer than a babe's… He swore, picking up his mug and taking a heady sip. "As soon as Gwen is able, she must return her to the time she belongs."

"Is the lass comely?"

Groaning, Aedan didn't meet his friend's penetrating

stare. Damn it. She *was* comely, more bloody comely than he'd seen for an age. Not that she'd looked overly appealing when she'd vomited on his boots. At least she hadn't gushed and thrown herself at him, nearly impaling herself on his sword, like so many other lasses. "No. I've never seen an uglier wench in my life."

His friend choked on his mead. "You jest, surely. I can't imagine Gwen not selecting a woman who would suit your tastes."

Aedan tore at the bread and scooped up the stew on his plate. "She did. The lass doesn't suit, and that's the end of this conversation."

His sister entered the room and searched out Braxton. She walked toward them, her hands clutched tightly in front of her. Aedan stood, noting the distress darkening her normally serene visage.

"What is it, Gwen?" he asked.

She smiled at Braxton and sat, piling her plate with food from the platter. "Abigail hasn't woken. I'm scared that grabbing her from her own time has caused her harm."

Aedan sighed and sat back down. "I'm sure the lass will be fine, Gwen. As for your well-being, that is another matter. Ye are not to use any magic for the foreseeable future. Do ye understand?"

"So ye don't want me to send her home, then?"

His sister grinned, and he fought to control his temper. She had a serious flirtation with death. "Do not push me, lass. Ye know what I mean."

Gwen rolled her eyes and commenced eating.

"I'm sure she'll wake soon, my love. It was probably quite a shock seeing the barbarian brother of yours for the first time. She'll come around. And ye never know, your plan to see her married to Laird MacLeod may work."

Aedan stood. "One more word about your ridiculous

designs for my wife, and I'll lock you both up in the dungeon."

"In the same cell?"

His sister giggled.

"Watch it, Braxton. My gille sharpened my sword today."

He walked from the room and headed toward his quarters. The tower stairs wound up past two floors before he came to his. He wanted the O'Cain clan burned to the ground before the first snows of winter fell on the Highland peaks. Fighting a clan battle knee deep in snow would kill them and the O'Cains and that was not how he wanted this war to end.

Therefore, he needed a wife, and soon. Wind blew in through the arrow holes in the walls and he shivered, the thought of marriage sending a chill down his spine. Not to mention the now added problem of an inconvenient woman from the future to deal with.

Perhaps he ought to kill her. The risk to those he held dear was immense. No one would miss the woman prone to vomiting on men. No one here knew her at all.

He entered his bedchamber and bolted the door. His bed was turned down already and a roaring fire burned in the grate, casting flickering shadows across the stone walls. The wind howled outside, the drafts seeking entrance through the smallest of cracks. Aedan sat and stared at the golden flames, the heat going some way to warming his core, but it wasn't enough.

The woman was a threat to their safety that was already in danger from the O'Cains.

He ran a hand over his jaw, itching the stubble that had grown over the last few days. That he would go to war over Jinny was in part his fault. He should have checked on her. Traveled the miles between them and demanded access to her, spoken with her alone to gauge her happiness.

But he hadn't, and now he must live with the guilt of his mistake for the rest of his life. No wife of his would be treated such. That was one thing he could promise his sisters. It may not be a marriage of love and affection, but it would be one of trust and respect.

He sighed. They had a sennight before the clans arrived for the Highland Games. A sennight in which to either send her home, or at least make her conform to his rules and play the part of a lady until they could send her back.

Gwen would never allow him to kill her. What he really ought to do was kill his frustrating sister. Had she, for once, thought through her actions, none of this would have happened.

Chapter Four

Abigail woke to the smell of wet wood, musty and damp. She leaned up on her elbows and looked around the room. She was no longer in the stone cabin where she'd first met Gwen. Far from it.

The room was square. A narrow window, with glass panels that didn't quite fit the small diamond frames, looked out to a valley beyond. Wind whistled through the small gaps and she shivered. Although a large fire burned in the grate, the room was cold.

Abby stepped out of bed and cringed at the icy flagstones beneath her feet. She made her way to the fire and stood staring at the hearth. Wood had been stoked to burn for some time and yet, it was the peat, added to increase the flame, that was making the room stink.

She looked around and conceded that for a historical bedroom, it wasn't so bad. The floor did have animal skins scattered about and the bedding itself had been warm. But the quiet, dark space, without power, or modern bathroom comforts, certainly hammered home the fact she wasn't in her time.

In her own room, her laptop and cell phone were never far away. Instinctively, she felt for her pockets in her jeans, that she wasn't wearing. They must have her clothes somewhere, along with her phone. Would it still work? Would they give it back?

Walking over to the small chamber pot that jutted out from under her bed, she noted that the bowl itself was plain, no colors or designs, but the inside was stained.

She cringed at not seeing a toilet, or anything resembling toilet paper, for that matter.

A knock at the door was followed by the muffled sound of Gwen's voice.

"Come in," she said, walking back toward the fire to keep as warm as she could.

"Good morning, Abigail. I trust ye slept well and are feeling better this day?"

The woman's vibrant, expectant visage eradicated what little anger she had left. No more arguing, she just wanted to be sent home. How hard could it be? She had managed to get her here in the first place.

Abby nodded. "I am. Thank you. Although I'm disappointed that I'm still here. When can you return me home?"

Gwen smiled, coming over to her and taking her hands. "As to that, I have news. My brother has agreed, since I'm unable to send ye home right away, that you're to stay as our guest. In a sennight, we have clans from all over Scotland arriving for the Highland Games. My brother will choose a wife from one of the daughters. We are to make ye a close friend of mine, from a distant family, if ye will."

Abby bit back the curse that wanted to fly out of her mouth. She took a deep, calming breath instead, and began setting the woman to rights. "I cannot stay another night in this castle. You brought me here, now you have to send me home. I refuse to play your games and pretend I'm some lofty lady I'm not." She glared, not allowing herself to react to the girl's crestfallen visage. What did she expect? For her to be happy here? There was no damn toilet paper in this time. Women could survive almost anywhere and in any time, but without toilet paper, well, that was a whole different scenario.

But that wasn't all, of course. Her whole life was in another time. Her home, school, friends, the few she had, were not in seventeenth century Scotland. What were they thinking right at this moment? Did they even know she was missing?

"I can't send you home without risking your life. To move through the time portal again, so soon after you traveled through it, could splinter you physically. I'm sorry, Abigail. I assumed you'd be happy to be here."

Abby stood. Never had she heard such a stupid thing in her life. "Why would I be happy to be here? I don't know any of you. You're strangers to me. Not to mention, there's no electricity, no running water, no bathrooms, no medicines. Nothing. It's barbaric. I won't survive here. Do you even have coffee?"

Panic threatened to choke the air out of her lungs. She started to pace, and for the first time she wondered who had changed her into this long flowing gown. "Who put me in this nightgown?"

"The servant, Betsy, who's assigned to look after you, dressed ye last eve. Please try and calm down, Abigail. I'm sorry about the situation ye now find yourself in. I know it's my fault, but it cannot be changed. I suggest, unless ye wish to feel the wrath of my brother, that ye heed his plan. We could all be in danger, if you do not play along."

Gwen came over to her, a small frown line between her dark blue eyes. Abby noted she was a pretty woman, and obviously too young to be playing around with magic. Magic she'd yet to master. "Wrath of your brother? What will he do to me, burn me at the stake? Hog-tie me behind a horse and drag me through the countryside?"

"Of course not. We're not evil villains. And what is 'hog-tie'? I don't believe I've heard that saying before."

Abby growled. "Okay. Fine. I understand that I can't leave…yet. But you must promise that as soon as I can, you'll allow me to go. How long does it normally take for a person to be able to travel back?"

"I promise as soon as I'm able, I will send you home. And as for the time, I'm not sure." Gwen looked sheepish, and Abby sighed. "You see, I've never brought anyone back through time before. You were the first. I didn't think it would be a problem, as I assumed you'd stay. My sincerest apologies for the distress I have caused ye, Abigail."

Abby couldn't form the words she was dying to yell at the woman. Gwen had never brought anyone back before? Did it mean she might never return home? Or if Gwen tried to return her to her own time, she could end up anywhere, perhaps blown to bits, or floating around space, even? *Holy shit!*

"Please leave. At this moment in time you're far from my favorite person."

"I'm sorry."

Gwen ran from the room, tears brimming in her eyes. Abby slumped on the bed, the furs creating a false sense of security. How would she survive in this time where disease, malnutrition, and non-hygienic practices were as common as fleas?

She itched her head at the thought. There was no running water and no pharmaceutical medicines—only herbal remedies and prayer. What if she fell ill? Caught some disease she hadn't been immunized against and died a painfully slow death?

Abby took a calming breath. She wouldn't be here for long, she reminded herself. They would send her back as soon as it was safe. And she was a tough woman. The past two years had proven that, since the death of her boyfriend David. All she needed to do was stay calm and in control. Maybe she ought to take Gwen's outstretched hand of friendship and clasp hold of it tight. She would need as many friends as she could get.

A servant entered bearing clothing and helped her get dressed. She looked down at the blue velvet gown with long sleeves that covered her hands when she held them at her side. It was very pretty. Silver stitching ran along the seams in an intricate pattern. All hand sewn. It would have taken forever to make. The workmanship was exquisite.

"I have a missive for ye, miss. The laird wanted me to wait for ye to read it, ask if you're in agreement, before allowing ye to break yer fast in the great hall." The servant handed her a piece of coarse paper.

Abby broke the wax seal and started to read.

Abigail,

If you agree to the terms as outlined by my sister Gwendolyn this morn, then please proceed to the great hall and join us in a repast. If you are unable to abide by our decree, you shall be locked in your quarters until you are dissuaded from the foolish course you've chosen.

Please give your answer to the servant.

Aedan MacLeod

Abby clenched her jaw, glaring at the words until her eyes crossed.

"What is ye reply, miss?" The servant looked at her with concern, but Abby knew she'd not stand a chance of getting past the woman should she go against the laird's decree.

"I'm in agreement with the laird," she said.

The servant smiled in relief. "Very good, miss." Stepping

aside to let her pass, she continued. "Laird MacLeod is waiting for ye."

Nodding, but with no intention of eating with any of them, Abby slipped on shoes made of rawhide, held on by a tie that zigzagged across the dorsal of her foot, and walked from the room . They were rather comfortable.

The tower staircase was steep and long, coming out into a corridor that housed the front double doors. Abby headed straight for them, needing to get outside and away from this castle.

The storm that had passed through overnight was lessening. In between the clouds blue sky peeked through, teasing them with better weather. Abby studied the courtyard that looked out over the Isle of Skye. People milled about. Some carried food from the few vegetable gardens she could see, others worked with horses or hauled water from the well, an array of activities that reminded her of stories she'd read in history books.

Shaking her head, she struggled to comprehend what was happening to her. Shouts from the front of the castle caught her attention, and she headed that way. She walked over a bridge that covered a small, slow flowing creek and saw the endless, lush forests that encased the castle like a cocoon. She turned and looked back at the castle itself, so different from the one that stood in the twenty-first century. There must have been numerous alterations and additions through the years.

A couple of guards with swords walked the castle perimeter. They looked at her, men who had seen death, caused death, and would likely take life without a moment's hesitation. Hardened soldiers who didn't take fools lightly.

Abby quickened her steps away from them and headed along a rough riding track. There were some outlying cottages scattered about the forest and shoreline, and people tended to pigs and goats that were housed in small wooden yards.

Fear crept along her spine that this could be her future. How would she ever survive living in this time? Although she had no family back in the twenty-first century, she did have friends, even if no longer close. Her own fault, after pushing them all away, cocooning herself in grief after David's death. But that didn't mean she wanted to walk away from her life and her twenty-first century comforts, most of all.

She may not have a lot of money and she may have to work for a living, but it was her life, and to have it snatched away wasn't right.

Anger replaced her fear, and she stopped walking. The sound of thumping hooves sounded behind her, and she turned to see Laird MacLeod riding hard toward her.

She hadn't been able to get a very good look at him when she'd vomited on his feet. All of her memories after that were hazy at best. *But whoa.* She doubted she'd forget him ever again.

Large, muscular arms urged the horse forward. His legs, his very bare legs, beneath a kilt that was doing anything but sitting down about his knees, flexed and held him astride his horse.

Abby's mouth dried up like the Sahara desert. Probably didn't help that her mouth was hanging open and tapping the ground. She closed it with a snap and stepped off the road a little in case he decided to run her over and be rid of her for good. The thunderous glare he was bestowing on her only supported that theory.

I'm dead meat.

The horse skidded to a stop, and he slid off in one fluid movement. He towered over her, making her kink her neck to meet his gaze. He was angry, the thumping of the vein near his temple proof of that, but a flicker of something else briefly passed in his gaze. Was he worried about her? Highly doubtful. He didn't even know her.

Abby pushed the thought aside and studied him instead. His shoulders were massive, built for sword fighting. A cloth looped over one shoulder and obscured part of his tunic covered chest. He was bronze-skinned, and the large muscles of his chest flexed with each breath. She bit her lip, not sure what to make of him other than the fact he was unbelievably hot.

Laird MacLeod stood with his legs apart, as if the package between them wouldn't allow anything less. He cleared his throat, and her gaze snapped to his face. Heat bloomed on her neck and across her cheeks. She should have looked away and immediately chastised herself for not doing so. For to look at him was to fall into sin in the most delicious way she could imagine.

He had a strong jaw with a day's growth of beard, a succulent mouth that begged to be nipped and kissed. Her hand itched to feel and stroke his wavy shoulder-length hair. Was it as soft as it looked? The fact he smelled of pine and clean soap wasn't missed, either.

But it was his eyes that again made this world spin for her. They were, without doubt, the most beautiful green eyes she'd ever seen. Dark as the heather that grew wild around their feet.

Damn it.

"What do ye think you're doing walking out the gates alone? Are ye daft, woman? A simpleton?"

She started at his words, not expecting such a harsh beginning to their conversation. "I beg your pardon. I'm none of those things. I wanted to go for a walk. To clear my head. Is that a crime?" Abby unclenched her hands at her side and made an effort to control her temper, which on occasion, had been unleashed on rude people like this barbaric Scottish ass.

"Scotland is not safe for a woman who isn't well-versed in current situations that encompass our land. Were you headed for the woods? Do ye have a death wish, lass?"

Abby pushed past him and strode toward the forest. How dare they pull her through time and then be all high-handed with her. She gasped when a large hand circled her upper arm and turned her about. She glared up at him, wishing she was a little taller so she could look him in the eye when she gave him what-for. Her hand burned against his chest, and she shoved him away, not liking the way her stomach clenched when she touched him.

"If I do, it's your sister's fault for bringing me here, and to marry you, no less."

"I'm only concerned for your safety. You were supposed to come down to break ye fast, not run away."

"I'm in front of your castle, and I didn't see the point of eating when I'm not hungry. Why can't I walk out here? Are you annoyed because I didn't join you for breakfast?" She didn't think he was, but still, Abby didn't really know what to think anymore. This whole situation was bizarre.

"Nay, Betsy told me you agreed to our terms, but when Braxton notified me of ye walking outside the castle grounds, I thought to check on ye."

"Well, I'm fine, as you can see. Is it always going to be this way while I'm here? Is this time that bad that I can't step a few hundred yards from the castle without being rounded up like a sheep?" He looked down at her as if she'd said the stupidest thing he'd ever heard.

"Women in this time are not always respected. I'll let ye decide as to what that means."

A cold shiver ran down her spine, and she looked into the darkened forest beyond, wondering who lay in wait for women, or anyone, she supposed, to use for their nefarious means. "I was only going to walk along the forest's edge. I wasn't going to enter into it."

"It makes no difference. Ye should not pass the bridge

beyond the castle itself."

His words brooked no argument, and she narrowed her eyes at his tone. "I don't know if it's escaped your notice, but I'm a big girl, and I'm not stupid. I can take care of myself." She hoped. Although, if the men lying in wait for women were even half the size of the one before her, Abby wasn't all that confident she could save herself.

"Really?" One eyebrow cocked up. "Do explain."

Not that he would understand... "I've taken self-defense classes. I've learned how to fight." She kept the confession that she'd yet to use her abilities in such a way, but still, under pressure, surely they'd come to the fore and save her ass.

"It is doubtful any fighting lessons you've been taught would save you from a knife to the throat before you're even aware yer foe's behind ye."

Abby swallowed, not liking the sound of that at all, or the fact he was probably right.

"Or an arrow strike to yer head."

"Are you trying to scare me? Why would you say such awful things?"

He shook his head, sighing. "Because I'd rather send ye home alive, than bury ye here. That's if we ever found yer body, of course."

"So where can I go that's safe? Surely, I'm not going to be stuck inside the castle permanently." The thought of having no sunshine, no fresh air away from the peat smoke or the smell of unwashed bodies, made her cringe.

"If you stay to the front of the castle you'll be safe enough. I have guards permanently stationed in that area, along with the castle servants who tend to the gardens and crops. I will have a servant accompany ye at all times to be safe."

"With all the guards around, like you said, I should be fine. I don't need a guard."

He crossed his arms. "Ye will do as you're told."

"You said I should be fine in that part of the grounds. I don't need a guard. I'm not royalty." Would this man listen?

"I will not repeat myself. You will do as I say." He made a growling noise, clasping his horse's reins, the conversation apparently over. "I don't know what my sister was thinking bringing ye here."

"Neither do I. Like any normal, sane person would want to travel from the luxuries of life in the twenty-first century to this hard, dirty, seventeenth century Scotland. If you think I'm any happier about this situation, you're wrong." Abby's hands shook as adrenaline started to pump through her veins. Oh, the audacity of the man. "You're an overbearing brute who I'd never consider marrying."

"I don't believe I ever offered."

"And I'd never want you to. And it's no secret that I don't want to fall in line with your little plan to act as a lady, either, but to save your ass and keep a roof over my head, I will. So, if I have to compromise on this, you can compromise about me having a guard."

He bared his teeth and she stepped back, not liking the savage look in his eye. "Verra well. I'll give ye that one wish, but be warned, I don't want ye this side of the castle. I may not get to ye in time, if ye disobey me."

Abby nodded, satisfied with this small victory. "We have a deal." She held out her hand for him to shake. He looked at it and did nothing.

"You will learn to fall in with my plans, lass, or I'll walk you into that forest that you're so fond of and remove you from this earth myself."

The murderous glint in his eye said he would do as he stated should she push him too far. Anger thrummed through every pore of her body. In this case, she would have to succumb to him. She would allow the brute to win this battle, but he wouldn't win the war. And if he wanted a sweet, delightful lady who would compliment his guests, he had another thing coming.

"I said I would. I'll fall in line, like all your little soldier men, but if you think for one moment that I'm enjoying myself, or that I'll go out of my way to please you and your guests, you can think again. I'd rather eat Haggis." Abby stormed back toward the castle and left the overbearing Scot behind her. She kicked up some dirt and one of the delicate shoes ripped. She rolled her eyes. Typical.

The thought of having to sit beside him at meals and play the lady irked her. This wasn't her time. To be kind to people who pulled her through time for their own nefarious means was wrong.

Chapter Five

Aedan ran a hand through his hair and mounted his horse. The obstinate woman from the future stormed toward the castle, and he took a moment to enjoy the view of her swaying hips and delectable rump as she did so.

Numerous curses, some words he'd never heard before, were coming from her mouth. Aedan shook his head. He couldn't blame the wench for being angry and upset. Had his sister sent him forward in time he would've reacted the same, if not worse.

He kicked his horse into a canter, and coming up next to her, he scooped her up and sat her before him on the horse. She screamed a high-pitch squeal that made his ears ring and then she clutched his neck.

"Hush, before the horse bolts and we both end up on the ground. Consider this ye first lesson. How to shut up and listen."

She glared at him, quite ferociously, and Aedan had an overwhelming urge to shock her further and cover her puckered mouth with his own. Her lips were red and succulent and her teeth where white and straight, much healthier than a lot of the women in this time. He contemplated a kiss, until the hellion slapped his face. Hard.

The action rendered him mute. His hand tightened about her waist, pulling her harder against his chest. She gasped, the color in her cheeks deepening to crimson. "I'll allow ye that once, lass, but try it again and I'll not be held accountable for me actions."

She pushed at his chest without success. "You would hit a woman? Why doesn't that surprise me?"

He chuckled and shrugged. "You're jumping to conclusions. I would never mark a woman with me hand or anything else for that matter." He smirked. "Unless she wanted me to, of course, but there are other ways to keep you in line."

"Urgh. You're barbaric."

They rode in silence for a time. Aedan admitted it was nice having a warm, delectable body snug against his chest. She smelled different from the other women he'd held as close. It was a sweet scent he'd never encountered before. He leaned in and realized it was her hair. Her dark locks had come free of the coiffure the servant had placed it in earlier, allowing her hair to cascade down her back unhindered.

Aedan's body tightened with need. With every jolt of the horse, her rump rubbed against his groin, causing a pain of the best kind to thrum between his legs. She was a tempting lass, made him yearn to turn the woman around, kiss her senseless, and see if she'd be willing to tup him where they sat.

She wiggled away from him, and he smiled. "Something wrong, lass?"

"Other than the fact you are rubbing up against me inappropriately? No, of course nothing's wrong." Sarcasm dripped from her every word.

"I canna help the movements of the horse. If you hadn't

tried to run away I wouldn't have had to chase ye in the first place."

She turned and her defiant brown orbs met his. "I wasn't running away. If it hasn't escaped your notice, your sister is my only means home." She paused, her breasts rising as she took a deep breath. "I merely went for a walk. How was I supposed to know your country is a death trap?"

"Mayhap you ought to thank me for joining ye before ye'd made the forest, as I may have been too late."

She paled and looked toward the castle. He dinnae like to scare women, but in this instance, it was necessary. Scotland was in a relatively peaceful period, but the forests often held men, bad men, who wouldn't blink twice at horrendous actions toward an unsuspecting woman. "Promise me ye won't go off on your own again and if ye won't do it for me, do it for yourself. We do plan on getting ye home. Alive."

She sighed. "I said I would, but if you want my promise, then I promise not to go there again."

The large tower to the left of the castle, a separate building to the others, placed them in shadow as they rode toward it. They crossed the bridge and Aedan stopped at the castle doors. Gwen stood waiting, the fear etched on his sister's face dissipating a little when she saw Abigail.

"Abigail. I'm so glad you're back. I was so worried about ye."

Aedan helped her down. She brushed down her skirts and walked past his sister without saying a word.

Gwen's shoulders sagged, and he felt a little sorry for his sibling.

"She really hates me for bringing her here. I don't know what else I can do to make things up to her." Tears welled in her eyes.

Aedan jumped off the horse and handed his mount to a waiting stableboy. He hugged her quickly and walked her indoors. "Be patient, Gwen, and take some comfort in the fact she hates me as well." His sister slapped his arm, and he laughed. "Give her a couple of days on her own. Don't try and tempt her outdoors or to meals. She'll soon get sick of her own company. Trust me, lass."

"Do you think that will work?"

"Aye. I do." Aedan walked his sister to the anteroom and the warmth of the roaring fire prickled his skin. He held out his hands to the heat. "And if she doesn't, she'll soon be gone, anyway. You need to stop fretting over the lass until it's time to send her home. Instead, concentrate on the games in a sennight. There's a lot of organization still to be done yet."

"I'll do as you ask and throw all my efforts into making the next Highland Games one of the best the country has ever seen, especially since you'll be announcing your betrothal on the final day."

Aedan raised his brow in surprise. "If I find the right lass, I shall. Dinna think I'll marry any wench with a saucy smile."

His sister laughed, and he smiled. "Oh please, if that's not the biggest lie you've ever told, I don't know what is."

"I only said marriage, lass, not sleeping with them." He heard his sister gasp as he walked from the room. "I'm going upstairs. I need a wash."

She waved him off, and Aedan looked into the main hall but didn't see the lass from the future. He climbed the circular stone stairs before coming to his floor and heading for his quarters. The castle was cold all year round and he hoped the servants had the fire well-stoked in his room. Movement at the end of the corridor caught his eye and he walked past his door, coming to the end of the passage that split in two different directions. He spotted Abigail standing at the narrow window overlooking the waters of the Isle of Skye.

He frowned at the sadness he read on her features. It was a sadness he could well understand; to be torn away from the only home he knew would be a veritable torture. His home, and Scotland in general, was a place deeply engrained in his soul and he'd be loath to part from it. In fact, he couldn't imagine living anywhere but Scotland. The country flowed as much in his veins as his blood.

Abigail slumped against the wall, sliding down until she was sitting, all the while oblivious to his presence. Silent tears ran down her cheeks and she swiped at them, as if annoyed by their presence.

Aedan backed away and went to his room. He doubted she needed to hear him telling her she'd soon be home and no harm done. There was a slight chance his sister wouldn't be able to send her back. Magic could be as fickle as the Highland weather.

Och, he hoped this wasn't so. The last thing he needed was a homesick lass with a temper as hot as his own. The games that were due to start next week were supposed to be peaceful, if not competitive. To have a woman skulking about wasn't what he had in mind.

His room was warm, the fire well-stoked, and he set the basin of water before the hearth and proceeded to undress for his wash. He was worrying for nothing. His sister was intelligent. She wouldn't let him down, and Abigail would be sent home safely.

Everything would turn out well.

Chapter Six

Abby stood beside doors that led out onto a courtyard. A thick stone wall ran the length of the grounds, and from where she stood it looked as if the sea itself flowed right up to it. An illusion of course, for the castle sat a fair distance away from the sea.

She slumped against the building, the cold stone at her back chilling her as much as the arctic wind that whistled through the yard.

This era was hard. Everything about it was coarse, dirty, and too different to comprehend. She shivered into a cloak her chamber servant had given her and watched a couple of kitchen servants weed a vegetable garden, their hands muddy, their clothing less than ideal for these weather conditions. Ski gear would be ideal…

Abby frowned. Above all else, the stench was the worst. Not everyone here was able to bathe, and the body odor coming off some of the populace was enough to make her gag. The animals, unfortunately, were penned close to the castle, and pigs, even if kept well, stank to high heaven. It was only at times like these, when the wind from the ocean hit her before anything else, that Abby could breathe the salty, unstinking air. What she wouldn't do to be back in the twenty-first century, warm in her modest apartment that smelled of clean linen, soap, and perfume. She didn't have a lot and was far from wealthy, but at least she had heat, hot water, and coffee.

She swallowed, refusing to cry anymore. She needed to be strong. Gwen had promised she'd return her home as soon as she could. She would have to believe in that. Trust the woman and her brother, who seemed only too eager to be rid of her.

"Abigail? May I speak with ye?"

She didn't bother to face Gwen as the woman came to stand beside her, instead she fought to control her emotions. She supposed the laird's sister would speak to her whether she wanted her to or not. "What do you want?"

"I'm going to be helping some of the village ladies prepare the needlework they'll sell throughout the games. Would ye care to help me?"

"What games?" she asked, having not heard of them.

"Castle Druiminn will host the Highland Games this year. My brother will compete and should the stars align, choose a wife."

Abby fought not to roll her eyes. From the small tidbits of history she'd read about the Highland Games, the strongest man won the fairest lady. "I don't understand your thought process, Gwen. You brought me here to marry your brother, so why go through all the trouble of hosting these games? Seems like a waste of time to me."

A slight blush rose on Gwen's face, and Abby narrowed her eyes. "I'm not sure how I'm able to do it, but I have the sight. I can see into the future. I've been watching you for some months and believed your strong nature, independence, and moral character would make a most promising match with my brother. I had hoped when you arrived that you would be happy, and willing to participate in the games and prove yourself to my elder sibling."

Abby's mouth popped open. *Prove myself?* The girl wasn't for the feminist movement, obviously. "As much as I love history and this castle, and the landscape is amazing, I don't want to live here. I don't belong here. And I certainly don't want to marry your brother. To parade around in an attempt to earn his favor is demoralizing. I want to go home. I don't know why you can't send me back already."

"I'm sorry. I thought you'd be happy about the gift I'd given you. The opportunity to live in a time not of your own, and possibly find love." Gwen led them toward the kitchen, a lone building that sat on the opposite side from the main part of the castle. The area was littered with piles of hay, and some small animals ran about freely. The smell again reminded of her why she wanted to go home. Burnt rubbish, musty and tinged with the hint of rotting flesh, permeated the air. Spying some type of dead animal hanging upside down on a nearby building, she swallowed and continued following Gwen as she led them toward a group of women who sat under a large, leafy tree, their laughter carrying across the slight breeze.

"I may be dressed like a woman of influence, but I'm not fooling anyone. I stick out like a sore thumb. I would suggest you save your necks, and as soon as you can, send me home."

Gwen sighed and motioned for her to sit. The ladies welcomed her with smiles, but their eyes gave away their interest as to who she was. "This is Abigail Cross, a friend from the Continent who's come to stay for a time."

"Hello," she said, sitting down. Abby took in the colorful plaid that was already woven, but was being sewn together. Reds and blues were the most prevalent, with a touch of black. "Whose plaid will this be?"

A young girl, no more than twelve, smiled up at her. "It's

going to be the laird's new plaid. We're also making a pleat for his future wife, whoever she may be."

"Oh." Abby met Gwen's eye and looked away. "It's charming. Do you want me to help sew?" She offered her help, although she hoped they'd decline. She'd only ever sewn the odd button that had come off a shirt or pair of pants, never an outfit that was going to be presented to a laird.

"Aye, the laird will be marryin', and soon we hope. He's a fine lad—man, I should say. He deserves happiness."

Picking up the plaid, Abby felt the woolen cloth. It was coarse beneath her fingers and no doubt would be itchy against the skin. "I believe there are other clans arriving in only a few short days. Maybe his future bride is among them."

Abby heard Gwen's name and turned to see the mighty laird himself, calling out to his sister. She watched him for a moment. He was a large man, not in weight, but in stature. The kilt hardly hid the great, flexing muscles of his legs, the plaid over his shoulder only accentuating his disgustingly muscled arms. His chin and chiselled jaw sported an unshaved shadow. She'd never tended to think of redheads as her type, but Aedan MacLeod wasn't a man to pass over.

Here was a man who oozed strength—a Highland laird with an army and a multitude of servants all willing to do his bidding. The women seemed to like him a lot, too, so she could only assume he was kind.

He caught her gaze and stared at her with unnerving indifference. Still displeased that she was here, he tolerated her presence with polite apathy. Well, she had not asked to be his unwelcome guest. She tore her gaze back to the women still hard at work. "Aedan MacLeod is a good laird, then? You all seem to regard him highly." Gwen continued to talk to her brother, and Abby thought to take the opportunity to learn more about the family.

"Oh aye, we do, Abigail, lass. Ever since he inherited the

lands from his father, he's ensured his people are cared for, his two sisters the most. Times are hard, but knowing our laird has our well-being in his thoughts makes things a little easier. Hosting the Highland Games this year will enable us to sell some of our chattels we've made and look after our families for the coming winter."

Abby started at the mention of another sister. "I haven't had the honor of meeting the laird's other sister. Does she reside here, too? Or is she married and living away?"

They cast furtive glances at each other and Abby's interest piqued.

The oldest woman met her gaze, a tinge of sadness in her eyes. "No, not anymore, poor lass. After being returned from the O'Cain clan after marrying one of the laird's sons, she's entered a life of solitude with the church."

"Well, I'm sorry I haven't met her." How odd. Abby knew they were holding something back from her, but what, she couldn't imagine. "Maybe she will return before I depart."

"A great wrong has been done to her, and she'll not be back. There are rumors the laird will declare war on the O'Cain clan after the games. And rightfully so," the older woman stated, her jowls wobbling in temper.

"What did the other clan do?" Abby thought back to what she'd read on the MacLeod family before being drawn back to their time. She couldn't recall what the older woman was talking about.

"She was handfasted, as I said, to one of O'Cain's sons, and for a year and a day she lived at their home. I do not know of what horrors she endured there, but I imagine there were many. The laird's sister returned blind in one eye, and to cause offense, they sent her home seated on a partially blind horse, led by a partially blind servant, and followed by a partially blind dog."

The other ladies mumbled their displeasure, and Abby

stopped sewing, wondering how people could be so cruel. "And you believe your laird will declare war over this?"

"Aye, he will. The rumors will prove true, I've no doubt. There isn't any love between the two clans, hasn't been for more than a hundred years. This marriage was our laird's last attempt for peace, and Jinny was thrown back in his face like a worthless pebble."

What husbands, brothers, sons would go off to battle and never return home? When it came to such actions, were there ever any winners? With her boyfriend David, she'd certainly been the loser when he'd died. A life cut short for no substantial reason at all. It may not have been a clan war David had battled, but a cop caught up in a gang war didn't end well, either.

"Are ye looking forward to the games, lass?"

Abby was happy for the conversation change, but the mention of the games left her feeling a little guilty for thinking marriage was the only thing that occupied the laird's mind. With talk of war, it was any wonder the clansmen were looking forward to the revelries.

Not to mention, these people relied on this type of activity to live, to make a hard life a little bit easier. "I am. I've never been to one before. And please, if you need any help, with anything at all, don't hesitate to ask me. I'd like to be useful while I'm here, if possible." As much as she hated being stuck in this harsh time, stuck she was, and she may as well be helpful, if she could.

"Oh no, my lady. You'll be busy enough with the Highland Games and entertaining the visiting clans to worry about our stalls and such. Being the laird's guest you'll have many a brawny, attractive Highlander looking to make ye his wife. I should imagine you'll be quite the popular lass."

She laughed, while also feeling a little sick at the idea of being courted. The last thing she wanted was to be carried off into the sunset on some laird's shoulders, his rank breath breathing all over her. "I'm not looking for a husband."

The women stopped what they were doing and stared at her as if she'd lost her marbles. "But you're a woman of means and of age. Why are ye not looking for a husband? Are ye entering the church?"

"As a nun? Oh, God no, but I'm young. I'm sure I'll marry one day, but not yet."

"Well, you're a wee sweet-looking lass, and next week when the games begin, you'll be courted, so ye better prepare yourself as best ye may." The older woman gestured to the woman around Abby's own age who sat across from her. "Who was that lad who visited some months ago?" She thought for a moment. "Laird Cullen of Clan Roxborough, I believe. If he doesn't turn every lady's gaze, I don't know who will, notwithstanding our own laird, of course. Our MacLeod will always be a favorite."

Abby smiled. It was understandable they loved their laird more than any other, and would never gainsay him in front of a guest of his, but she was still deciding what she thought of him. Handsome yes, but as prickly as a cactus bush in Arizona he most certainly was.

"So what will happen at these games exactly?" The women stared at her, and Abby made a mental note to try and remember not to stand out like a nitwit who knew nothing of their life.

"How can ye be a guest of the laird's but not know anything about a highland game? You must have traveled a great distance to be here and lived a verra sheltered life."

"You have no idea." Abby chuckled, placed her sewing down, stood, and dusted off her skirts. "And you're right, I'm not from Scotland or England, so I know little of the ways here, but I look forward to learning as much as I can before I return home." She nodded and walked toward Gwen, who stood talking to a man she hadn't seen before today. The slight flush on the woman's cheeks made it easy to surmise Gwen felt something for him. Abby came and stood next to them and smiled.

"Abigail Cross this is Braxton MacLeod, the clan's best swordsmen and distant relative to us all. He's also competing in the games."

Abby held out her hand to shake his, and he jumped back as if she were about to grab his nether regions. Heat seized her body, and she dropped her hand quickly. "Forgive me. I meant to shake your hand. It's how we greet people in my country."

He threw her a quizzical look, but smiled a little. "I'm honored to meet you, Abigail. Any friend of Gwen's is a friend of mine."

Abby smiled at Gwen, knowing what the play was between these two. She would lay money down that the two were in love. "Good luck next week, Braxton. I'm sure you'll do well."

"I truly hope so. I have high hopes my future will be settled at the completion of the games."

She nodded and left them alone. It was obvious by the longing gazes between the pair that she was only a third wheel. She walked toward the castle the same way Gwen had taken her earlier, but spying a staircase leading up to the stone bridge near the front, she changed direction and went that way.

The courtyard was still abuzz with servants. She nodded to those who made eye contact, and tried to be as friendly as possible. If she was stuck here for the foreseeable future, she needed to have as many friends as she could muster. These times were dangerous enough, without creating enemies.

Abby entered the castle, the damp, cold stones making her skin prickle with gooseflesh. She rubbed her arms as the small passage opened up into the Great Hall. Trestle tables with long wooden benches filled the space. At the end of the room, a larger table, the dais, ran in the opposite direction to those before it, obviously where the laird sat each night.

She looked up at the wooden beams that spanned the roof. A large window sat at one end, while near the dais, a roaring fire burned behind the table. A minstrel's gallery ran the length of the room, and from here she could see two servants dusting the dark wooden railings.

Abby walked over to the roaring fire and warmed herself. She watched the wood burn for a moment before a servant came up to her and bobbed a curtsy.

"Will ye follow me, mistress Cross? Laird MacLeod would like to see ye in the anteroom."

"Me?" At the girl's large beckoning eyes, she sighed. "Okay. Show me the way." The girl visibly relaxed and headed toward a passage behind the main dining table. She hadn't been in this part of the castle before, and the lower ceiling made her feel a little claustrophobic. The walls were bare, and a lone narrow window stood at the end of the corridor, before they stopped near a door adjacent to it.

The girl gestured to the room, and looking inside, Abby saw Aedan sitting behind a large desk. He was studying some scrolls—one laid out and held open by what looked like smooth rocks.

She entered, but was startled as the door slammed closed. Still, he didn't acknowledge her presence. Abby narrowed her eyes and looked about the room, instead. The walk to his office had seemed cold and menacing, yet this room was warm and welcoming. Tapestries covered the walls, and being a corner room it housed two windows, allowing plenty of light to enter. A large fire burned in the grate and an assortment of candles sat atop, giving off more light.

The room looked softer compared to the rest of the castle.

As this was his domain, did it reflect his personality? She had to concede from what the villagers had said about him he was a fair laird.

"Sit."

The curt order put to rest the nice thoughts she was having about him. "What's the magic word?" she taunted, not willing to do what she was told.

"Excuse me?" He did look at her then. Well, maybe look was the wrong word. Glare? Dismiss as an idiot, could come a close second.

Abby would allow him this win. She sat and raised her brows. "Never mind. I don't expect you to get it." She paused. "You wanted to see me?"

He studied her a moment, his features unreadable. "I did. I wanted to talk to you about the games next week and what is expected of you. We need ye to be prepared for the questions that will be asked, and ensure you know how to answer them appropriately. I don't need any trouble brewing between the clans who'll be meeting here. They're volatile enough without witchcraft and a time traveling wench making them ill at ease."

"Wench? Really?" She sighed. "So, what is it you want me to know? Perhaps we ought to start there."

He pulled out a piece of paper and skimmed it quickly before saying, "You'll be a family friend from abroad; France, perhaps. That would, at least, explain your strange accent."

"It's not strange, it's American. I thought your sister would've explained that to you since she's the one who brought me here." Sarcasm laced her tone, and she questioned why he aggravated her so. She wasn't normally snappy and cross, but he seemed to bring out the worst in her. That he made her nervous, didn't help. She looked up to him glaring at her again, his piercing green eyes like a beautiful, angry sea.

"I think she may have mentioned that." He looked back

at his paper. "Now—"

"Does your concern over my behavior in front of the clans have anything to do with your sister, Jinny?"

His gaze snapped up. "What do you know of Jinny?"

"Just that she lives away in solitude due to her mistreatment from Clan O'Cain. That they blinded her in some way and threw her away when she was no longer useful." He regarded her for a moment before leaning back in his chair.

"It will be helpful to keep the visiting clans my allies rather than foes. I'm hoping they'll stand with me against the O'Cains when the time comes."

Abby could understand that. She may not like conflict or the outcome it brought with it, but since she also needed many friends in this time, Aedan's similar need made sense. "I am sorry your sister was treated in such an abhorrent manner and because of it, I can promise I'll not cause you any harm with the clans. I may not always say or do the right thing, but I'll try my best." Abby doubted she'd ever shocked someone more.

"I'll be grateful to ye, if ye do." He cleared his throat. "Now, getting back to who ye are in our time, you have no family and know no one here. We've never met before your arrival and you're not married, nor have you ever been. You're a maiden, and while you're here, you shall act like all the other young women looking to marry."

She snorted. "You want me to act like a maiden. Tell me exactly how a maiden acts. Is it different from any other young woman?" Abby smiled, enjoying his discomfort over her questioning. But he was such a by-the-rules, no-nonsense kind of man who really ought to stop worrying so much.

He frowned. "I do not need to instruct ye on the ways of a maiden. You're a woman, you should know such things."

"I'm not a simpering miss and even though I promised to behave myself, I'll not act like a woman without a brain." At his confusion she added, "I'm not a maiden and haven't been for a few years, so I won't act virginal, even if you demand it of me. Do you understand what I'm saying? I'm not going to beg for the attentions of all the Highlanders with skirts—"

"They're kilts."

"Whatever. You have another think coming." She sat back and crossed her arms over her chest. His gaze honed in on that spot and she realized the action made her breasts look ready to bust out of her dress. She folded them onto her lap.

"Are ye telling me you're not a virgin?"

He looked shocked and not a little repulsed. She smiled. "I'm twenty-two. You do the math."

He sat back, and she wasn't sure what he was thinking. He was a man who didn't give a lot away, and for his role as laird, that was probably a handy trait. She changed tactics. "Are you a virgin, Aedan MacLeod?"

At her question, a flicker of a smile touched his lips. The action made her pause. Over the last few days she'd become used to his scowl, especially around her, but that small smile left her wondering what he'd look like laughing, happy, carefree. His deep green orbs, aristocratic jaw, and perfect nose told her he'd look pretty darn good. She swallowed.

"I am not."

"Well then," she said. "Now that we've gotten that out of the way, perhaps you ought to continue on with what's important to keep your family safe from the charge of witchcraft."

He nodded and seemed to shake himself from his thoughts. "Of course. We also need to discuss your role as a member of our clan. Even though we know you're no lady, you still need to act like one."

Abigail choked over her words. "What the hell do you mean by that?" She stood and leaned over his desk. "If I'm not mistaken, you're no gentleman, either. No doubt you've pleasured many female servants in many a location, so unless you don't want to continue tupping as a pleasurable pastime, I'd watch what comes out of your mouth, before your man bits are shoved down your throat."

He stood and towered over her. She lost some of her nerve, as he made her feel like a dwarf. Bloody tall Scotsman.

"You do not speak like a woman of class."

His tone fired her blood to boiling. "I think you're forgetting I didn't choose to be here. I may have Scottish ancestry, but I'm certainly not what *you* would term a Scot. Nor am I a lady of a castle. I apologize if I've made a mess of your perfect life, but you need to take that problem up with your sister." Abby paused, taking a deep breath to calm her temper. "I won't cause any problems, as long as you get me home as soon as you can."

He slumped back in his chair and rubbed his jaw. "If you can promise me you'll not the lady, cause no offense to the clansmen coming to stay, and try to look like you're enjoying my home and hospitality, I'll apologize for my unkindness."

"As to that, you'll apologize now." His jaw flexed, and she knew he didn't like being told what to do by a woman.

"I'm sorry," he said through clenched teeth.

She smiled. "Apology accepted," she said, sitting back down.

...

Aedan took a calming breath. The woman was a hoyden and going to be the end of him, literally, if she didn't start to cooperate. What his sister had been thinking bringing the lass here was beyond him.

Abigail Cross was trouble if ever he knew it.

"There are numerous clans coming for the games. Each clan's laird and close family members will be housed in the castle for the duration of their stay. We will have shelter erected for their clansmen near the fields where the games will be taking place. I'll leave the ladies of these great houses in Gwen and your capable hands."

"Won't the games themselves be entertainment enough?" she asked.

"Must you fight me on everything I say? Why can you not entertain some women?" He ran a hand through his hair and wondered what it was exactly his sister had seen in the lass that would suit him.

Aye, she was bonny, there was no doubt about that, with her rich dark strands of hair that fell about her shoulders. Her eyes were the same color, giving her an earthy appeal. Her skin was flawless, not a freckle graced her nose or cheeks, unlike so many of the Scottish lasses. Her figure wasn't anything to dismiss, either. The strange trews she'd arrived in, tight-fitting across her ass, had made him want to run a hand across her soft flesh and squeeze.

He shifted on his chair and frowned. The sooner he procured a wife, the better. It had been too long between lasses as it was. He should probably find a willing miss...

Abigail's words about bedding wenches in different locations turned his gut in pleasurable guilt. Not that he'd ever admit it to her, but yes, he'd indeed slept with some, and no doubt would again. As a man, he was permitted such activities. It was the way of the times. She'd soon be gone and his life would return to normal.

"Fine. I'll do everything you ask, but on one condition."

"And that is?" Her jaw jutted out, and he noted her lips. Supple, nicely shaped, a lovely shade of—

"That you return to me my phone and promise me that the moment your sister is able to do so, that I'm returned home."

He nodded, meeting her eyes. "We've already agreed on

this, and you have my word. As for the strange device you came with, I think it is best that I keep that until you depart. To be found with something so odd would only bring forth questions neither of us wish to answer."

"I will keep it hidden, I promise, but please return it to me. It was fully charged when I left, and if you're interested I could show you a little of my time, give you a glimpse of my life. Please, give it to me."

Aedan didn't wish to hand it over. Hell, never had he seen anything as odd as the metal object that she'd arrived with, and it was a dangerous move to allow her to keep it. But, mayhap, if he did give way on this one rule, she would stop being so prickly toward all that he asked of her. "Very well, I will give ye the object, but be mindful, I will take it back, break it into a million pieces, if I see it out around my people. Do ye understand me, lass?"

She held out her hand, nodding. "I understand perfectly."

Aedan stood, gesturing toward the door. "I will bring it to your room later today."

"You can't give it to me now?"

"'Tis hidden, and I do not wish for ye to know where. So, as I stated, I shall bring it to your room, later."

She stood and walked toward the door. "Fine, but I'll be waiting, just so you know."

He stopped himself from smiling at her audacity. "I'm assuming by the fact you're about to walk out the door that this conversation is over?"

She looked confused and then laughed. He didn't want to admit what that carefree, larger-than-life laugh did inside his chest.

"Yes. Unless there is something else you wish to discuss?"

"No, there is not. You may go."

She waved over her head and was gone. He walked over to the window, looked down on the castle courtyard, and watched as their head cook, Mrs. Turner, dug in the garden for herbs and vegetables for the evening meal. He wasn't fond of Abigail Cross, and the sooner his sister could send her back to her home and rightful time, the better. She wasn't like the women he knew. Too opinionated and strong willed. She was a woman who could get herself into all sorts of trouble.

Trouble that he would have to settle. Hopefully, not with a sword.

Chapter Seven

Abigail couldn't do it. She adjusted the bow and tried to find a more comfortable way of shooting the arrow. There wasn't one. Her arm didn't seem strong enough to pull back the tight string.

"It isn't working." She held it at her side and looked to Gwen who stood beside her, giving her instruction.

"We may have to help build up your arm muscle, but this is a woman's bow. I'm sure you must be holding it wrong. Here let me show ye again."

She sighed and again watched Gwen lift her own bow and demonstrate how to use it. Abby raised hers and tried to copy her actions. "Maybe I've been given a bow that is supposed to be used by a male?"

Gwen chuckled. "You haven't. Now keep trying."

I am she wanted to scream. Instead, with all her might, she pulled hard on the string and let it go. It worked that time. Now all she had to manage was placing an arrow in there and firing it off toward the target. Easy. *Yeah, right.*

During the past week, Gwen had been showing her all

different types of activities that she would have to attempt with the ladies who were to visit for the games. Today's lesson on archery wasn't a favorite.

Nor was yesterday's when she'd had to learn the basics of stitching. The whole castle now knew never to ask her to fix a garment. Abby shook her head at the irrationality of it all, and most of all, how silly it was that she'd been upset at not being able to do the basic chores that were expected of these women.

She was all for women's liberation, but to know how to sew, even a hem, would be a handy ability, even in her own time. She couldn't even stitch in a straight line. It was easy to say she wouldn't win *that* competition.

"Right, now let's add an arrow and see how ye go."

Abby grabbed one from the small leather satchel at her feet and placed it against the bow, threading the nock into the string. She pulled back as far as she could, trying to keep the arrow against the bow and not veering off into the air.

"Use your fingers to guide the arrow and keep it in its correct position before firing. Now look at the bullseye and let go."

She concentrated on her mark, pulled back, and set the arrow free. It flew through the air and landed a few meters in front of her. "I suck at this. Tell me again why I have to learn archery? Can't I just hand the ladies a bow?"

Gwen chuckled. "It'll be fun. And think, no one else in your time can say they took part in a Highland Games in the seventeenth century."

"That's true." Abby grabbed another arrow and tried again. She managed a little farther than the last time, but still she didn't seem to have the knack for the sport. At this point in time, she didn't seem to have a knack for much at all. If only they could see what a whiz she was in front of a computer, or how fast she could text. Now there she had skill.

"Will your brother really choose a wife based on how well

she does with these different activities? In my time, women do everything that a man can do. There are no limits to our greatness."

Gwen laughed and turned to look at her. "What do you mean?"

"I mean we do all sorts of things." Abby lowered her arrow and turned to face Gwen. "Most women will marry for love, not for stature or to increase a family's connections, although, you know, there are always some who still do that. But most women want someone who's kind, understanding, supportive, and compassionate, inside the bedroom and out."

"That's a lot of qualities." Gwen grabbed her flask of water and took a sip, holding it out to offer her some.

Abby shook her head, not thirsty at the moment. "I suppose it is, but why would you saddle yourself with someone you don't know or can't stand? Women are independent in my time. We work to earn money. We can be anything we want, be it a doctor, lawyer, farmer, or horse wrangler."

"Your era sounds so wonderful. I'm glad with the passing of time it's changed for women."

A sense of pride overwhelmed Abby at Gwen's words. It was good that women were closer to being equals, no longer a commodity to be bartered with between men. Even so, they still had a long way to go with some things.

Gwen fired an arrow, and it pierced the bullseye on the tree. "I wish Aedan would choose a wife in such a way, but he won't. Both of our parents are dead, but it wasn't until after father died that he changed. He used to be so carefree—he loved life and had made the most of every day. I'm not sure why he changed, but he became so serious. It was like overnight he changed into someone even I, sometimes, cannot recognize."

Abby frowned. "I can't imagine him being so lighthearted. He's extremely serious all the time." And a little scary.

"Aye, he is, but once he wasn't." Gwen sighed. "And now

he's after the most perfect wife he can find to run this castle and his lands."

"I wonder why you thought I would make him a suitable match." Abby sat on the grass and watched Gwen, who continued to fire arrows at the bullseye without trouble. "I'm not sure if you've noticed, but we seem to clash."

"I've noticed, and it still hasn't changed my opinion of you. You, Abigail Cross, are exactly who my brother needs. He needs a woman who's not afraid to tell him off, to argue and play with him. He needs to learn to live again, and how is one to do that if the person one marries enables you to stay in the shell you've formed around yourself?"

Abby lifted her face to the sun. The day was still young, and lunch would soon be served. The wind whistled through the trees and the clean, fresh air filled her lungs. There was magic in these hills, she was sure of it. For how else could a place so beautiful exist? "I know I've been angry with you, Gwen, and I want to apologize for that. Your home, for all of its terrible plumbing, is very beautiful. Especially when one is upwind from the pigs."

Gwen laughed. "I'm glad ye like it. And I'm happy you're here. Will ye tell me more about your home?"

There wasn't much to tell. What a sad fact that the people who lived more than four-hundred years before her were wealthier and had more assets than she did. "There isn't much to say. Sometime in the eighteen hundreds, my family emigrated from here to America. I'm still in college, although I'm not sure yet what I want to do. I've been taking anthropology and history, because I may want to be a museum curator."

"That sounds most interesting. What exactly is a curator?"

Abby stood and dusted off her skirts. "A curator manages the acquisition, preservation, and display of museum artifacts. I would also authenticate the age and origin of pieces that are brought in for display. It was one of the reasons why I was so desperate to come to Scotland. The history here is beyond anything we have at home."

"And now you'll be able to look around our home and marvel at all the historical pieces of the future."

She chuckled and started to pack up her bow and arrows. Not that she had to walk very far to gather them. "You're right. Maybe before I leave I could put some historical piece in my pocket for a keepsake." She paused as she waited for Gwen to collect her own arrows. "I do have a question, though. What is happening back in my time while I'm here? Does time slow down? Stop? Or does it continue on as normal?"

"It continues on as normal, or maybe it slows or stops. Actually," Gwen said, waving her arms about, "I'm not really sure, to be honest." She threw her a guilty look. "I'm sorry if ye have family or friends who may be concerned, but it won't be for much longer. Each day the magic wears off on ye, and I'll be able to send ye home soon."

They started to walk back toward the castle. Gwen spoke to some of the field workers and women who passed them on their way, none of which Abby understood as it was spoken in Gaelic.

"How do you know the magic is wearing off? Can you see it?"

"Aye, I can. It's like a glow that hovers around you. My mother and grandmother both had the gift. I hope, should I be blessed with a daughter, she will as well."

"It's quite fascinating now that I've calmed down, to appreciate the time I'm now living in. I really can't believe I'm here, experiencing all this, but you needn't worry about anyone missing me at home. I'm an only child and my parents have both passed away. Other than a few college friends, no one would be overly concerned and I am away on vacation. Like you said, I'll be home soon. They'll never know."

Gwen smiled. "As you say."

...

Later that night, Abby sat at the dais in the Great Hall with Gwen and her brother. Gwen was busy talking to Braxton, their heads close together in whispered speech. The room took on another life when animated with speech and laughter, the clan gathering for the meal. Aedan had given her cell back and now it sat snugly in between her breasts, hidden by the fabric that she wore. What she wouldn't do to take a selfie right now.

Abby looked around the room, watched the dogs weave in and out of the diners' legs, looking for food. Groups of people ate the stew and bread with vigor. Some cast inquisitive looks her way, but most kept their own company and savored the nightly meal. Abby would enjoy it more if they actually had cutlery and didn't have to use a spoon or their fingers for everything.

"Did you enjoy the rest of yer day, Abigail?"

She swallowed her mouthful of mead and nodded. "I did. I found some parts of it a little trying, but overall it was good." She met Aedan's gaze. He seemed pleased with her answer and oddly, she was glad of it. No use bickering at each other all the time.

"Gwen tells me you're very good at archery."

She choked on her spoonful of broth and threw a surprised look at Gwen who grinned. "Good wouldn't be a word I'd associate with my archery."

"What, then? Competent?"

Abby grabbed a bread roll and pulled it apart. "I would probably term it as crap. Your sister has grossly over-exaggerated my talents." Aedan sipped his mead, and her attention snapped to his lips and his throat as he swallowed.

"I don't believe it. She said you did very well."

"I didn't. Trust me." At that moment, a man came up to the table. He was dressed in a kilt and tartan the same colour of Aedan's. They spoke quickly and to the side. The man's accent was thick and hard to follow.

"The men on lookout have sent word they've seen the banners of Clan Grant traveling through The Red Hills. They should be here within the hour."

Aedan ran a hand over his jaw. "Send word to Mrs. Turner and tell her to prepare the bedchambers in the eastern castle quarters. They'll be tired after their long journey."

"They're early, Aedan. They weren't due to arrive until two days hence."

Abby cast an inquisitive look to Gwen at the vehemence she heard in the woman's voice. It was the first time she sounded less than pleased with the Highland Games, or the guests who were taking part in it.

"Plans change." Aedan continued on with his meal and didn't try to converse with her again. Abby sat between a scowling sister and silent brother and wondered when she would be able to excuse herself to go upstairs.

Just when she was going to make her exit, the hall doors opened with a bang, and a rotund elderly man walked in. He had a long white beard and, instantly, Abby thought of Santa Claus. A younger man, one she assumed to be his son, entered behind him. He was tall and built well, like Aedan. But where Aedan's features had been softened by the luck of good genetics, this man's hadn't. He looked as hard and as rugged as his muscled arm.

The large man waddled forward, his arms out in welcome. "MacLeod. 'Tis good to see ye, lad."

Aedan stood, came around the table, and hugged the man. Abby took a calming breath. This man, for all his jolly appearance, was as housetrained as a lion, but something about him gave her pause.

"I'm very happy to see you again. I hope your travels were not wearying."

"Aye, they were, but I'm hoping the journey was not for

naught."

A young woman entered the hall, and Abby felt her eyes widen. She was tall and yet still petite. Her long auburn locks were held back in a delicate type of knot. Gwen stiffened beside her, and Abby turned to see her glaring at the woman.

The young lady gave a small curtsy before Aedan. Surprisingly, he took her hand and pulled her in against his side. They spoke for a little time, the meeting between her and her family like a well sought after reunion, but if the seductive looks the woman was throwing at the laird were any indication, the girl had the hots for Aedan.

"Who are they?" she asked Gwen.

"Clan Grant from the Highlands. The old man with the beard is the laird, his son Evan, and daughter, Aline accompany him."

"You say her name like it's poison on your tongue."

Gwen took a sip of her mead and shrugged. "It is. They traveled through here last summer. Her father declared her too young to marry, and it was the only declaration that made her stay palatable. This year our family won't be so lucky."

The young woman laughed and for the first time, Abby saw Aedan laugh, as well. For all his sister's dislike of the girl, Aedan seemed to like her. Abby shifted on her chair, wondering why that made her feel...odd.

But that feeling was nothing like the one she felt seeing his face animated with happiness. He was as devastatingly handsome as she imagined. Perfect straight teeth, smile lines beside his eyes. His throat worked as he laughed, his whole persona drawing every eye upon him like a magnet.

Holy shit. He is hot!

"What did Aline do that upset you so much?" Abby spooned more broth into her bowl. It was some sort of meat soup with an assortment of vegetables bobbing about. It was a plain meal, but delicious.

"She tried to entrap Aedan in a compromising position. Luckily, my chamber servant is loyal to me and told me of the plan the girl had thought up, and needing the help of another, it was only fortunate she'd chosen my servant for the role. So, on the night she was to be caught bedding a man before taking her vows, it was me who walked into her room and explained to her that Aedan wouldn't be coming, that night or ever."

Abby chuckled. "You know, Gwen, we may not have started off the best of friends, but I'm starting to really like your gumption. Unfortunately, by the looks of how they're together right now, I think she'll end up your sister-in-law, whether you like it or not."

Gwen watched them as they walked toward the hall doors. A flurry of servants were going in and out with an assortment of luggage.

"Aedan will be kind to her, but I do believe he thinks her too young to marry. I hope the lass doesn't try any more conniving schemes."

Abby patted Gwen's arm. "I'm sure she won't," she said, not entirely sure of her own words.

...

Aedan walked Aline out toward their carriage. He knew the girl's ploy and shouldn't be alone with the lass, but she'd wanted help finding a bracelet she'd dropped coming inside. He caught something shimmering in the rushes near the doors and he leaned down and picked up the small keepsake.

"Thank ye so much, Aedan. I don't know what I would've done had I lost it."

He smiled and helped place it back on her wrist. She clutched at his arm, and a cold sweat broke out on his skin. He was a good many years older than her, ten at the least, and the attention she marked for him although not unpleasant, was a little suffocating.

"I'm starved after the journey. May I break my fast at your table?"

"Of course. 'Twould be a pleasure." He helped her toward the dais and noted Abigail was in deep conversation with Gwen and Braxton. He held out the chair for Aline and smiled as she sat, her attention never wavering from him.

"Would you care for some bread and soup?"

She nodded. "Thank you."

Aedan caught the gaze of Laird Grant, and he nodded. The old man looked pleased he was dining with his daughter. He turned his attention back to the girl. "I hope your travels were not too arduous."

"Nothing is too much trouble if I know we're to visit the MacLeods."

A hand reached out in front of him and he sat back, frowning at the intrusion.

"I'm Abigail Cross, a guest of the MacLeods. I'm very happy to meet you."

Aline didn't take Abigail's proffered hand, but only stared at it. Aedan quickly introduced the two women and didn't miss the annoyance that passed over Aline's features before she smiled in welcome.

"I'm very pleased to meet you, but pray, what am I to do with your hand? Why are you holding it out to me?"

Aedan clasped Abigail's hand and placed it back in her lap. Her fingers were long, and her skin softer than he thought possible for a woman. Had the girl ever worked a day in her life? Most women's hands here were a little calloused, either by sewing, gardening, or riding, but not Abigail's.

He placed her hand palm up on her leg and ran his hand over it. Not a callous to be found. Fascinating.

A discreet cough from Gwen pulled him to his senses, and he snatched his hand back. Abigail, thankfully, ignored his lapse and continued to try and converse with Aline about the forthcoming Highland Games.

"I understand your brother will be competing in the games. What are his strengths?" Abigail asked.

A dismissing laugh escaped Aline as she sipped her wine. "My brother excels in all challenges, not just one." She smirked. "I haven't seen you before today, Abigail. Tell me, how is it that you came to be here?"

"We invited her," Aedan said, meeting Abigail's eyes. "She's a life-long friend of the family's. 'Tis only right she comes to stay with us for the foreseeable future."

"You intend to stay?"

He didn't miss the shock in the girl's tone, yet why she would be threatened by Abigail he couldn't fathom. He had always seen her as a sweet girl, but nothing beyond that. He'd certainly never wished to tup her. Abigail, on the other hand, was closer to him in age, with curves in all the right places and a woman he'd certainly tup, was she not so aggravating.

She leaned across him, and the action afforded him a sweet view of her bosom. Her breasts would be a good handful, and her skin, pale and freckle-free, looked as soft as her palm. His body hardened, and he took a sip of mead. 'Twas fortunate his kilt, with its many layers, covered him well.

"For the moment, yes, but it won't be for a long duration. As much as I love the Highlands, the beautiful country and most welcoming hospitality of Laird MacLeod, I won't be trespassing on them for too much longer."

Abigail blinked up at him, mischief in her gaze, and his lips twitched. "Just so," he replied, taking another sip of mead.

"'Tis probably for the best. The Highlands in winter can be hard for a foreigner. Where are you from, if I may ask?"

"France," Abigail said, motioning to the servant for more whisky.

"Oh, you poor thing. It's any wonder you've come to stay

with your relatives. France is a ghastly place to live."

Aedan inwardly smiled as Abigail bristled at the derogatory remark. From what his sister had told him about the future Abigail hailed from, "ghastly" wasn't one of the words he'd associate with her way of life. Gwen had explained marvelous industries, suitable housing for all, and plumbing that involved more than a bucket and window to throw it out of each morn.

Abigail's time sounded almost divine compared to the hard life they lived now. "Abigail is well cared for. I expect nothing less for a friend of mine." Aline's eyes widened at his stern tone. Whether Abigail was wanted here or not was irrelevant, and no matter his feelings on the matter, he wouldn't have her treated with little respect. It wasn't her fault she'd been pulled through time and plonked in his. His sister had a lot to answer for, and he would have to watch her more closely in the future to ensure she didn't try anything so dangerous again.

"Clear the room. I have a need for dancin' this night," boomed a voice from the other end of the hall.

Aedan laughed at the Laird Grant's declaration and his daughter's resounding blush at her father's drunken joviality. What was life without a little fun?

"Will ye dance with me, lass?" he asked Aline. She smiled and nodded, only too happy to dance, no matter her embarrassment.

He pulled her from her chair, but not before leaning down toward Abigail, enjoying the wariness that entered her dark eyes. "You're next, lass." She raised her brows in obvious challenge, and his skin prickled in awareness—an emotion he'd not felt for a while. 'Twas refreshing to feel anything, after feeling nothing at all for so long.

"I look forward to it," she replied, not taking her gaze off him until he turned away.

Chapter Eight

Abby clapped to the bagpipes and singing from the two clans. The great hall echoed with laughter and joy and resembled what Abby assumed a medieval night club would sound like, should there ever be one. Whisky and wine flowed freely into goblets, and people danced, kissed in corners, and enjoyed the gathering of two great families, with little worry, for this night at least.

Gwen stood and pulled Braxton to the floor, and Abby laughed. The way the two looked at each other, was similar to lovestruck couples in the twenty-first century. It was strange seeing love, true love in this time. She'd always assumed historical marriages that involved affection were limited to the works of fiction and hearsay, but there was nothing fake about what Gwen and her guy felt for one another.

She caught sight of Aedan dancing with Aline, the young girl laughing up at him with large doe eyes. He, too, seemed to be enjoying himself, and he was actually smiling, not scowling at everyone.

A young man, one of the guards she'd seen outside the

castle, bowed before her. "Would ye dance with me, Abigail, lass?"

Abby nodded. "I would love to. Thank you." He took her hand and helped her down the dais. The dancing seemed to be going from large circles and then back into lines, the women weaving in and out of the men. She tried to copy, and managed not to embarrass herself most of the time, but for most of the dance it was a pretty mess.

"Yer doing wonderfully well, lass," her dance partner said, laughing as she went to move in the opposite direction to everyone else. "Yer making me look the veritable expert. I'll have to dance with ye again, me thinks."

Abby laughed at his attempt to shade light on her dreadful dancing skills. "I do apologize. I'm not used to these sorts of dances." And she wasn't. The dances she was used to happened in nightclubs. Lots of people grouped together, grinding against each other, getting wasted with friends, hoping to find someone to get their rocks off with.

Dancing like she was now, with meaning behind the music's tune, and the clans coming together in celebration in a form that hadn't changed in centuries, made the ways of partying in the twenty-first century seem ridiculous. How stupid these people would think them should they see how they carried on. Like a bunch of drunken idiots, who were in competition to see who could vomit first.

"Ye doing fine, lass. Perfect, in fact."

She smiled and laughed as he pulled her against him, dancing down a line of people. They turned at the end and went back the way they came. The music seemed to grow in volume with people almost yelling the lyrics. The atmosphere became unlike anything she'd ever known.

These people knew how to have fun, to enjoy themselves. "Thank you, but without your expert help I fear I would've failed miserably," she yelled over the noise.

"Och, never. I don't let any lass fail."

"Stop flirting, Kyle. You'll make Abigail blush."

Abby stopped dancing and looked up at Aedan's laughing gaze. "Kyle was merely being a good partner," she said in his defense.

The young soldier clansmen laughed and bowed. "With a woman as handsome as ye are, I'd never do anything other than behave."

He *was* flirting with her. Aedan clapped him on the back. "May I steal her away for a time? It's only fair we all should have the pleasure of dancing with Abigail tonight."

"Of course." Kyle bowed. "Mistress." He smiled and danced off toward a group of young kitchen servants who stood huddled near an arch beside a storeroom.

"I must warn you, I'm not the best at these types of dances," Abby said, placing her hand in his. His skin was warm, and his hand much larger than hers. Aedan pulled her against him, and the scent of soap and something that was only him, assailed her senses. Taking a deep breath, she fought to calm her nerves at his nearness.

Why did he have such an impact on her? No one she'd ever met before had sent her into such a dizzying spiral of awareness. What's more, his arrogance when they'd first met wasn't something she'd forget. The instant dismissal of her as someone who was nothing but trouble for his well-planned life had annoyed her. But then, the worry he must have over the O'Cains and his other sister, would be a heavy burden to bear.

His hand skimmed down her back, and she bit her lip. "This dance seems to go for an awfully long time." She was blabbering now, trying to think of anything to say that would take her mind off what his presence was doing to her body.

"Aye, 'tis." He weaved them through the other couples and laughed when she made a mistake. "It's one of the longest dances I know. Don't tell me you're already sick of dancing with yer laird."

She met his gaze and raised her brow. "My laird?"

He grinned and again her stomach flipped at his physical charm. *Who is this man? And what did he do with the surly, authoritative, and anal Laird MacLeod?*

"You're an intelligent woman, and I've been watching your conduct over the last week and I've come to a decision."

He was serious again, all laughter wiped from his visage.

"Okay. What is it you want?"

He pulled her to a stop and moved to the side of the room. "As you know, I'm making use of the Highland Games to find a wife, but not in the conventional way. This is where you come in."

"Me?" Abby crossed her arms over her chest, not liking the sound of this. "How so?"

"I need ye to help me pick the most appropriate, even-mannered, accomplished young lady there is on offer."

"On offer." She nodded. "You do understand it sounds like you're about to purchase a horse and not a wife. Don't you think your heart should have some input into your decision?"

He looked appalled, and she fought not to roll her eyes. This man really had not one ounce of brain. Not when it came to happiness in the marriage bed, at least.

"Nay. The heart has no impact on my decision. This is an important step in my life. It must be right."

"Hence, why I suggest you use your heart." She sighed and pulled him farther away from the gathered throng as their conversation was starting to pull inquisitive eyes. "Listen, if you choose your wife based on her abilities, what happens when you go to lie with her each night? If you don't want a woman who'll tempt you every hour for the rest of your life, or if you do not love her, your attraction will wane. It'll end up being the worst kind of marriage."

"And you're an expert on this, how?" He stood tall,

seemingly mocking her average height. He crossed his arms, the muscles in his biceps bunching; a fine vein of blue running through one.

Abby snapped her eyes back to his. "I'm an expert because after my parents died, my foster parents had such a union, and believe me, no one should be made to watch the train wreck that that was."

"What's a train wreck?"

"A type of vehicle." She waved his question aside. "Anyway, it doesn't matter, you asked me to help and this is me helping you. Not by scoping out the women for you."

"Please, Abigail."

Damn it. She hated when people begged, it always made her cave and give in to their demands. "This so goes against who I am, but fine. I'll help you, but on one condition."

"Only one?"

"Make that two," she said, wanting to smack the condescending smirk off his face. The man really did have it coming to him. Perhaps she ought to let him marry an asshole and he could rot in the marriage forever and a day.

She caught the hopeful look of Gwen from across the room and knew as much as she thought such things, she wouldn't let Aedan make such a catastrophic mistake. It wasn't in her nature to be mean.

"What are yer conditions?"

"That you'll listen to what I say without judgment. If you want my help, be willing to consider what I have to say, without interrupting me and dismissing my opinions."

"I asked for your advice, why would I dismiss yer opinions?"

"Because you seem to like the sound of your own voice." Abby grabbed a goblet of mead from a passing servant and took a sip. The fruity drink wasn't her favorite, but at least it afforded her some time while the laird digested her words.

"Your tongue is sharper than my blade, Abigail, lass."

He stared at her. She wondered if he was thinking of how to be rid of her, instead of making use of her while she was stuck here.

"What's yer second condition?"

"That your choice will be based on at least a fraction of what your heart desires. You must feel more for the woman than admiration over her skills at stitching or archery and her family's value to your plans. You have to desire her."

"Ye place a lot of merit on feelings, Abigail. Why? You're not married, from what I've been told."

Abby stepped toward him, bringing her nose equal to his chest. She glared up at him and poked him in the rib as hard as she could, ignoring the solid mass that her finger met, and that the action actually hurt her digit. "I may never have been married, but that doesn't mean I'm an idiot. And anyone with an ounce of common sense knows a union without love is never going to last. You're welcome to marry without affection, go right ahead, but don't look back on the day of your decision and wince when you've married a block of wood that doesn't care for you, your lands, or your people, and only your purse."

He scoffed, and she poked him again. "And need I remind you, that *you* asked me for help, not the other way around." Abby turned him about and looked over his many guests. "I tell you what, why don't you walk up to Lady Aline and ask her to marry you? Since you're so bloody smart, why not marry the first woman who's shown an interest in you?"

His face turned thunderous, and Abby wondered if she'd overstepped. But damn it, he couldn't keep being contradictory. He had to choose a path and go with it. She was only trying to help him not make one of the biggest mistakes of his life. Why did he have to be such a Neanderthal?

"Very well, I'll consider what my heart is telling me, but be warned, I don't take nicely to being talked to so dismissively or without respect."

"And neither do I, so from now on, we'll not do it to each other," Abby said, patting his arm. "I would like to help you, Aedan, but you must be willing to help yourself, as well." Abby spied Gwen, who was gesturing to her to come across the room. "Now, if you'll excuse me, I have mingling to do."

Abby walked quickly toward Gwen, all the while feeling her back burn with the heat of his gaze. It was no surprise he was pissed off, but he'd pissed her off, too, so they were even. Laird or not, it was his sister's fault she was here, and she'd be damned if she'd cower to him.

Abby hadn't put up with such treatment in the twenty-first century, and she wouldn't in the seventeenth, either.

•••

Aedan took a deep breath and relaxed his fisted hands. Revelry continued, unaware of the seething temper a lass with dark brown locks and knowing eyes had brought forth in him. With a defiant tilt to her chin, she joined his sister and didn't even look to see if he was watching.

He was watching. Couldn't take his eyes off the bonny chit. The fact that he'd wanted to follow her across the room and berate her for her rudeness was another matter entirely. Berate her and possibly something else. Kiss the wicked mouth silent. But he couldn't. As to why, he didn't want to think about it, but he had asked for her help. Not the other way around.

Abigail was a woman who could help him. A woman who was strong of character, had lived a life free of restraint that he could only imagine. Having been made the laird at the young age of sixteen, he'd not dallied with the lasses like Abigail seemed to have with the boys of her time.

Of course, when he'd grown a few inches, and his body had

filled out, the lasses had soon rectified the lapse. He certainly knew what to do with them now. His gaze traveled down Abigail's form, the dress in no way hiding what delicacies were hidden beneath.

She was bonny, probably the bonniest woman he'd ever met. Her skin was flawless, not marked with childhood scars or illness. Her eyes were clear and bright as the stars, and her breasts, pert, a good handful that begged for a man's touch.

His touch.

He ground his jaw and tore his attention elsewhere. He shouldn't be thinking about her like that. She wasn't Scottish enough, nor of his time, notwithstanding the fact she wanted to go home as soon as she may.

Her words flittered through his mind. No. His heart couldn't be used in the decision of choosing a wife. As long as he lusted for his future wife, there wasn't a need to be any more emotionally attached to the woman. There were plenty of marriages where such an agreement was entered into, and they still procured offspring.

He caught sight of his sister laughing at something Braxton said, her eyes alight and looking at his best swordsman with affection. She, too, would be married soon, and although she would have a marriage of love, he would not. A laird's first and foremost role was to ensure his people were well cared for and safe. Having a wife he loved would distract him from that role. To care was dangerous.

He walked over to a servant, and giving the red-headed lass a wink, took a goblet of wine from her tray. He captured Abigail's eye and nodded. Aye, he'd let the lass think he'd include his heart, if only to keep her happy and quiet. He'd use her advice, and then she would be gone. His life would resume order and peace with a wife who knew her role and responsibilities and no more.

He inwardly smiled. 'Twas a good plan, sure not to fail.

Chapter Nine

The following day after lunch, Abby found a secluded, vacant plot of land far enough from the castle so not to be found, and started to practice with the bow and arrow. She didn't like anything getting the better of her—a trait she'd picked up as a young child—and it seemed archery was proving difficult.

She loaded the arrow into the bow and tried to hit the large oak about fifteen feet away. Again, the arrow refused to behave and sit against the string. She swore, took a deep breath, and tried again.

"Are ye having trouble, lass? Do ye need help?"

Abby turned and narrowed her eyes on the laird, cursing his timing to see how useless she was at this sport. Typical of her luck. He'd probably lord it over her that he could do archery standing on his head. "No. I'm fine thank you. You don't have to stay."

He raised his brow, but didn't turn to go. Her gaze raked his form, his chiselled cheeks and strong jaw drew her eyes to his mouth. She'd be a liar if she said his presence or his body didn't affect her.

Aedan MacLeod was hot, and probably knew it. He cocked his head to the side and grinned. She glared back. Oh yes, he knew he was good-looking and no doubt thought she'd fall under his spell as well as any other.

Fat chance.

Liar…

"Are ye alright, lass? Ye seem to be staring at me." He looked himself over, touching his cheeks as if to check for food or something. "Do I have some of me lunch on my face?"

"Not at all. I'm just stunned silent by the honor of your presence."

He shook his head. "You're very good at sarcasm, but it still doesn't help when you're as good as useless with an arrow." He walked toward her, reaching for the bow. "Here, let me show ye."

She sighed as he turned to stand behind her. His arms came around her body, and he helped her hold the bow and arrow in the correct position. Awareness swamped her, his heat and scent washed over her like a rain shower. She ground her teeth and tried to concentrate, but it was almost impossible.

"If ye hold it slightly raised, it'll be less likely to hit the ground when you fire. And always keep your eye on the target, forget everything about ye, and focus."

His whispered words grazed her cheek, and her breath stuck in her lungs. He held her outstretched arm, his large hand covered hers, and kept it locked about the wood of the bow. Heat coursed up her neck, and she cursed her inability to stay unflustered by him.

Focus my ass. She'd be lucky not to go cross-eyed with desire.

She wanted to pull away, to step away, but her pride wouldn't allow it. She couldn't let him know he affected her. He was just a guy. No different from any of the others she'd met.

What a load of crap. He did affect her and deliciously so. Even now, with his other hand helping her pull the string back, keeping the arrow hard against the bow's wood, all she could think about was his chest hard up against her spine, the deep timbre of his voice, soothing, coaxing…

"Let go, lass," he said faintly.

The words sounded like a double entendre but she did as he advised and watched in amazement as the arrow sailed clearly through the air and imbedded itself into the tree. She stepped out of his hold, laughing. "Oh my gosh. I did it." She turned and smiled. At his intense stare, her smile slipped a little. "Thank you for helping me. You seem to know what you're doing."

He shrugged. "I've had a lot of years to learn." He walked over to the tree and collected the arrow. "Try again," he said, handing it to her. "Let's see if you can do it on your own."

Abby followed his previous instruction, and Aedan, true to his word, tweaked her stance, her hold here and there, but allowed her to do it herself. That she missed the tree entirely wasn't so bad since she hit a small one a little farther away. "Maybe I'll enter the archery competition and best all the lasses vying for your hand."

He laughed, collecting the arrow again for her. "Does that mean you're going to vie for my hand? You're comely enough. You need to learn your place and a few manners, and then you'd be a contender."

"Are you serious?" Abby rolled her eyes. "As much as I've enjoyed you teaching me this afternoon, and being kind…sort of, I'm not doing this to earn your favor. And I'll certainly never 'learn my place' to gain a husband. Do you have any idea how annoying it is to hear a man speak about a woman in such a way?"

"'Tis the natural way of things. I don't understand why

you're so upset." He crossed his arms, pulling her gaze to them.

Damn it. She tore her attention back to his face and focused on his eyes. "You're putting women in a box. Making them think they'll never be anything other than a servant who's taken a vow and married a man." She paused, firing off another arrow, hitting the oak dead center. "Just imagine if my only need of you was sexual."

Abby walked up to him, walking her fingers up his chest before gliding her hand over his skin. A muscle worked in his jaw, and she half smiled. "How would you feel if you wanted to marry me because you loved me? That you couldn't imagine your life without me, and I turned around and said, 'I'm sorry, I may have sex with you, but there'll never be any emotions involved. You have a job to perform and you better do it good, or I'll find someone else who can."

He watched her quietly for a moment, before sighing. "Are ye trying to tell me, lass, you'd like me to tup ye?"

"What? No!" she said, stepping away and laughing in spite of herself. "I'm trying to explain to you how making your future wife go up against other women is foolish, not to mention, mean. You should pick a wife with your heart, not your head."

"And why's that?"

"Because I fear your head is beneath your kilt at the moment, and not thinking clearly." She paused. "You're going to be with this woman for a long time. There has to be affection, because the lust will wane."

"I cannot marry a simpleton who's good in my bed but has nothing between her ears. My wife must be accomplished in all things."

"And I understand that. I do. But don't marry a perception of what you think is perfect, marry the perfect girl for you. I know you're a laird, and with that comes certain obligations and standards that are expected. But most of the time you're here, with your people, and no one is watching. And if you don't like your perfect wife, what are you left with? Do you see where I'm coming from?"

Aedan scooped up the spare arrows near her feet, silent for a moment. "Aye, I see yer point," he said. "But such thoughts are foreign to me. 'Tis not how it's done, not the way I was brought up to think. If we're to work together, and make what little time ye have here peaceful at all between us, ye must concede to my way of thinking as well."

"That's a fair point, and I promise I'll try." She asked for an arrow and took another shot. It embedded itself into the ground. "Why do you need to have a wife from one of these visiting clans, anyway? From what I've seen of your people and your home, you don't seem to be low in coin. Everyone seems well fed and looked after."

He sat down on the ground beneath a nearby tree and watched her. "I'll need many men to take down the O'Cain clan. The horrors they put Jinny through I dinna even want to imagine. A strong marriage that will unite two great homes is what's required to succeed."

Pain crossed his features, and she knew he was thinking of his sibling. "You feel guilty about it, don't you?"

"Aye." He nodded. "I do. Verra much so."

"You cannot be held responsible for other people's actions, Aedan. Whatever happened to your sister under the care of the O'Cains is their cross to bear. Their error of judgment. You were trying to gain peace. How would anyone know they would use your act of goodwill in an evil way?"

"I should not have bartered my sister. It was a mistake that'll haunt me for the rest of my days."

Abby came and sat beside him, leaning back on the tree as well. She looked out at the sheer beauty of his lands and sighed. In a lot of ways, the man beside her reminded her of

David. A man with an ingrained need to protect others, risk his life and limb to keep those he loved safe. She pushed the thought aside, not wanting to remember how it had all ended, nor did she want to start having feelings for a man who could be killed at any moment. "You're a good man, Aedan. If not a little pigheaded at times, but then, no one's perfect."

He laughed, and their gazes locked. A warm ache fluttered in her stomach, and she looked away, not liking her reaction to him when he was charming.

"Well," he said, standing and pulling her up to join him. "Like I said before, should ye wish to compete for my hand, you're welcome to it."

She smiled; glad his words changed the tension in the air to one of ease. "Maybe I will. Maybe I won't."

"I'm betting ye won't."

Abby grabbed the bow and arrows, anything to distract her from his devilishly cute grin, and started toward the castle. "I think you'll probably win that bet."

They walked for a little time in silence before Aedan cleared his throat. "Abigail, lass, I've been meaning to ask ye for some time now, and since we're alone, this may be the perfect time. I wanted to know about yer home. What yer life was like before coming here?"

Abby searched Aedan's gaze and could see he was serious about the question. She thought about her home, of all the amazing things she'd had available to her: medicine, transport, living conditions, technology, and her college education.

She looked at the castle, a magnificent edifice beyond the trees they now walked beneath, knowing no two places could be farther apart, if they tried. "I suppose it's a lot faster paced than how people here live. Everyone's in a hurry to be somewhere, to do something. This, of course, is helped by the fact that people can travel around the world in twenty-four hours or so."

"What of horses? Surely, they still exist?"

Abby laughed, nodding. "Of course they do, but the cart has been replaced by what we call vehicles, no horses required. People can travel by air, and yes, I do mean we can fly, but not literally."

He looked at her as if she'd lost her mind, and she supposed should she be in his situation, she would've had a similar countenance. "Do you want to ask me anything?"

"You fly?"

She smiled. "They're called airplanes, and they hold one-to three hundred passengers at a time, and yes, they fly, over mountains and oceans alike. I must admit, I'm not a huge fan of air travel, but it's a lot quicker than walking or by boat."

"But how? It doesn't seem possible." Aedan frowned, looking up at the wispy clouds. He had a handsome profile, and she smiled.

"The airplanes take off down the runway at a great speed, and their wings produce an upward force called lift, and they go up into the air. It's hard to explain, and I'm not a scientist, but that's the gist of it." Abby accompanied her words with hand actions and he smirked.

"Let's move on from the flying, it's too bizarre to warrant thought." Looking up at the sky, he continued, "So what else made up yer life?"

Abby didn't want to tell him studying and her part-time work in a supermarket was what made up her life. The daily grind to earn enough money to pay her college school fees had felt like a noose about her neck sometimes, not the liberating career path she'd envisioned. And then, Aedan probably wouldn't understand why women worked or were allowed to go to school. But, he did ask...

"I'm in school learning to become a museum curator. I've always loved history, and the stories behind beautiful paintings, or Roman sculptures, or a ring, or a bracelet. To look for items for a museum, catalogue and piece together their history, is everything I've ever wanted. Maybe it's because I know very little about my family, having been raised in foster care…" At Aedan's confused frown, she went on, "I was orphaned very young and lost my parents. Piecing together history, making sense of it and showing it to the world, is satisfying."

"You're a very fascinating woman, Abigail, lass."

"Not really. I'm an ordinary woman in my time. Here, I may seem a little eccentric."

"What about a husband or lover? Did ye have one of those in yer time? Please tell me my interfering sister didn't pull ye away from yer family."

Abigail laughed. "No, I have no husband." Was that relief she noticed on Aedan's face. Abby wondered at it before she said, "I did have a serious boyfriend, and before he was killed we spoke of marriage. But that's over now, obviously."

"I'm sorry for yer loss, lass. I'm sure, to have captured yer heart, he was a good man."

Abigail met his gaze and read the sincerity behind his eyes. "He was a good guy." But even after all the time she'd known David, never had her body reacted as it did right now, standing next to Aedan. Abby didn't want to delve into what that meant, and she stopped as they came before the castle outer wall. "We're back," she said to change the subject.

"Aye, and if you'll excuse me, I have some work to do before the evening meal. I thank ye for our chat today, lass. 'Tis always good to learn a little bit about people."

"Very true." Abby gestured for him to go, and unable to help herself, focused on his ass as he walked away. *Yowzers, they don't make men like that anymore, and if they did I've never seen one.* How sad she had to travel back four hundred years to view a guy with such sensual attributes.

• • •

Abigail stood between Gwen and Aedan at the front of Castle Druiminn, as clan after clan arrived for the Highland Games. Each day there was a new arrival, and each introduction and explanation of who, what, where, when, and how she'd come to be here had taken a toll. Before the games had even begun, she was exhausted.

Her answers had become curt, with little embellishment to smooth over inquisitive noses. Aedan had pulled her aside and reminded her of their deal. It had annoyed her a little, but a deal was a deal. And she wasn't one who went back on her word. Not to mention the fact that, as the days passed and a truce formed between them, her stomach had an unfortunate consequence of somersaulting whenever they spoke.

But he'd become a Scottish Neanderthal again in front of his Highland lairds, and all the softening emotions she had developed disappeared. At times, he tarnished her ideals of what all Scottish men of this era were like. Never again would she read a romance novel and think Scottish lairds were swoon-worthy men she'd love to sneak into her bed.

"We're heading down to the field where the men are practicing the different events for the competition. If you would accompany me, I'm in need of your advice."

Abby sighed. Not in the mood to help him pick his bride, especially one from Clan Grant, who were at the field already, going through their own preparations for the competition. "Can't we talk at dinner? I've about had enough of listening to all the clans boast about who's the strongest and who's sure to win."

He took her arm and placed it around his, and she ignored the thrum of awareness that coursed through her veins. Surely it was only because he was so vexing at times that she reacted to him. It couldn't possibly be that she found him attractive. His mouth, which was smiling down at her, may be smooth and nice looking for a guy, but as soon as he opened it, she had a totally different reaction.

"You promised, and I'm going to hold ye to that promise. Now come," he said, pulling her along.

Abby followed. They walked down a grassy bank, little stone steps buried into the side of the small hill that led to a large field. It looked like the Murray and Scott clans had also come down to practice, the men busy with whatever they thought would give them an advantage.

There was one consolation. The lack of clothing the men had on certainly made delectable viewing. Large shoulders rippled, their backs glossy from sweat, glistened in the sun. Well-built sword-wielding arms clapped each other on the shoulders in welcome, their smiling features making her wonder if she'd been too quick to dismiss all Highlanders as Neanderthals.

"Enjoying yourself?"

His hardened tone snapped her out of her perv fest, and she looked up at him. He was frowning down at her, the line between his brows quite severe. "Actually, I was. You didn't tell me they were going to practice with only their skirts on."

"They're kilts." The word squeezed through his teeth.

Abby laughed. "Whatever." She chuckled and felt him stiffen. "Now, as for the women we're supposed to be discussing, who is it exactly you want me to advise you on."

He looked over to where a group of ladies stood, some giggling into their hands and looking away shyly from the men, while others openly ogled them. "She's from Clan Murray. Her name is Mary. I saw you talking to her after dinner last eve. What was she like?"

Abby looked to where the girl stood and shrugged. "I like her. A lot. She isn't a simpering idiot like the Grant lass." She could feel him staring at her, and she tried to ignore it before the extended silence got the better of her. "What?"

"You don't like Aline?"

"No, I don't. She's as cold as Loch Ness in winter." A cool breeze picked up, and she cuddled into him, seeking his heat. "I may not like you very much, either, but anyone as a wife would be better than her."

He huffed out a breath, half laugh, half scoff, and looked back toward the women. "What else did you find out about Mary?"

"She seems learned. Her brother recently married and would like her to become someone else's problem. She let it slip that he's low on money, something to do with a land dispute."

"She said all that to you after one night?"

The look of awe on his face made her smile. "Well, of course. You did ask me to scope them out and that's what I've been doing. If you take an interest in people, eventually they open up and start blabbering about all sorts of things."

"You seem to be doing a great deal of chattering now. So your summarization seems correct."

"You're such an ass."

He laughed and walked toward Mary, the first woman he'd shown an interest in. As he greeted her, it was all smiles and easy conversation. Abby stood back and watched how the women all simpered around the very handsome Laird MacLeod. And he really was particularly nice to look at in his kilt and sporran. Somehow the colors of red and blue only highlighted his captivating eyes.

Eyes that reflected merriment and enjoyment. She hoped he wasn't playing a part, a part that would end as soon as he married. Aline pushed her way into the conversation and clasped his arm. Abby's eyes narrowed, not missing the way the little minx rubbed her breast against his arm, or how Aedan looked down at her with something akin to shock... or was it desire...

Well, it was a dangerous game he was playing, and

women, more often than not, didn't play fair when marriage to a wealthy laird was on the table. She smiled. The poor man was almost being led to the slaughter, and by her, no less.

"I see ye found my favorite Highlander and placed him in the bonniest circle in the Highlands." A large hand clapped her shoulder, and she stepped forward to stop herself from falling over. "I've never met ye before, but I'd like to. I'm Benjamin Ross from clan Ross. Most people call me Black Ben."

Abby looked up to the towering form of muscle, long black hair, and huge biceps. She felt her mouth pop open. Never had she seen such a huge guy. "I'm Abigail Cross. A distant friend of Laird MacLeod and his sister."

He smiled, showing teeth stained with red and in need of a good cleaning. What had he been eating?

"Sure ye are, lass." He called to Aedan. "Hey, boy. You forgot to greet me like the good host you're supposed to be."

Aedan turned and came over to the man, hugging him tightly, both of them clapping each other on the backs. Abby joined the women and let the men have their reunion in private. They spoke animatedly, laughing and talking at the same time.

"I see ye met Black Ben, Laird of Ross. He's the best longbow shot north of the Scottish border. Tower of a man, but just as kind as Aedan MacLeod. They were both under the tutelage of my father from clan Scot for a few years."

Abby smiled at the young woman. "I'm Abigail Cross, by the way. I'm sorry, I've forgotten your name. I've met so many people these last few days."

The woman smiled in turn. "I'm Mae. 'Tis lovely to meet ye, Abigail."

Aedan met her gaze across the short distance, his eyes taking in her form while the other gentleman spoke and looked at her as well. Heat suffused her cheeks, and she looked back to Mae. "I noticed when I spoke to the Laird of Ross that his teeth are red. Why is that?"

The woman laughed, causing those close by to look at her with interest. "They're not normally so, I would think he's been partaking in too many Rowan berries. There are a few trees scattered around the castle. Surely you've seen them on your travels."

"I must admit I have not." Abby paused. "Are you looking forward to the games?"

"Aye, I am. Because the sooner they start the sooner they'll be finished. I didna want to come here, but my brother, future Laird to Clan Scot, insisted." The woman's brow creased as her attention snapped to her brother, who had now joined Aedan and Black Ben.

"You can tell me to stop being nosy, but why didn't you wish to come here?" For a woman of her age and living in this time, not to be interested in this type of entertainment and socializing was odd.

Mae cleared her throat. "My brother wants me to marry a man that I do not love when my heart has already been given to someone else. I will not be forced into marriage — by him, or anyone. I have promised myself to a good, kind, honorable man. I will not be swayed."

Sympathy for the girl consumed Abby. The poor woman, living in a time where the men in her life could dictate to her, make her marry someone she neither knew nor cared for. She shook her head. Thank God times had changed for women in the twenty-first century. "I hope you can marry the man you love. If there is any way I could possibly help you, please let me know. I, too, would hate to have an arranged marriage."

"Thank you," Mae said, clearly astonished and relieved Abby had said what she did. "I will not forget your kindness."

"You don't owe me anything, truly. And I really don't mean to be nosy, I don't know anyone other than Gwen and

Aedan, but I'm curious, who does your brother wish you to marry?" Maybe it was Aedan, and by at least knowing that she wasn't interested in him she could advise him, in case he was looking at her for a potential wife.

"He's from Clan Kirk. They're not here, but we're to travel home past their lands. My brother will break our journey for a day or two at their castle." She shook her head. "He's the worst of men. There are rumors the woman he was betrothed to disappeared. An English woman that no one past the border would care for, so easy to be rid of."

"That's terrible. Do you think he murdered her?"

"I don't know, but I certainly don't want to marry him and find out for myself how dangerous he is. I can't believe my brother is even considering the alliance."

"Maybe Aedan could speak to your brother and help sway him to see that such a marriage is not wise."

Mae clasped her hand, squeezing it. "Would you do that for me? I would be eternally grateful. From the few times I've met the Laird Kirk, I've been left with a revulsion that has stuck with me for days. I do not like him, and I certainly couldn't marry the man."

"I will do whatever I can. I promise."

At that time, Gwen joined them, letting them know luncheon was served up at the castle. Abby walked with Gwen and Mae and watched as Aedan and his friend Black Ben walked in front of them, their muscular thighs hers to look at.

She shouldn't ogle Aedan. He wasn't someone she should be looking at in any way. This wasn't her time, nor were these the people she'd grown up with, hung around, or called friends. And although they were friendly, Gwen especially, and had tried to make her experience here as smooth as possible, it didn't change the fact that she was in way over her head.

Aedan might be kind, a good laird, but medieval

Scotland wasn't for her. There was a reason why society had evolved over time, people lived longer and were increasingly intelligent. Who wanted to live with no access to medicine or die from trifling illnesses like colds? Social media, technology, and electricity were non-existent. Everything she knew, her entire way of life, was foreign here.

The thought of never having ice cream again, watching a chick flick on TV, or going out for drinks with the girls, was awful. Women in this time had no rights, in many cases were seen and not heard, and basically used as bartering tools between men, a fact of which she'd been made well aware. Not to mention, throwing all her years at college down the drain and never using the degree she had worked so hard for. No, it wasn't an option.

Aedan bent over and her attention snapped once more to him. On the other hand, what harm was there in admiring the man's form while she was here? He'd never know that she was taking in his strong legs and muscular arms that she imagined would flex nicely when leaning over someone in bed. She'd be a liar if she hadn't thought about him in that way. Of what he'd look like thrusting into her, his intense eyes meeting her own at the crux of orgasm. Of what he'd sound like finding pleasure within her.

He laughed at something Black Ben said. There was certainly no doubt he had a definite charm, well, maybe not so much charm, but his body certainly had appeal.

Abby bit her lip to stop herself from laughing at her own thoughts. She was in a bizarre position, so it was only fair that she enjoy herself.

•••

Aedan sat next to his oldest and closest friend Ben and broke a piece of bread apart. His time traveling houseguest sat next to Gwen and Mae from Clan Scott, her laughter continually pulling his attention toward her.

"Stop looking at the lass. The other women will become jealous."

Aedan scoffed at Ben's words, but did as his friend advised. After Ben's arrival, he'd told him everything that had happened over the last few weeks. Ben was privy to Gwen's abilities, but his hilarity over the current situation wasn't helpful. "I was merely keeping watch to ensure she didn't cause trouble or offend any of my clansman."

"Leave her be. It's yer sister's fault she's here in the first place. You ought to be nice to her. She could be of help, knowing what's already transpired in history and all."

Aedan frowned, having not thought of that possibility. His gaze, with a life of its own, sought her out again, and he wondered what she did know of the past. Of what was going to happen to his beloved Scotland over the next few hundred years. He wondered if she'd ever heard of Clan MacLeod and what had happened to his people and home.

"Now look what you've done, the lass from Clan Grant has spotted yer marked attention to Mistress Abigail. I don't know why you're always needing to cause trouble."

Aedan laughed. "If any one of us causes trouble, 'tis you, not me." He took a sip of wine, spooning more stew into his bowl. "Ach, there's something about the lass that—" He paused, wondering if he should tell his friend how much the woman haunted his dreams. Worse was the fact he'd wake up, sweating and aching for her touch. Something told him with her life experiences, she'd be no lady when it came to sleeping with a man.

Perfect for tupping.

He shifted on his seat, his body hardening at the image the thought conjured in his mind. Damn it. He needed to find a wife, a suitable woman who'd do her duty, run the castle, and produce his children with little fuss. He needed to stop thinking about Abigail. He needed to stop wondering what the repercussions would be should he throw all his ideals—the determination to marry well, to a woman who could bring him more power—over the battlement's walls. Blast it.

"She seems nice enough to me. Why not look to her for yer wife, since you're so adamant you require one."

Aedan ignored his friend's mocking tone. "Aye, and ye need one as well, might I remind ye. Perhaps ye ought to look for a wife while yer here. It's about time someone pulled ye into line to produce some lads of yer own."

"Aye. Mayhap I'll seduce yer lovely Abigail, if yer not going to. Ye wouldn't mind, would ye? She's not planning to stay, 'twould fill in me time well having her warm my bed at night."

Every muscle in Aedan's body hardened to stone. Just the thought of Ben and Abigail together caused a red haze to pass over his vision. He met his friend's contemplative gaze and felt panic rise in his chest. Did he truly mean to seduce her? "Don't touch the lass, Ben. We've been friends a long time, but she's not for you. Do ye understand?"

Ben smirked and then grinned. "Aye, we're friends, and I see how 'tis between you two, even if ye don't. Not yet, at least. I'll not touch your lass, I promise, but if you're interested in the girl, you need to tell her. Now, while she's here, before she's not."

"I'm not interested in her." The words turned his gut for the lie they were. Deep down, even he realized that Abigail Cross was unlike any woman he'd ever known. Other than his sister, she was the first person he'd been honest with about his wishes for the future, his plans. She may have not agreed with how he'd set out to achieve those goals, but she was willing to help him, in any case.

In fact, her strong will and independence attracted him

the most. She didn't cower around him, wasn't scared to share her opinion. *So why do I want a wife who is the exact opposite...*

He frowned, delving into his meal with zest, not wanting to debate why he'd think such a thing. He never used to. What he said and thought were always the same, but since Abigail's arrival, everything had turned upside down.

Again, the word "trouble" floated through his mind.

"She's a beautiful lass. She actually reminds me of someone, but I can't think of who at the moment."

Aedan looked at Abigail and then to Ben. "She's never been here before, you know that. Why would ye think she reminds ye of someone?" He paused. "Have ye been talking to Gwen?"

Ben shrugged, taking a sip of mead. "I'd have to agree, but that's not it. It'll come to me, but like ye said, it matters little. We know she's not native."

No, she wasn't. She stood up from across the table and bid the ladies good night. Aedan rubbed his jaw, the stubble on his chin reminding him to see his servant about a shave. Perhaps he ought to seek out his man before it became too late and the instruments wouldn't be brought up to his room in the morning. "Excuse me for a moment."

He stood and walked from the hall. Soft footfalls sounded ahead of him on the stairs, and he took them two at a time to catch up with Abigail. His eyes widened when he caught her pulling at the strings of her bodice before she'd even made her room.

"What are ye doing, lass? 'Tis hardly a private location."

Abigail gasped and jumped against the wall, knocking her head. "Oww." She rubbed her skull. "Don't sneak up on me like that. You scared me half to death."

Her bodice gapped, and the smooth, plump mounds at the top of her breasts were visible. He swallowed and shut his eyes, willing the vision to disappear from view, only to be bombarded with the reminder in his mind sight. He forced his eyes to reopen. "I apologize," he said, meeting her gaze and holding his attention there and not lower on her person. "I wanted to catch my servant before it was too late. He's old, I don't use him at night normally."

She started up the stairs again. "Well, good night then."

Aedan fisted his hands. "Did ye find out anything interesting with the lasses today? Anyone appropriate that may be suited to be my bride?"

She came down the stairs and stood on the one up from him, placing her at eye level. He wanted to clasp her hips, pull her against him, do a lot of things he shouldn't want to do.

"I did. I met Mae from Clan Scott today. She's sweet, but unfortunately in love with someone else, so you'll have to content yourself to being her friend only. Actually, her brother wants her to marry someone she's not fond of, and we'll need to discuss this at another time."

He ran a hand through his hair, the smell of jasmine wafting from Abigail's skin. Hell, she smelled sweet. "Aye, well that's a pity, but I didn't much like her openness and straightforward manner."

"What do you mean?" She was frowning at him again, the action only making her more tempting.

"Mae Scott is very opinioned. I doubt such a woman would raise the amorous feelings you're so adamant I use when choosing a wife." Aedan didn't know why he was teasing the lass so. Did he want her to react to him, to chastise him, remind him he was among the living but letting life pass him by?

He never used to be so dull. When he was a child he would've been in the thick of things, ready to do battle and protect his own. What a fool he'd been.

Inheriting the land, being Laird MacLeod, was not a light burden to carry. He'd sworn on his father's grave to bring order, rules, and peace throughout his lands. That he would never allow the threat of others to impact his clan's people, if he could help it. A laird guarded with his trust, guarded with his heart and home, and never allowed anything to threaten that peace.

And he'd lived by that decree to this day. Right up to the moment Abigail Cross had entered his life and brought nothing but chaos to his secure, regimented world.

She placed her hands on her hips, the action lifting her breasts closer to the top of her gaping gown. "That's it, from now on, whatever stupid thoughts are flying about in that brain of yours must stop. How are you going to know if you have feelings for a woman if you don't even talk to her, have fun, learn to be their friend and confidant? Never mind kissing the girl to see if you enjoy it."

"So now you want me to kiss all the women I think could be a suitable bride? I don't want to be married to all of them." Not that this would occur, if he was careful, but still, kissing a lass when one was a laird wasn't as easy at Abigail seemed to think. Many clans would demand a handfasting ceremony without delay.

"Do you even know how to kiss?" Her gaze flicked to his lips and his body tensed. "Have you ever kissed a woman? And I mean, really kissed her, as if she was the world to you?"

"Don't be daft, woman. Of course I've kissed a lass, but had I kissed her like that I would be married already." He'd even enjoyed the action a time or two, especially with the kitchen wenches who were more than willing and wanted no promises in return.

"And when you kiss, do you allow yourself to take pleasure in it? Do you let that stoic character of yours relax, and fall into the moment with abandonment?"

He raised his brow. "Are you going to start spouting poetry next?"

Her hands came up and lay on his shoulders. Her touch burned through his tunic, and he fought not to give in to his desire, the fire that blazed in his gut threatened to consume him.

Her fingers glided into his hair, pulling him close. Her lips were a lean away, their breathing intertwined like the moon and stars in the night sky.

"If I started reading poetry would you listen to me?"

He clasped her hips, unable to keep his hands off her. She didn't pull away, or start at his touch, if anything she came closer, teasing him with the notion of tasting her. Of kissing her.

"Perhaps," he said, losing the point of their conversation.

"And if I kissed you, Aedan MacLeod, do you think you'd enjoy it? Or are you scared you'll suffer from that terrible, scary notion called regard for the wrong woman for your perfect plans."

She was teasing him, making fun of his rules and regulations, but as her tongue came out and wet her pink, soft bottom lip, all he wanted was to devour her, damn if she didn't care for it. "Shall we find out?"

Their gazes locked, and he could see the excitement and determination in her golden brown eyes. Then their lips touched.

The lightest melding of mouths, a brush, no harder than a flutter of a feather. He stood motionless for a moment, completely shocked to his core by what her miniscule touch did to him.

A hunger he'd never known roared inside. A hunger that was no longer willing to be denied. He brought his hand up around her nape, the skin on the back of her neck soft and smooth, and pulled her mouth hard against his.

He angled her head and deepened the kiss. She gasped, and he used the advantage to slide his tongue against hers. Desire exploded through his veins, hardening every ounce of his being. He kissed her long and deep, the feelings, the emotion her kiss ignited in him addictive and new.

Aedan knew in that moment, when she kissed him back with as much force, with as much need and desperation, that he wanted her. Only her.

They didn't move, but kissed to the point of madness. Both of them clinging to each other, a mating of mouths, with small bites that were driving him insane.

Where had she come from? Well, he knew where, but by God, how was he to survive her time here when after tonight everything would change? One kiss would never be enough. He wanted more. Much more.

He tore away and stepped back, giving them space. She swayed and caught the small stone railing on the wall to steady herself. Her lips were wet, swollen, and red from his kiss.

But he couldn't speak. Couldn't think, for that matter. It was all about that kiss, and the woman in front of him who'd proven how much trouble she was going to be.

"See, Aedan? When you give yourself up to the act, it can be quite fun. Nothing to it. I'm sure if you kiss the woman you find yourself wanting as your wife, just like you kissed me, you'll be married in no time."

Her dismissal of what they'd shared irked, and he narrowed his eyes. "Aye, thank ye, Abigail. I'll be sure to give ye a full account when I do."

"You do that," she said, turning about and walking up the stairs and out of sight.

Aedan leaned against the wall, the cold stone doing little to diminish the fire burning inside him. He wanted to follow her, tempt her into his bed so the need, the want of her, was sated.

But he didn't. Instead, he turned and walked back down the way he'd come, needing the company of his clan and old friends to distract him from seducing a woman who had no part in his future.

Abigail Cross was not for him. Not in this life or the next.

Chapter Ten

The next day of the games began with congenial weather. The nights were still cold, dew sat on the trees and ground, the roofs of the cottages that dotted the lands looked wet, but the sun that rose in the east promised warmth, and clear Highland air.

Abby sat on a wooden platform that gave the women and a few older clansmen a good view of the field and settled in to watch the day's competition. Abby welcomed Gwen as she came to sit beside her, the woman's excitement over the forthcoming event almost palpable.

"Is Braxton competing today?" Abby asked, knowing already he was. In fact, he was going up against Aedan and his team of clansmen in a tug of war. Little lads she'd seen about the village were busy throwing buckets of water into a pit, while others sloshed about with their feet, making it as muddy and slippery as possible.

"Yes. He's competing with Clan Ross and Black Ben since they were short of men. Apparently, he has a plan that will beat my brother. Of course, I hope he does. I'd love to see

Aedan fall in a puddle of mud."

It was obvious that Gwen adored her brother. Abby laughed, knowing she spoke in jest. "That's not very sisterly of you. How could you think so cruelly of the man who, for all his perfectionist qualities, loves you dearly?"

Gwen scrunched up her face in thought. "Seeing him fall in mud, getting dirty, which he hates by the way, does not make me love him less. But it won't hurt to see him live a little, too. He's so serious. He could use some fun in his life."

Abby couldn't agree more, and yet, the thought of their kiss, how much *fun* they'd had the night before, bombarded her mind and she shifted on the seat, feeling a little warmth on her cheeks.

Last night after she'd made her room, she'd done nothing but pace for a good hour. No matter how much tread she'd worn on the wooden floor, it didn't change the roiling emotions he'd created within her.

She watched him on the field, the men about him listening intently, some flapping their arms about in preparation for the tug-of-war to come. They were all so serious. Anyone would think they were about to go into battle.

"Are they playing for anything of value today?"

"Aye." Gwen nodded toward the front of the platform where a man stood beside a wooden square box. "'Tis a bag of coin. The clans place an equal amount each into the winnings, which is distributed evenly between the events. If a clan were to win all bouts, they'd walk away with a wee fortune. 'Tis nothing to sneeze at."

"Well, no wonder they all look so serious." The crowd started shouting as the men in the two teams took their positions on either side of the muddy hole. "So every clan will have a turn and eventually, the two strongest teams will compete for the prize money?"

"Aye."

The tug-of-war started and shouting ensued, not only from the people sitting around her, but the two teams. Feet slipped, arms strained under the pressure, faces turned bright red as the men, all of similar weight, tried to pull one another over.

Abby's attention snapped to Aedan's legs, his kilt doing nothing to hide the strong, corded muscles that ran up their lengths. His arms flexed, tightened, and it was hard to imagine he'd held her against him with nothing but care and softness.

The bout went on for some time; both teams feeling the strain, as they seemed well matched in strength. But a member of Clan Ross slipped onto his bottom near the front, making some of the men lose their footing. It wasn't long before Aedan's team used the men's disadvantage and pulled them over the allotted line.

Gwen swore as Braxton landed on his ass, his kilt covered in mud.

"That'll be a bastard to wash," her friend said, making Abby laugh.

"I should imagine so."

Aedan clapped his men on their backs, joining them in ribbing the following team that they'd be next to end in the mud pit. Abby laughed and found herself enjoying the day immensely. What wasn't to like? She was in the Highlands, surrounded by good people, even if they weren't of her time. Everything was crystal clear here, the air, the people's morals, likes and dislikes.

It was quite refreshing and not a little addictive.

Aline ran up to Aedan, her enthusiasm over his team's win seemed a little overdone, even for her. The young woman gushed, practically re-living the event, while smiling up at Aedan with obvious longing.

Abby inwardly cursed the girl before putting a stop to such thoughts. Why shouldn't Aline look at him like that?

He was a good-looking man, certainly one who pulled many female gazes his way. He leaned down and said something in the woman's ear, her face flushing a little, making her more attractive than she already was.

Abby looked away and concentrated on the hills in the distance. She should be happy he was forming an attachment to another woman. She wasn't staying to fill the position. As soon as she could, she'd be returning home, back to her own life.

It may not be the most extravagant life, but it was hers, nonetheless. The thought of her tiny apartment in Salem, and the amount of friends she could count on one hand, made her a little sad when surrounded by people born centuries before, who seemed to have hundreds of people who cared, loved, and looked out for one another.

Her parents had died before she even knew them, and her foster parents had never really bothered to exert themselves too much. And she'd never had what others would call close friends. Laughter pulled her attention back to Aedan, and she watched as Black Ben slapped him on the back, Ben throwing an odd look toward Gwen before both men walked off toward a group of tent-like structures that'd been erected for the games so that men could change and warm up, and women could relieve themselves. Abby narrowed her eyes on Ben's retreating back. What did that look mean toward her friend? Did Ben seek out Gwen in some way? Want her approval or attention?

"He doesn't fancy Aline, you know."

Gwen's statement startled her. "Who?" she asked, already dreading the answer. Was her attraction to Aedan obvious? Did she even have an attraction? She'd have to pull her libido in line if she wanted to remain anonymous.

"My brother has known the Grants all his life, and while he may flirt and tease the ladies of the house, he wouldn't trifle with any of them unless he was intending to ask for their hand."

"I told him to kiss the next woman that intrigued him enough to feel the smallest amount of affection. Do you think he'll listen to my advice?" Had she made a mistake asking him to do such a thing? Would he take her suggestion and run with it? Kissing anyone who was female, attractive to him, and in need of a husband? The thought of his lips on hers, how he'd ignited a fire that, damn it, wouldn't go out, not even hours after it had occurred, drove her wild with jealousy.

She was being irrational.

Gwen snorted. "Highly doubtful, but it may occur. A stolen kiss is harmless enough, I suppose, but I couldn't see him doing that without a lot of prior thought. He wouldn't want to give the women the wrong impression."

"He seems taken with Aline, though. What makes you think he's not?"

"As much as a match between them would be advantageous to both clans, she's far too young for him and would drive him mad within a month. Aedan's always liked more mature women. I think he realizes that should he marry the lass she'd drive him to the point of madness within a year."

Abby agreed. The young woman did seem a little immature and not overly friendly toward her own sex. She'd be a jealous wife, but then Abby was a jealous nothing-at-all. "What about Mae? I know her brother is looking for a suitable husband for her."

"Aye, but I don't think the word suitable should be associated with the man he has planned for her. Rory, the laird of Clan Kirk, is an awful man. Cold, distant, and cruel, as his ancestors were. Clan Kirk are not known for their kindness, but iron fists. To be married to such a man would be hell on earth."

Abby caught Mae's gaze and waved to the woman. She

looked happy among these people, a young woman who wanted what everyone did. Love, a happy, fulfilling life. That she could possibly be placed in danger because her brother was determined to be rid of her, filled Abby with dread and she frowned. She would tell Aedan of the man Mae loved and see if he could say something to her brother.

"I know what ye thinking, Abigail, and don't go gettin' involved. Clan Scot don't like bein' told what to do, and with any luck, the laird of Kirk will find another to tempt him and leave Mae alone."

"And if he doesn't?"

"They'll not be much we can do."

Abby stood and walked from the platform, as another two teams picked up the tug-of-war rope out in front of the gathered spectators. She walked toward the tents, wanting to go back to the castle, needing a little time to plan. She would speak to Aedan and see what he could do. She certainly couldn't stand around while an innocent young woman was led to her potential slaughter.

An arm shot out in front of her and pulled her into a tent. She blinked quickly to adjust her eyes to the dark, but the reaction of her body told her who had pulled her inside. "What are you doing?"

"Ye look fetching today, lass."

The deep baritone pulled at something profound in her chest and she relaxed. Today she'd dressed in a dark purple gown with white trim, wanting to look as nice as she could. She'd told herself it was pride that led her to have a servant help her with her hair. That the Highland Games were something she'd never see again, certainly not like these, even if twenty-first century people tried to re-enact them. She didn't want to admit the thought that Aedan may see her, like what he saw, and wish to steal another kiss.

"Thank you. Congratulations on your win."

Grinning, he nodded and her stomach flipped. "Maybe the fair lass will grant the winner a boon?"

"A boon?" she frowned, pretending she didn't know what he meant.

"A prize," he said, his hand sliding across her hip to sit against her back.

Abby bit her lip. Her body was on fire. His hand stroked across her spine, playing her like a musical instrument. Her clothing suddenly felt tight, constricting, and she needed air.

"What did you have in mind?" She hated how he made her voice sound breathless, full of need and desire. That it was exactly how she felt didn't matter. He wasn't for her. Not only was he a laird living in seventeenth century Scotland, he was too old for her, if she were to count the years between his birth and hers.

"I'd hoped," he said, leaning closer, his lips but a hair's breadth away, "that you would allow me to kiss ye again."

With a will of their own, her hands slid up his naked chest, his skin warm and soothing against her palms. She clasped the nape of his neck, leaned up on tippy-toe, and kissed him. "Like that?"

He smiled, keeping her hard against his body. Her own body flew into overdrive. Never before had she felt the kaleidoscope of feelings as she did with Aedan. Somehow, in some way, she finally knew what chemistry meant with another person, true, life changing emotion. And it was good.

He stared down at her, his eyes smoldering with desire and she shivered. "Aye, exactly like that."

Her fingers pulled him down for another kiss, and for a moment she forgot where they were. The kiss was nothing but raw hunger, a need that consumed them both. Hands clutched, bodies meshed, and mouths fused as the kiss turned hot and demanding, both of them wanting more, but unable to get close enough.

He hitched her higher against him, and through his kilt she could feel his desire. She wanted to weep, to wrap her legs about his waist and beg him to put them both out of their misery and take her here.

Instead, she gave him one last taste, and pulled back. "Good luck with the rest of the day's games, Aedan."

His breathing was rapid, his eyes a little shocked. She could understand the latter because so was she. If only he lived in her time they would have a lot of fun together, but he didn't, a fact she had to keep reminding herself.

"Where are ye going?" He clasped her arm to stop her from leaving.

"Aedan, I'm not for you and you know it. And while I enjoy kissing you—very much—I'm not lining up to be your wife. You need to leave me alone, and try and make a connection with a woman who is here."

He let her go and she saw the shutters come up, his defenses back in place. That man she could handle—the cold, calculating one who did everything by the rule book. But when he lowered his guard, and showed the real man inside, one who was considerate, gentle, kind, and so damn passionate, she had no chance at keeping her feelings from getting involved.

"I never asked ye to be my wife."

His words were like a slap, cold and harsh, and she knew why he said them. She'd hurt his pride. Hurt his heart a little, even, but wasn't it better to keep him at a distance now, than form attachments to each other, the kind that would make her want to stay and never return home?

"I know." She turned to leave and pulled back the canvas. "Don't waste your time on me, Aedan. It won't end well for either of us." She left and tears pricked her eyes with each step she took toward the castle. No longer did she have the stomach to watch the day's games. All she wanted was some peace and quiet, a chance to gather her wits and decide on what to do the next time she ran into him.

Just the thought of him made regret eat her alive. She wanted to see how their chemistry developed, where it would take them both. To a future together? A family, perhaps? Who knew? But it was something she'd never find out. How typical of her luck that she would meet a man who made her feel, for the first time since David's death, and she couldn't grab him with both hands and never let him go.

She'd always thought she'd been born under an unlucky star, and now she was damn well positive of it.

...

Aedan ground his teeth and stormed out onto the field, the games going on about him as he walked in no direction at all. He shook his head at his own stupidity. He should have left the lass well alone. She wasn't of his class, and certainly wasn't what he required in a wife. He needed a wife from a strong, proud family like his own, with access to a large army, that would be willing to support his cause against the O'Cains. Abigail Cross had none of those things.

And her archery was atrocious.

He stopped and ran a hand through his hair. It didn't matter that she was the first lass he'd ever felt anything for. In the short time he'd known her, she'd woven her special magic around him, each day pulling him a little more into her world. A warm, bright, open, and happy world full of laughter and joy, a light that beckoned him from the dark places being a laird of a clan often took him.

He wanted to join her there, to be a part of such a carefree life, but as laird it wasn't possible. Abigail was right. It was foolish of him to want her, and perhaps he should refrain from kissing her. It would, after all, only turn out to be nothing but desire, a passing lust brought on by being chaste for too long.

Aline smiled at him, and he headed toward her. It was time he listened to the lass from the future and secured his own in the past. No more desiring things that would never be his. The bonny Grant lass sidled up to him, and he whispered how pretty she looked.

She tittered up at him, and he supposed she was very beautiful, if not a little too sure of the fact. And if she proved herself in the arts befitting the station of laird's wife, then he'd marry her, as soon as any other.

After all, what did it matter, as long as the woman warmed his bed, produced heirs, could sew, and make order of his home? What difference did it make if his chosen was vain? There wasn't a consequence for that.

● ● ●

Aedan sat chewing the game bird Cook had covered in bread crumbs accompanied with an assortment of hot, steaming vegetables, and it tasted like cow dung in his mouth. Aline, seated beside him, kept brushing her breast against his arm in an attempt to seduce him, and normally he'd take pleasure in the flirting banter of the lass, but not tonight. This evening, his attention kept snapping to Abigail, deep in conversation with Black Ben. Their laughter, the guests around them laughing and enjoying themselves more than he, was starting to grate on his nerves.

He'd never wanted to smash the skull of his closest ally and friend like he did right at this very moment. In his wisdom, he'd changed the seating arrangements and ensured Abigail was placed in the main hall, beneath the laird's table, to dine with his clansmen, like the commoner she was. He hadn't thought Ben would be only too pleased to take a seat beside her.

As for Aline, seated next to him for what seemed too long already, she played the role of future laird's wife very well, gloating over his people, smiling smugly at Abigail whenever she could. The crowing actions of the lass made him loathe her. She would never do, and it had been a mistake to allow her to believe she did.

He was a fool.

"Thank ye again for having me join ye tonight, Aedan. I so like the company of my equals."

He raised his brow and took a sip of wine. "'Tis my pleasure. I'm honored to have yer company." Gwen, seated beside him, scoffed and tried to hide her reaction with a cough. Throwing her a glare, he took another sip of wine and hoped Aline hadn't heard her.

"I'm looking forward to tomorrow. I love riding."

The way she said "riding" gave him pause and he caught her eye, not missing the seductive tease hidden in their dark depths. *Has this woman, too, slept with a man and knows of the delights a couple can have together?* He nodded, "Aye, a ride about the lands will be good for the ladies of the house. Ye be sure to let me know how it goes."

"Are ye not coming then?" She frowned; her bottom lip pouting a little with the knowledge the men wouldn't be joining them. "I didn't think we'd be unaccompanied."

"Ye won't be. I'll have men with ye to ensure your safety, but there are clan matters I must attend to that would only bore the womenfolk, so best to keep ye happy and occupied."

Aline made a whining sound, and Aedan knew in that moment he could never marry the lass. He wanted a biddable wife, not someone who would grate on his patience after only a few hours. He pinched the bridge of his nose, feeling a slight thumping above his eyes.

"Well, I'm sure that's appropriate, then. And, of course, I'll have Gwen and your pleasant houseguest Abigail to keep me company."

She paused, her hand coming to sit on his knee. He stilled.

"What a shame it is that the poor lass is so unfortunate with her looks. Why, I believe you'll find it almost impossible to marry her off to anyone, unless she's blessed with a fortune."

Aedan ground his teeth, hating that the viperish words were spoken out of jealousy. Abigail Cross was the last woman he'd ever call unfortunate looking, and that Aline made such a rude, untrue statement only made the beautiful lass seated beside him more ugly than a rotting corpse. "'Tis luck that it'll not be you then who'll be saddled with her." He smiled at her shock before she laughed to cover her unease.

"Quite right. To wake up next to that sight each morn would be torture indeed."

Aedan refused to be caught in any more of her nonsense. Instead, he turned his attention to his clansmen before him, one table in particular. He willed Abigail to look at him, to smile, nod, anything, but she ignored him.

Black Ben picked up her hand and kissed it, her laughter ringing out, both of them enjoying the night immensely.

The sound of his chair scraping against the flagstone floor finally caught her gaze. That she looked at him with little affection or care shouldn't annoy, but it did. In fact, the sooner he left, the better. No one wanted to see a laird throw a woman over his shoulder and carry her from the room.

Not bothering to pay his regards to his dinner companions, he headed toward the anteroom. Fury at himself, at Black Ben, at Abigail, made his vision glaze over with red. Once the door closed and he was alone, he poured himself a large draft of whisky and downed it in one swallow, before repeating the action numerous times.

Anything to take his mind off the fact he wanted to murder and kiss to madness the lass from the future who wouldn't be tamed.

Chapter Eleven

Her ass hurt. The fact that the horse in front of her kept letting off disgusting smells and popping noises didn't help, either. Abigail shifted again in the saddle, trying to alleviate the uncomfortable ache that had settled there after the first mile, but nothing seemed to work.

How much longer were they expected to ride? All the way to bloody London?

Right at this moment she hated Scotland with a passion, and coming in a close second was the idiot who'd thought riding horses would be a good idea. Namely, Aedan.

The women around her chatted and laughed, every one of them enjoying the outing. She wasn't. All she wanted to do was go back to the castle where she could rub her bottom in the privacy of her room.

"Are ye alright, Abigail?"

She cringed. "Not really. How much longer do we have to ride these beasts?"

Gwen laughed and pulled her horse alongside Abigail's. "Only another mile or so and we'll break for lunch. Aedan has organized a light repast for us all on the northern hill overlooking the keep. Some of the men not competing today will be there, too."

"So your beau will be there." It wasn't a question, just a statement of fact that was obvious by the loving look on Gwen's face at the mention that Braxton would be present.

"Perhaps." Gwen grinned, quiet a moment before she said, "But really, are ye well? You seem to be in pain."

"I want to walk. My bottom is so sore. I've never ridden a horse before."

"I'm so sorry. I never even thought. I assumed you'd be used to it, but, of course, you're not." Gwen rubbed her back in an attempt to comfort her. "I promise, 'tis not too much longer."

Abby smiled. "It's okay. I'll survive."

And she did. Only another half hour and they arrived at the designated picnic spot. The view on top of the hill overlooked endless miles of heather-covered fields, the purple blossoms shimmering like water on the top of a loch on a windy day.

The closer they came, the more Abby's bottom hurt and her desire to be off her mount became almost unbearable. Climbing the last few feet to the top of the hill, her horse seemed to slow and she had the urge to kick it into a trot, anything to get there faster and dismount.

She stopped beside a man she'd seen take the horses from the clansmen at the castle, flipped her leg over the back of the horses rump, and slid off the side. Not used to the position she'd been sitting in the last couple of hours, or the fact her bottom had become numb, her legs gave out on her as her feet touched the ground and she landed on her rear with an *oomph*.

A pair of strong arms came around her from behind, eliciting a shock of awareness through her body. "Are ye alright, lass?"

Aedan's words, kind and soft enough for only her to hear, whispered against her ear. She shivered as he helped her to stand. Abby turned, meeting his concerned gaze, a gaze that also held something she didn't want to acknowledge. "I am, thank you. I'm merely a little saddle sore."

"Aye, I can see that." He stepped into her space, bringing them almost nose to nose. The horse beside them ensured a little privacy, but not a lot. "Let me know if ye need any help feeling better."

Her breathing increased, her stomach doing a little flip. What she wouldn't do to be able to take him up on such an offer, to lean into him, touch him, allow him to rub her sore bottom until it felt better. Instead she patted him, trying to ignore how her hand wanted to run up his chest and curve about his nape to pull him down for a kiss. "Thanks for the offer, but I'll be okay. A short break from the horse is all I need."

He reached around and patted her ass and she gasped. "Let me know if ye change your mind."

Abby felt her mouth open as he winked at her and walked off to join a group of men. Had the stiff-upper-lipped Aedan just smacked her on the ass? And why would he, when only last night all through dinner he'd sat at the dais glowering at her and flirting with Aline?

Not that she didn't deserve his daggers. She'd purposely teased him, laughed at everything his friend Black Ben had said, and had pretended she was enjoying herself immensely. What she'd been feeling inside was another matter entirely. She hated seeing the snobbish, spoiled little Aline seated beside him—looking up at him with doe eyes and wandering hands. Aedan had placed her at the table before the dais, practically putting her in her place, and she'd done everything in her power to make him regret that choice.

Never in her life had Abby been so jealous of another. Aedan MacLeod was turning her into a deranged little green monster. Her behavior was shameful, and regret pierced her with its jagged edge. Aedan wasn't for her, how many times did she need to repeat that mantra before she understood it? Believed it, even.

She followed him and sat beside Mae. The women were talking of the games that would continue tomorrow and what the competition would be. Eating a piece of bread, she listened with only half interest when she noticed Gwen wasn't anywhere to be seen.

She caught Aedan looking about as well. He seemed to have noticed the same.

And then Gwen walked from behind some trees, and she chuckled at Aedan's glower at his sister. Well, at least she wasn't the only one getting in trouble by the man. It made a nice change.

"Who do ye think will win the caber toss tomorrow, Gwen? Ye know, your brother holds the record for the longest throw," Aline said, smiling.

"Aye, I did know that," Gwen said, as she rejoined the group and sat down.

Abby desperately tried to think of what sort of competition caber toss was before the conversation went any further, but failed. "Can I ask what the caber toss actually is?"

Aline snorted, but didn't answer.

"'Tis where the men toss a large tapered caber or pole and see how far they can throw it," Gwen said, handing her a cup of mulled wine.

"Aye. No doubt the men will be sporting a few splinters tomorrow eve," Aline said, sighing for dramatic effect that only brought out the bitch within Abby.

"Lucky the men have you to see to their wounds, Aline." Abby took a slice of ham and added it to her bread, ignoring the girl's glare. She looked at the food that'd been packaged for them and would've given anything for a jar of mayonnaise to be included. "Does tomorrow's contest earn prize money as well?"

Gwen grinned, her lips a lot redder than they had been when they'd arrived. "Whatever man wins gets a kiss from a lucky fair maiden. It's all very proper, don't look so scandalized, Abigail."

Abby's eyes widened. "Is that allowed? It's one thing for a kiss to occur in private, but in front of everyone. Won't the fathers of these girls be outraged?"

Aline chuckled, the high timbre of her voice grating on Abby's nerves. "Why would they? It's only a small kiss, like you'd give a family member."

Mae scoffed. "Well, I'll not be putting my name down as a possible candidate."

Since the woman was already in love Abby understood why. Mae would never betray the man she intended to marry, no matter what her brother said. Abby hoped the woman received her wish.

"I will be," Aline said, throwing a heated gaze toward Aedan. "I have high hopes as to who the winner will be."

Gwen scoffed. "I do not doubt it."

Aline glared at Gwen and Abby smiled, taking another bite of her sandwich. "You were saying the event causes splinters. How bad can they be?"

"Quite nasty. The wooden poles they're throwing have not been smoothed, so it's a hazard the men must deal with. Last year, Aedan had one that had to be cut out. He required stitches afterward. Ghastly looking wound, if ever I saw one."

The thought of blood and bits of wood sticking out of skin turned Abby's stomach and she put down her lunch. "It sounds barbaric."

Aline sighed, rolling her eyes. "Abigail, if you're to live

in the Highlands, wounds, in most cases more severe than a mere splinter, are as common as the heather on these hills. You best get used to them."

Gwen glared at Aline but Abby nodded. The girl was right, but it didn't change the fact that she'd never been good around blood. "Well, all I can hope is tomorrow no such wounds occur, but then, since you're such a capable woman who will tend the wounded with great enthusiasm, the competitors are truly fortunate that you're here to help, aren't they?"

Abby didn't hide the sarcasm in her tone, which unfortunately seemed to be lost on Aline as she only nodded and smiled.

Not long after, they began to pack up the lunch, the leftovers were given to the men who had looked after the mob of horses to finish off.

Her mount, a placid mare that stood at her head height, looked more imposing than when she'd first mounted it back at the castle. She pulled the animal over to a fallen tree and stood on the wood to help get her foot in the stirrup. With one foot in, she jumped to gather momentum and felt a hand clasp her ass and push her into the air, and onto the saddle. She sucked in a startled breath.

Where Aedan's hand touched, her skin burned. Her body longed for more of the same. For his hands to slide over every ounce of her flesh and touch, tease, learn every curve of her being.

Damn the man. She couldn't be like this with him.

"You shouldn't touch me like that. Someone may see."

He watched her, the heat in his eyes making her ache.

"And if no one was watching? Would ye let me touch ye then?"

And there it was. The proposal of what he really wanted. *Her*.

Abby pushed a flyaway piece of hair from her eye and

looked between the horse's ears, anywhere but at the man who consumed her every thought, inflamed her every need and desire.

There was no doubt he could fulfill her every requirement in the bedroom, and expertly, too. She fiddled with the reins. "Does it really matter what I'd allow?" She did look at him then, his face the most appealing one she'd ever seen. Strong bones and eyes of deep green to make the grass weep with envy.

"It does to me." His hand came to sit on her foot, his fingers sliding up her ankle to clasp the back of her calf.

Abby took a calming breath. The man was dangerous. "Right now there are three women who'd make a good match for you. All of them with breeding that surpasses my own. Not to mention, they're born in this century."

"I don't give a blast about the other women. I want you."

Her mouth dried at the words. Aedan moved closer still, his hand sliding farther up her leg, his fingers massaging her flesh. His touch felt wonderful, and she wondered what else he was good at. Abby shut her eyes, her body thrumming with suppressed desire. "Stop it," she said, no conviction in her tone. "We could be seen."

"Meet me in the anteroom on ye return. There are things we need to discuss." He stepped back and she immediately felt the loss of his touch.

She wanted him next to her, touching her, looking only at her, as if she were the single most important person in his life, and the thought gave her pause. She nodded. "Fine. I'll meet you there, but it won't change anything. Surely you understand that."

He didn't reply, but slapped her horse on the bottom, sending it walking forward. Abby followed the other riders, her mind lost in thought. In only a few hours she would have to tell Aedan yet again to leave her well alone, to look for another and stop wasting his time with her.

It sounded so easy.

But it was so not.

To tell Aedan that she wouldn't sleep with him when her body totally wanted to do just that was near impossible. Truth be told, having some sexy good times with Aedan was all that occupied her mind. Each time she saw him, her eyes seemed to be glued to his ass or abs. Although she'd never had a short-lived fling before, she could have one now. At least she'd never have to worry about running into Aedan in the future and having that awkward I-didn't-think-I'd-see-you-again conversation. And what was wrong with having a little fun with the man before she left?

Nothing, when she actually considered it…

•••

Abigail hadn't turned up to their arranged meeting, nor had she come downstairs for dinner that eve. He'd sent word to Cook to send a meal up for her, and was informed she'd requested a bath.

He couldn't blame the lass for wanting to soothe her muscles. Gwen had informed him she'd never ridden before, and when organizing the event for the ladies, he'd not given her comfort a second thought.

But that thought had soon been overrun with another. That of Abigail, soaping her alabaster skin, running the soap over her breasts, her stomach, her…

Black Ben slapped him on the back. "I've not seen that look on yer face for many a year. Tell me which lass has been lucky enough to capture the attention of Laird MacLeod."

Aedan sat back in his chair, meeting his closest friend's knowing smile with a dismissive laugh. "Ah, there are many a lass here that have captured my attention, why should it be only one?"

Ben scoffed, the sound mocking, and Aedan frowned. "Ye lie. I saw ye the other eve, glaring at me like ye wanted to put a knife through my gullet. I'll not be forgettin' it, ye know. After all the years I've known ye, to think that I would steal a wee lassie away from ye was deeply upsettin'."

"Do ye actually expect me to believe what ye're saying?"

"No," Ben said and laughed, "but it sounded good and ye know I like the sound of me own voice."

The tables were pushed to the side, the gathered clans preparing the area for more dancing. "I will find a wife at these games, and must keep my options open." A servant ran up the stairs, and Aedan wondered if she was calling on Abigail. Was she well, or was she sore from today's ride and needed a tisane? He looked for his sister. He'd have Gwen take something up to Abigail to make her feel better.

Aedan stopped his thoughts before they became any more alarming. Aye, the lass was bonny, made him feel things no lass had in a very long time, but she'd made it perfectly clear she wasn't interested in him. That her body and her beautiful eyes told him something else was beside the point.

Black Ben nodded, taking a sip of mead. "In all seriousness, Aedan, she's a pleasing lass, young enough to give ye bairns, and bonny enough to keep ye loyal for a time. You'd be wise to stake a claim before someone else does."

Like you? The thought left him angry and not a little ashamed. His friend was clever enough to know not to touch Abigail, and certainly not to seduce the girl. His hands fisted at the thought of anyone laying claim to her, of touching her sweet flesh, kissing those lips laced with sin.

He pushed back his chair and stood. "I'll see ye tomorrow."

"Aye, have a good night." The salacious smirk on Ben's face required no reply.

Aedan strode from the room, taking the stairs two at a

time. The night was cool, the passage that led to his room darker than it ought to be, since the sconces hadn't been lit. A servant shut Abigail's door and bobbed a curtsy as she passed him.

He stopped at Abigail's door, contemplating whether to knock or not. He should keep going, leave the lass alone, let her go…but something kept him standing there, not allowing his body to stride the remainder of the way to his room.

The sound of sloshing water sounded behind the wood and he leaned his head on the door, wishing it was open so he could see her. His imagination ran wild with the thought of what she'd look like naked, water wrapping about her like he wished he could.

He'd never been more jealous of an inanimate object in his life.

Fool.

He walked off, then changing his mind, turned about, and strode into her room just as she stood, one long arm reaching for a drying cloth on a chair beside the tub.

His imagination hadn't done her justice. She had magnificent breasts that would fit in his palm nicely, thin waist and legs that went on for miles. Water dripped from her, the little droplets running between spaces he could only dream of tasting, licking, kissing…

"Perhaps you'd like to take a photo, Aedan. It'll last longer."

He didn't understand what she'd said, but by her tone of voice he knew she was being sarcastic. Instead of looking away, he crossed his arms and continued to admire the view. "If a photo means I could capture how you look for all time, I'd only be too willing to do so."

A rosy blush ran up her chest and onto her neck and he smiled. He shut the door, and walking over to her, helped her out of the tub.

She contemplated his outstretched hand before taking it and stepping out. Whether the gods were on his side, he'd never know, but Abigail slipped, and the lass, forgetting all decorum, grabbed his shoulders as he clasped her waist.

Her very naked waist…

His body roared with need. The smell of lavender and something else that was only Abigail, assailed his senses. Of their own accord, his hands slid over her smooth, unblemished flesh, tracing up her spine, until he pulled her closer than he ought.

Her labored breaths pushed her breasts against his chest, and he cursed the fact he still wore his tunic and kilt. The need to have her against him, skin on skin, was unlike anything he'd ever known. His hand slid over her bottom and he clenched one buttock, eliciting a gasp from her.

"We shouldn't do this," she said, leaning closer and kissing him softly.

His cock hardened, and he lifted her, undulating against her core. He moaned, taking her lips in a searing kiss, wanting her with a need that scared him with its intensity.

His body burned for her, his mind in chaos over what he felt for the lass in his arms. She wrapped her legs about his waist, her body hard against his. "Aye, we should." Aedan walked over to the bed, kneeling on the animal furs as he laid her down and came over her. Her dark locks spread out about her face like a halo, an angel sent from heaven to tempt him into sin.

And if sin was where Abigail was taking him, he'd gladly follow. Her fingers slid up his chest, up his neck, to clasp his nape. He kissed her long and deep, and she matched him with every stroke.

He was enthralled.

Aedan pulled away and ripped off his tunic, his kilt soon followed, before he stood at the end of the bed and looked at her, enjoying the beautiful woman who was willing to give herself to him. She lay open to him. No modesty, only raw need. Her glistening mons begged for his touch and so he knelt at the end of the bed, slid her down until he was able to taste and tease the very essence of her.

She was sweet, clean, and delicate. He flicked his tongue across her excited nubbin and grabbed her thighs to keep her still. Again and again he lathed her flesh, delving as deep as he could with his tongue, before teasing her with long, soft glides of his lips.

He nibbled her thigh, kissing his small love bites before making his way up her body, her flat stomach, breasts, her beaded nipples, taking his time to pay homage to such greatness.

"Aedan," her soft plea made him as hard as a rock, but when her hand clasped his flesh and stroked, he lost all sense of control.

"Aye, like that, lass." Pleasure rocked him. Her touch was soft but sure, driving him almost to the point of completion, but with enough control not to.

And he wasn't going to come on her hand, when what he really wanted was to be inside her. Take them both to where their second kiss had brought them.

It was like their meeting was written in the sands of time, was meant to be.

He slid his tongue up her neck, kissing beneath her ear. She shivered beneath him, breathing heavily. He settled himself between her legs, undulating against her wet core, teasing them both with his touch.

He grabbed her hands, holding them above her head, their fingers entwined. Her breasts pushed out and he leaned down and kissed their rosy peaks. Wanted to make tonight memorable, pleasurable for her. She was beautiful, the most beautiful woman he'd ever met.

He couldn't get enough of her.

•••

Abby moaned as Aedan's tongue stroked her breasts with a care she'd not thought possible of him. It seemed opposite to how he was in everyday life. A man of no-nonsense, duty, and honor.

And it was this softer side of him she was afraid of seeing, of getting attached to. He was above her and she opened her eyes, their gazes locking as inch by delicious inch he pushed into her.

She strained against him, wanting to free her hands to bring him down for a kiss. She moaned his name, a plea for him to do more than fill her. She wrapped her legs about his hips and pulled him into her.

He stayed where he was, ignored her silent appeal, and continued to take her with long, slow strokes.

She'd not had a very good look at him before he took her, but by the feel of him, the delectable sensations sparking through her body, this Highlander was perfect in *every* way.

"Let me touch you." Again she pulled on her hands and this time he let her go. She tugged him down onto her, needing to feel skin-on-skin, the graze of his chest hairs against her breasts. Feel the sheen of sweat that covered both their bodies.

His back tensed beneath her hands, the muscles flexing with every thrust. A mirror above them would be perfect right at this moment. He would look so hot reflected in that way, demanding delicious things from her body.

His lips took hers in a searing kiss, and she lost all thought. All she was left with was an overwhelming feeling of rightness. Shivers rocked her body, her core thrumming with the promise of a fantastic orgasm that was building within her with every stroke.

Abby sighed as his thrusts increased, his hands clasping her ass and pulling her higher against him. He was so deep, pushing against that special spot inside that so few men had ever reached. Her fingers scored down his back, holding him to her with a desperation that scared her.

"Don't stop what you're doing." Her body trembled with the first shocks of her orgasm and she moaned. "Aedan, keep going."

He did, kissing her deeply, matching his tongue's movements to that of his cock. And then there was no control, he took her with little regard, demanding that she, too, reach the completion he was so close to.

And she did. She broke the kiss as her orgasm tore through her. For a moment, Abby couldn't breathe, so powerful were the tremors that took her breath away.

Aedan continued to take her, her body wrapped around him like a second skin, before he pulled out and emptied himself against her mons, the action making her jump, her body still so sensitive from their love-making.

He came to lay beside her, pulling her against his chest, his hand idly stroking her back as their breathing slowly returned to normal. "Are ye alright, lass? I wasn't too rough, I hope."

She smiled against his chest, kissing a little mole that sat in the middle of his breastbone. "Not at all. I feel quite sated."

...

He chuckled and jumped from the bed. She squealed as he picked her up and walked over to the bathtub, stepping in and sitting down with her on his lap. The water was tepid, but with the fire roaring in the grate it was far from cold.

Aedan searched beside his legs, before he found the soap he was looking for. He lathered it between his hands and then began to wash Abigail. With the friction of the soap and water, her body felt like silk, all smooth lines and his to relish.

His hand captured a breast, making sure to wash them well. Her head rested on his shoulder, her breathing more heavy with every minute that passed.

"You're so beautiful. I don't think I've ever seen skin as unblemished as yours."

She turned to face him, resting her chin atop his chest. "You know, when you're not going on about what constitutes the perfect wife and are instead enjoying yourself, you're quite likeable." She chuckled, and he basked in the honest sound of it. His feet tangled with hers, their bodies sliding against each other in unvoiced need. He bit back a groan as she pushed against his swollen manhood.

"I'm glad ye think so, lass. And I must declare, when you're not arguing every point I make, you're less vile yourself."

She flicked water on his face, and he pulled her up to straddle him. Her eyes widened when he slid against her core, teasing them both for what was to come. She tipped up his face with a finger and caught his gaze. "What we're doing here changes nothing. You know I can't stay, don't you?"

"Aye, I do."

"And you're all right with that? I mean, doesn't it go against your principles to be with a woman and not marry her?"

Sliding his hand up her back, he pulled her close. "You're not like all women. And secondly, I've been with plenty of women before and not married them." She studied him for a moment, her features not giving anything away. He didn't want to delve into the reason he wanted to know every thought she possessed, her ideals and beliefs. Or why the thought of her leaving left him a little panicked.

"I'm portraying a guest of yours, so this will have to remain a secret. No one can know what we're doing together."

He grinned. "Are ye saying this is going to continue?"

Hell, he hoped so. Just the thought of stolen moments with this lass set his blood to burn. The castle had a lot of different places built for such trysts. She'd never be safe from him.

"I hope it does." Her teeth bit her bottom lip, and he stifled a groan. He pushed against her, her hands threading at his nape. "I think I could get used to this type of pleasure quite quickly," she said.

Lifting her, he guided her upon him. She fit him perfectly, her body clamping around him like a vise. They both moaned as he took her mouth in a powerful kiss, their tongues mimicking their bodies. He helped her to ride him hard and deep, not allowing either of them the time to breathe.

She pulled at his hair, her fingers scoring his skull, and he loved it. She leaned over him in the tub, riding him, taking his mouth as she pleased. He lost himself in her golden brown eyes; eyes that pulled him into her soul and beckoned him to stay there forever. Heat rushed to his groin and pleasure exploded between them as she rode him to orgasm, taking her pleasure without reserve.

He panted, his breaths coming in quick succession and still he hadn't had enough of her. The word "trouble" floated through his mind, and he smiled.

If Abigail Cross was trouble, then he was going to get himself into a lot of it.

Chapter Twelve

Abby didn't think watching men throw a tree trunk could be so alluring, and yet, seeing Aedan's muscles flex, the strain on his body, reminded her of the night before. Of him above her, enjoying her as much as she'd savored him.

She sighed and received a curious look from Gwen. She smiled, not wanting to tell anyone of their affair. Wanting to keep the dirty, delicious little secret all to herself. She may be stuck in medieval Scotland, but she was definitely having a little fun while here. And last night had been very amusing, lots of times.

In the small hours of the morning, they'd agreed their affair was just a little entertainment, a way in which two people who found themselves attracted to one another could relieve some stress, enjoy each other's company. Have lots of hot sex.

This type of relationship would at least make what little time she had left here easier to bear. With the implant in her arm, she was covered from getting pregnant, and although there weren't any condoms available to use, Aedan had assured her he had no illness. It was a risk, and one she wouldn't normally take, but with Aedan, all bets were off. She may go to hell for it, but she wanted him. Her attraction wasn't going to be denied any longer, and all she could hope was that he was as healthy as he seemed.

Gwen sidled up next to her and sat. "You're happy today. Do tell me the Highlands have finally wrapped around ye soul and held ye captive."

Only the Highlander on the field, laughing and taking pleasure in the competition, was holding her captive. "I must admit I am having a good time. I may even thank you for it one day."

Gwen laughed. "And I'll gladly say you're welcome."

Another competitor took the wooden pole and started to jiggle it in his arms, trying to find a comfortable position to throw it from. When he did cast it out in front of him, it was a long way off the distance Aedan had reached.

"Your brother seems to be winning this event." Abby looked at the men to follow the last competitor. All were brawny, muscular types, but they lacked Aedan's height, his large broad shoulders, and strong thighs. Or maybe she was biased now… Either way, Aedan would surely win.

"Yes, and so he'll have to steal a kiss from a willing lady."

Abby frowned, having forgotten what the prize was. Excitement thrummed in her veins that Aedan might touch her again. That she'd get to feel those soft, sinfully addictive lips once more. Last night seemed so many hours ago. "What if the lady doesn't wish to kiss the winner?"

"She'll either give him her hand or cheek and it'll be over." Gwen grinned. "We'll have to wait and see."

The remainder of the competitors finished their throws. Black Ben came to sit with them as Aedan was announced the winner.

"Now we'll see who Aedan has taken a liking to," Ben

said, smiling at Abby, which made her wonder if he knew of their hook-up.

Abby nodded, feeling a little queasy that the time had come for him to choose. And what if it wasn't her? "Who do you think he'll pick?" She couldn't help but ask, and even though she knew she shouldn't care, she did. Aedan kissing anyone but her left an awful simmering anger in the pit of her gut. She pushed away the thought that she was jealous. She was definitely not that. They had agreed their liaison was to be of a short duration due to her going home. No emotions. Just sex.

"I'm not sure. I've seen ye two whispering in dark corners a lot, maybe it'll be you." Gwen grinned and looked back toward the field. Abby didn't think it would be her, even though a little part of her hoped it was. Clansmen slapped his shoulder, others yelling and lifting goblets of mead in celebration that the day's events were over.

Aedan walked toward where they sat, an array of clan members looking on with interest. He looked over the crowd and her stomach fluttered. But instead of coming to her, he bowed before Aline. The young woman stood, staring up at him with awe, and Abby went from hope to devastation in an instant. Watching what was about to take place was like a slow motion horror film. She was a deer before headlights, mesmerized by the sight of something that could kill her... figuratively speaking.

He leaned down and kissed her quickly on the cheek, but true to her character, Aline wasn't content with such mediocre affection. She jumped into his embrace, hands wrapping about his neck, and took the kiss to a whole new level.

The clansmen shouted out, making bawdy remarks and Abby stood, having seen enough. "It's been a long day, Gwen. I'm going to head up to my room before dinner." Out of her peripheral vision she could see the kiss had ended and Aedan was walking Aline toward her father.

"Are ye alright? You're not feeling ill, I hope."

"No." She shook her head. "I'm fine. Just tired, I think. I'll see you in the hall later."

Abby threaded her way through the crowd and made her way up to the castle as quickly as she could. She blamed the lump in her throat on a forthcoming cold. It certainly wasn't from seeing the man who'd left her bed only hours before, kissing another woman.

Well, he wouldn't be sharing her bed again, that's for sure.

...

"So, is ye plan working then, lass?"

Ben watched with amusement as Gwen turned toward him and smiled smugly. "I do believe Abigail Cross is as jealous and green as the grass. Did ye see the devastation on her face the moment Aedan kissed Aline? My plan is working out perfectly."

Ben chuckled, shaking his head. "So the lass has agreed to stay?"

Gwen squirmed on her seat, a slight blush on her face. "No, I haven't had that assurance from her as yet, but I shall. Why, she's half in love with my brother already."

Ben watched Abigail storm back toward the castle, a proud tilt to her chin. "If Aedan keeps kissing other lasses like that, I doubt you'll see any wedding other than Aline's take place. She's a minx."

Gwen sighed. "Aline is definitely a problem. She needs a husband but has, for whatever reason, fixated on Aedan. If only she had someone else to occupy her time."

A cold chill swept up Ben's spine. The heat of Gwen's gaze burned up the side of his neck, and he refused to meet her gaze. "Perhaps," is all he managed as a reply.

She clasped his arm. "Look at me, Ben."

He fought the pull of her beautiful features as long as he could, before, like when they were kids, he was unable to deny her anything. "No."

She smiled, laughing up at him. "Please, dearest. You're perfect for the position. Just think of all the fun ye could have."

"No." He clenched his jaw, refusing to do her bidding. Seduce a maiden. By God, he was a man, but not an idiot. "I won't do it."

"Just kiss her, then. Ravish her to the point that she'll forget about my brother."

"My ravishing didn't make you forget Braxton." The moment the words were torn from his mouth he wished them back. She paled and pulled back. Damn it. "Forgive me, Gwen. I dinna mean…" his words trailed off when nothing witty or defusing came to mind.

"We would not suit, Ben, whereas Braxton and I have an understanding."

He nodded, clenching his jaw at the thought of Gwen marrying a man so worthy of her it made his temper fire. If only Braxton was corrupt in some way, abusive, anything that would give reason to kiss her again and steal her away from him. But he was not. He was as good as men got.

"Just kiss her, ye say?" Her eyes lit up with joy, and he knew he'd never be able to deny her anything. "Nothing else?"

"Nay, nothing. Just show her what it is that beckons her to others. Show her that Aedan isn't all there is to sample and enjoy."

Ben cursed, but nodded. "Aye, I will. Mayhap my kisses will affect her more than you. She could be my grand match."

Gwen laughed, kissing his cheek quickly, leaving a trail of heat that shot to his chest. "I wish you all the best. Thank you, my friend. I'm forever in your debt."

He stood, needing some distance from her. "No, you're

not. I'll do this out of friendship." *And love...*

•••

Later that night, Abby paced her room, counting down the minutes until she headed downstairs. Her stomach rumbled, reminding her, yet again, she was starving. She hadn't eaten much at lunch, and then seeing Aedan kiss someone else had turned her off food altogether, but now...now she was pissed.

How dare he?

A knock sounded on her door, and she opened it to find Gwen standing there. "Are ye ready?"

"Yes." They walked down to the great hall in relative silence, and Abby wondered where Aedan's new favorite lass, Aline, would be seated, probably on his lap, knowing the forward little chit. Although, after what she'd done with him the night before, she hardly had the right to call Aline forward.

If anything, Abby had been the one who'd crossed the line. She should never have slept with him. He was a product of his time and she should've remembered that, before getting involved. A man who took pleasure when and where he could, before moving on without a backward glance.

She stopped mid-step and Gwen halted a little way ahead, looking back at her with concern. "Are ye alright, Abigail?"

Abby nodded, but she wasn't all right. She was jealous. Not bunny-boiling-mad-jealous like Glen Close in *Fatal Attraction*, but still jealous of anyone who dared get close enough to Aedan and kiss him.

The emotion wasn't welcome. For crying out loud, she was a modern, twenty-first century woman. A future museum curator, a smart, educated woman and damn it, she couldn't allow herself to develop feelings for this man. Perhaps, if she'd been more liberated with her sexual exploits and had indulged in a few one-night stands, this complicated situation with the laird might be more simple.

But the truth of the matter was she'd always been in relationships with the men she slept with. As modern as she was, sex wasn't just sex for her. It meant something. Even if that something was minimal. But in Aedan's case, it didn't seem like his emotions were engaged at all.

Shit!

Rallying herself, they continued on into the bustling hall, some clansmen already well on their way to being blind drunk. Normally, the sight would make her laugh. After all, she wasn't a prude, it was good to let your hair down every now and then, but tonight wasn't one of those nights.

Tonight, she was annoyed with Aedan *and* herself. Everything people did aggravated her more than it should. She didn't want to be rude, and she knew her face sported an unwelcoming glower, no matter how much she wanted to snap out of the temper the kiss between Aline and Aedan had caused. She liked the blasted laird more than was safe.

Aedan sat at the dais, Black Ben seated to his right, both of them eating and laughing at something Aline had said, who was, predictably, seated to Aedan's left.

He had to choose a wife, so why not Aline? It was never going to be Abigail, no matter how much she feared she wanted him. If only she'd been born in a different time, then perhaps, she could be his wife.

The ache in her chest told the truth, that seeing Aedan with another hurt like hell. At that moment, she regretted sleeping with him, allowing herself to get close enough to care.

Damn it.

"You're sitting here with me tonight," Gwen said, motioning to a table on the hall floor. Abby sat and thanked a young serving girl who ladled out some broth, another pouring her wine. As much as the food smelled delicious, the wine sweet and refreshing, it all turned to sawdust in her mouth. She didn't like that her and Aedan's time together was a secret and had to remain so. Abby wanted to stand and shout from the rooftops that he was hers and no one else's.

A ridiculous, fanciful idea that she dismissed.

She clasped the table to stop herself from doing anything stupid. Aedan had been truthful from the beginning about what he wanted, what his clan needed. And so, too, had she been honest, stating that no matter what they did it wouldn't change anything. Never had he included her in the long-term and vice versa.

She ate with haste, hoping to finish dinner quickly. Abby conversed as much as she could with a clansman from Clan Ross. He was an older gentleman, and had many a tale about his laird, Black Ben. Abby listened, finding the conversation a good distraction from what was taking place up on the dais, where laugher rang out with nearly every breath they seemed to take.

When the older gentleman rose and walked out the castle doors, Abby took the opportunity to leave. There was no way in hell she could put herself through this torture any longer.

She stood and made the mistake of looking toward Aedan. Dark hooded eyes watched her, a cup of ale loosely held in one hand while Aline and Black Ben spoke to each other around him. His gaze was intense, heavy with desire, and she frowned.

What is he doing to me?

She walked away, and once she got to the safety of her room, she made sure to lock the door, sighing with relief when the bolt slid home without incident.

•••

"So we're to go to war?" Black Ben sat back in the chair in Aedan's anteroom, deep frown lines between his eyes.

"Aye. Clan MacLeod will declare war on Clan O'Cain as soon as the games end. I'll not have those bastards get away with mistreating or demeaning Jinny as they have. They'll pay for their abuse of her, and by my sword."

"You know you have the backing of Clan Ross." Ben paused a moment, gathering his thoughts. "How is Jinny? I haven't seen her since I arrived."

Aedan rubbed his face and poured himself another whisky. "She's decided to stay at the convent for the foreseeable future. She's ashamed and thinks the people here no longer see her as pure or a lady." He scoffed. "Our clan would never see her as anything but the best of people." He glared down at the amber liquid in his goblet. "I'm going to enjoy cutting down the man who mistreated her. He shall feel as much pain as she has endured."

"Nay," Ben said, sitting forward to lean on his knees. "Do not fight with anger or revenge in your belly. It'll make ye weak. You must enter this fight with a clear mind and strong heart. When ye return home safely, then ye can give your emotions free rein."

Ben was right. To enter a war, a ghastly, hard battle like the one they were about to embark on, without a clear mind would ensure he met his maker a lot sooner than he hoped. It wasn't a war he wished to fight, but he couldn't allow the slur against Jinny to go unpunished.

"And what about a wife? If ye should be killed at this battle, who'll take over the MacLeod lands and home?"

He shrugged, not wanting to imagine such a thing. "I have a male cousin who'll return. He's only young and currently under the tutelage of Clan Stewart. Gwen will ensure he learns all he needs to know to take my place."

"Have ye told your sisters of your intention?" Ben met his gaze. "'Tis likely they'll want to flay ye alive over your course."

"They may disagree, but they'll understand why I must do this."

"And will ye go to war before Abigail is returned to her time? 'Twould be wise to have her safely stowed at home, in case this castle falls and Gwen is unable to secure her well-being."

It was a thought he, too, had pondered. A thought that had left him cold, empty, and without purpose. He would miss the bonny lass when she left. In truth, he didn't want her to leave, not after having her warmth, her care, and affection bestowed on him, but he couldn't be selfish. Her well-being and wish to return home had to be paramount.

"Abigail will leave the day I depart. I'll not have her put in harm's way, not when her journey here was not of her doing." He stood, snuffing out the candle on his desk. "It's been a long day. I'll see you in the morn."

Ben laid down on the animal fur before the fire and made himself comfortable. "Aye it has," he said, grabbing a nearby cushion for his head. "Wish the enchanting lass Abigail good night for me."

Aedan started at his friend's words before continuing on, ignoring the knowing chuckle that followed him up the passage toward the hall.

•••

It was later than he'd hoped when he made his way back to his room. The castle had long settled into quiet slumber, save for a few men who lay snoring on the hall floor. The meeting with Ben played on his mind as he climbed the tower stairs. The decision to go to war was not one he took lightly, but it was also an action he wouldn't be swayed from.

His sister deserved retribution.

As he approached Abigail's room, he noted no light

flickered from beneath her door. He stopped and looked about, pushed the door handle down and found it steadfastly locked.

He stood looking at the door with a smile on his face. Shaking his head, he continued on to his chamber and headed for the tapestry that hung beside his bed. The castle was built with many hidden passageways and tunnels through its massive edifice. He pulled it back and slipped into the dark and musty-smelling corridor, taking a few steps before pushing another tapestry aside and slipping into Abigail's room.

A slither of moonlight pierced the room from the window. His eyes adjusted to the darkened space, and he could see her small form huddled on the bed.

He stood there a moment, watching her. She was deep in slumber, her long brown locks lying about her face and over her shift. He quickly undressed, letting his kilt fall where it may and slid in next to her. He started at the cold, sharp blade that came up against his neck.

"What are ye doing, lass? 'Tis me, Aedan." He felt her relax a little before she skittered away from him like he had the pox.

"How did you get in here? I locked the door."

No longer was her voice soft and welcoming. Instead, it was as hard as stone. Aedan didn't like how it made him feel, like he'd lost something irreplaceable. He sat up. "There's a hidden corridor that connects our rooms. You are, after all, staying in the room my future wife will use."

"Well, aren't I lucky?"

There was no mistaking the sarcasm that accompanied her words. He quickly found a candle and getting up he walked to the fire and lit it. "Something troubling ye, lass? Tell me what it is."

"Oh, you're interested in me now. I wouldn't have

guessed that after the way you treated me today." She threw the blankets off her legs and jumped out of the bed.

Her light shift did little to hide the siren body that teased him. His mouth dried at the sight of her, hair flying about her head in temper, her thin arms waving about angrily. She really was quite remarkable to watch. But her next words brought him back to reality.

"Maybe you should tip-toe down the hall and knock on Aline's door. I'm sure she'd adore fawning over you some more. You enjoy it so well."

He leaned against the mantle, ignoring the cold stone at his back. Abigail glared at him, her breasts rising with each breath, her cheeks pink with temper. He laughed. "You're jealous."

She crossed her arms, the action accentuating her breasts even more, not that she needed to. Her sweet, pink nipples puckered against her shift, and his body hardened, the need to taste her again, to kiss those delicious peaks, roared through him like an avalanche on the Highlands mountain range.

"I am not. You may do as you please. I don't give a shit. But what I don't like is being used and then ignored. You acted like an ass today and now you can leave."

He raised his brow. He had no intention of going anywhere. "Explain."

She scoffed at him, going to stand by the window. It was the worst thing she could've done as the shift became transparent in the moonlight. He bit back a groan.

"You, *Laird*," she said, accentuating his title, "didn't even bother to speak to me, had me sit away from the dais, like some common whore with no right to eat beside you. Never mind the fact you kissed another woman."

He joined her at the window, hating that he'd upset her, but also, wasn't this what they had agreed? "We made no vow to one another."

She huffed out a breath. "That's all you have to say for yourself? You didn't make a vow?" She jabbed him in the chest. "Listen here, you medieval ass, where I come from it doesn't require a man to declare a vow after such an act. If the guy has any honor, any slither of respect for the woman, he'll speak to her again, ask her out again. Not ignore her like a lowly whore you'd pass in a dark alleyway."

"If ye must know the reason I kept me distance from ye, I didn't think I could trust myself. Blast it," he said, running a hand through his hair. "Every time I look at ye I want to haul you against me and kiss ye senseless—take ye away from the games and do with ye as I please." He stepped toward her, the tips of her breasts touching his chest. "Even now, when you're angry with me, I want ye. All of ye."

Excitement thrummed in his veins. She looked up at him in surprise, her delectable mouth partly open. He wanted to kiss her, wanted to feel the soft glide of her tongue against his, to hear her moan against his lips as he drove deep into her core. "'Tis also become noticeable by some of the clans that I've taken a keen interest in ye. That I seek ye out often and talk to ye more than I should."

He slid a finger down her neck, revelling in the most perfect skin he'd ever beheld, before slipping the shift off her shoulder, exposing one breast. "The clans are expecting me to marry a woman from one of their families. They won't look kindly if I spend the majority of my time staring at you. And as ye said, you've no intention of fighting for my hand, so…"

Her eyes went wide at his words and she sighed. "I have no idea what we're doing."

No longer able to deny himself, he kissed her shoulder, sliding his tongue along her collarbone. Gooseflesh rose on her skin, and she shivered in his hold. "'Tis the truth, lass. No more or less than that." He kissed his way up her neck. "I'm sorry I hurt ye. It was never my intention," he whispered into her ear, relaxing as her arms came to sit on his hips.

"I shouldn't care. I know what we're doing has no future, but seeing you today, having that feeling that I'd been used and discarded, hurt. Don't do it again, Aedan. I won't be so forgiving a second time."

He met her gaze, running his hands down her back, pulling her fully against him. "I promise ye I won't. You have my word, but we need our association to be of a private nature. Trust me, whenever I'm speaking to another, I'm thinking of you."

Aedan wasn't sure if she believed him, but her arms pulled him close and he took the opportunity to hold her against him, to feel her warmth and revel in it. "You smell very sweet." He rubbed his jaw against her hair. "What is that scent?"

Her chuckle against his neck made him ache. "Jasmine. Your sister showed me where the cooks make up soap and they had some spare for me."

He pulled her back to look at him and slowly bent down and kissed her. Just like a flower, she blossomed in his arms, and opened for him.

Their kiss turned hot, heady, and desperate. All day he'd thought of her in an array of secret locations, his to seduce and enjoy. His body burned, wanted her with a need that didn't seem to abate, but only increased in its ferocity.

She kissed him back, her urgency matching his. A knock at the door sounded and he broke the kiss, saying a silent prayer that she'd locked the door after all.

"You must go," she whispered, pushing him away.

He didn't move. "I dinna want to."

She bit her lip, her eyes darting to the door and back again. "It could be your sister or a maid and if anyone sees you in here with me they'll have us married before you can put your clothes back on."

Now that Abigail mentioned it, he was naked. She wiggled

out of his hold and this time he let her go.

"Who is it?" she called, his sister's muffled voice sounding outside to let her in.

Aedan sighed, swiped up his clothes from the floor, and kissed Abigail good night, lingering over her lips, savoring her as much as he could, before she laughed and shooed him from the room.

He left through the tapestry and made his way back to his chamber. Normally, his quarters were welcoming, a place he could relax, to think, but tonight it seemed barren, empty, and cold. Unlike the woman next door, who was warm, as bright as sunlight, and as refreshing as a northern wind in this damp, ancient castle.

Groaning, he lay on his bed and stared up at the wooden rafters on his roof, wondering how long his sister would take to leave. And what on God's good earth was she still doing up? She had a knack for turning up at the wrong time. He settled in for a long wait.

Chapter Thirteen

Aedan never came back that night, even when Gwen left after a visit that had no purpose at all. Abby had waited patiently, even pushed back the tapestry and looked to see how he'd entered her room, but the dark passageway that probably had too many spider webs to count, had been too scary to contemplate and she'd gone back to bed.

And had failed miserably to sleep. She'd tossed and turned all night, her mind longing for what their earlier kiss had promised and yet never delivered. It wasn't right to stir up a woman to such a point and then leave her hanging unsatisfied. She wanted more…

She went downstairs for breakfast and noted Aedan seated next to Aline. She ground her teeth and went to sit beside Gwen. As soon as she sat she could feel the tension radiating from her friend. Normally, Gwen and Braxton were a lovable pair, spent more time gazing into each other's eyes than talking, but this morning, there was tension that thrummed between them that didn't seem right.

Abby leaned close to Gwen and whispered, "Have you

had an argument?"

Gwen shook her head, frowning. "No. 'Tis my brother. He's being foolish."

For a moment, she wondered if someone knew about them. Had someone seen him try to enter her room last night? She'd heard his attempt and had ignored it, but what if a servant or guest had watched him? Abby poured herself a mug of mead and took a large sip. "How so?"

"There is talk that he's going to declare war with the O'Cains for the slight against our family and Jinny." Gwen ripped a piece of bread in two and bit into it with little etiquette. "I cannot believe it."

Abby looked up and met Aedan's gaze. His lazy smile did odd things to her insides. She smiled back, wondering how much she should say about what she knew of the family and their history.

She had, after all, been staying in the area, reading up on the history of the castle before being brought back in time. It wasn't until now that she realized what a profound moment in history she'd landed dead center in.

And she wasn't sure she should say anything. Wasn't there an unwritten time travel law that travelers touch nothing, kill nothing, talk no one out of wars, decisions, or anything that could possibly change the future? She dipped a piece of bread into her porridge. The butterfly effect or something...

"Braxton is going to talk to Aedan about it and see if he can garner the truth. Should Aedan even be considering it, it could put all our lives at risk. The Scots aren't known to back down and Clan O'Cain would certainly enjoy another battle."

A cold knot formed in her gut that Aedan, his clansmen, Gwen's love, Braxton, could be injured or killed. "I'm sure there's no truth in it. I mean, why would he? It doesn't make any sense when Jinny is now living happily at the convent, or so I was told. Have you heard from her? What do you think she'd say?"

"Honor is at stake and to war we will go, even if it's a war we cannot possibly win." Gwen sighed. "Jinny would think the same as me. Although angry and upset over her failed marriage, and the disgraceful treatment she endured, she's happy now. She's never been like me and Aedan, she never wanted to marry or have children. The quiet solitude of church life suits her, and she'd not condone this battle."

"But if it does happen, is the clan prepared? How large is Aedan's army? Surely, you're not without hope?" Abby put down her breakfast, her stomach turning in knots as she tried to remember what happened in this battle. What had happened to the family, this home and lands?

"We are prepared, but the fight will be long and hard."

If this was a Facebook post, Abby would press the dislike button. Abby read the worry on Gwen's face and it made her pause. Aedan was about to marry, was right at this moment looking for a wife to secure his future. To go to war seemed an illogical thing to do.

And if he died, what would happen to the family? The thought left her cold, and she pulled her shawl about her arms. She looked up at the dais and noted Black Ben and Aedan deep in discussion and something told her that in only a matter of days, a declaration would be made and the future course of this family would be set.

Just as history dictated.

Abby bade a quick good-bye to Gwen who was heading out to the day's events, then followed Aedan who'd walked toward the anteroom. She found him seated behind his desk, reading a letter. She shut and bolted the door, in case he kissed her again and she forgot she was trying to act a lady.

"Good morning," she said.

He smiled and beckoned her over. She went, willingly, almost too willingly, to be back in his arms. As his arms enfolded her waist, pulling her onto his lap, it felt like the most natural thing in the world to do. There was no other place on earth she'd rather be.

"'Tis now a very good morn." He kissed her quickly, pushing a lock of hair from her face and placing it behind her ear. "I missed ye last night."

She smiled. "I didn't think your sister would ever leave."

"Why did you not join me in my room? My bed felt barren without ye in it."

He nuzzled her neck and she chuckled. "I pulled the tapestry back, but when I saw all the spider webs I thought better of it. You'll have to have the corridor cleaned out or your bed will remain empty. Unless you join me, of course."

Abby shifted on his lap and felt a telling hardness against her hip. "Why are you in here this morning? I thought you'd be joining the games. Isn't it sword fighting today? And the ladies turn to show our archery skills?"

"Aye, it is. I had some correspondence I wished to look over 'tis all." He leaned back in the chair, closing his eyes and sighing.

He looked worried and she wondered if his concern stemmed from the rumors circulating the clan. "Is something wrong?" she asked.

His hand idly rubbed her back, massaging it. "Just some trifling concerns, nothing for ye to worry over."

"You mean the rumors that are circulating about you going to war against the O'Cains?"

He sat bolt upright and she almost slipped from his lap. "Where did ye hear that?"

"Last night, your sister was discussing it with Braxton who'd heard it from someone else. I questioned her about it at breakfast."

He stared at her a moment before rubbing his jaw. "If Braxton knows, then most of the clan does, not to mention our guests." He swore.

Abby clasped his hand and caught his attention. "Why is it you've never asked me what I know of your history? I'm from the future. I know, should our roles be reversed, I wouldn't hesitate to ask." If she'd had the ability to know and change David's future, know of his impending death, she would've done all she could to stop it.

He shrugged. "'Tis probably best that I don't know, wouldn't ye agree?"

"But what I could tell you could possibly help with your decision. It could help your clan and save you from making a mistake. Or save your life."

"And is this one of those mistakes?"

Abby bit her lip, not sure if she should say anything or not. "You know that I was on vacation in the area before your sister brought me back here. I know a little about what happened to the family, the clan. You may not want to hear, after all."

His face paled, and she worried that she was crossing some mysterious line of time travel etiquette.

"What do you know?"

It was the most bizarre conversation she'd ever had in her life. Abby said a little prayer that the future would remain as is even after she opened her mouth. "If it's the battle I'm thinking of, the one you're about to embark on, it's known as the last clan battle between you and the O'Cains in Scotland. The history books state it took place in 1601 and was called *Coire na Creiche*. Both clans suffered heavy losses and the battle was one of the bloodiest ever told, but I cannot remember anything more particular than that."

"And does my home fall to the O'Cains?" His voice was hard, cold, and for the first time the calculating mask of a Highland warrior settled on his features.

"This castle still stands today, and there is a laird, but I'm not certain if he's a direct descendant of yours. I know there are massive casualties on both sides, Aedan. Something you can stop now, if you don't go ahead with this." Abby cringed. Telling Aedan this could possibly change the future. Who knew what disasters she'd wrought already?

He stood, leaving her to stand at the desk. "War is a risk." He paced the length of the room, his stance one of thrumming tension. "But I canna let this go. The O'Cains will pay."

She frowned. "And if you die, they win. Why fight, Aedan? Just stay here, enjoy your life, and the wonder of your Highland home."

"What's to stop them from doing this again? What if it's a woman not as strong as Jinny? What if they kill the next woman they claim and not just maim her beyond repair? Our life is not as simple as *enjoying* the magnificence of Scotland and nothing else. I will not let this go."

His voice brooked no argument, and she slumped down in his chair. Abby wasn't sure if she should be horrified or pleased by his words. And the thought that she could lose Aedan in a similar fashion to how she'd lost David was too horrific to contemplate. "No one wins in war, and Gwen seems to think Jinny wouldn't want this."

"Don't ye think I know that?" He paced the room, running a hand through his unbound hair. "But I cannot forget the fact that Jinny left here, hale and whole, and returned a broken woman with one eye missing." He cursed. "What horrors did they inflict on her that she would lose her vision? It makes me sick to my stomach to imagine."

Abby cringed, having not known her injuries were so bad. She had no family, so to worry, to care so much for a sibling was something Abby had never experienced. But seeing the pain etched on Aedan's face she understood the love he had for Jinny and Gwen a little more. "I understand your anger, and I can see why you'd seek revenge. But what of everything you hold dear? You could lose everything. Your home and family. The wife you're so determined to find. What's the point of these Highland Games, if you're only going to go off and fight a war?" He glared at her and she returned the gesture. "Don't you think the O'Cains may be baiting you for a war? Perhaps they used your sister to spark your ire? I know you love your sisters, but I don't think you should do it. I'm sorry, but that's my opinion."

"Well, 'tis good then that I didn't ask for your opinion on the matter, isn't it?"

Abby walked over to him, clasping his hand to stop his pacing. "You have a good life here, Aedan. Jinny is happy where she is. You should think of Gwen, of your people, and yourself. It's time to let go of this hatred. Forget the O'Cains. I don't want to leave and be worrying about you back here." The anger she sensed thrumming through him abated a little and she smiled.

He shook his head. "So ye'd worry about me, lass? Perhaps I ought to declare war just so I know you're thinking of me."

Abby laughed at his teasing that edged toward real feelings. Something she couldn't let happen. Aedan needed to be kept locked away in the "holiday fling" box, and nothing more. "I think you know I'll never forget you, or my time here, and of course, I'll worry about you when I leave. But your future is about to start, and it's a future that although it doesn't involve me, also shouldn't involve war."

Her reply caught his attention like she knew it would.

"I find my need for a wife has waned and certainly a wife who's biddable—who is seen and not heard—is no longer what I desire."

A warm glow spread within her. "You're not allowed to fall for me, Aedan. It's against the rules."

"How can I not?" He clasped her jaw, tilting her face up to meet his. "The thought of ye leaving me rips my soul in two.

I cannot imagine not seeing you next to me in the morn, to watch as you walk around the grounds, taking pleasure in my home as much as I adore you."

Tears burned her eyes, and she blinked to clear her vision. "Don't say that." She pulled away, needing space from the man who consumed her every thought. *Damn it. I'm never going to be able to keep him in a box.* "Getting back to what's important, I don't think you should declare war on the O'Cains. I think it's a mistake you'll live to regret."

He pulled her close to him again and nodded. "I'll think on yer advice and I promise I'll not act hasty or without thought."

He kissed her softly, the barest touch that left her longing for more. He was saying what she wanted to hear, placating her.

"Come, we must join the games," he said, walking toward the door. "A good sword fight is just what I need."

She smiled, sensing his troubles were far from over. "Actually, now that you mention that, I need to ask something of you."

"What is it?" he asked, walking over to where he kept his swords and a varied amount of knives.

"I need you to lose if you happen to face Clan Scot."

Aedan slowly turned toward her, confusion marring his brow. "And why is that?"

"I haven't told you this, but Mae Scot's brother wants her to marry into Clan Kirk, some laird named Rory. Well, apparently, he's horrid and she's in love with someone else. The prize today is money, isn't it?"

"Aye." He crossed his arms, giving her his full attention.

Abby tore her gaze away from his magnificent pecs and back to his eyes. "If they win some money, it may grant her a little time. She's petrified she'll be left at Clan Kirk's estate on their travels home."

"I can understand her concern." Aedan turned back to his swords and picked up the two he wished to use. "I'll see what I can do. I canna promise ye I'll lose, though, lass. It's not in my nature to do so."

"Well, there are some large men lined up for this competition today. You may not even make it past the first round." Abby grinned at his glower. "Are you sure you're up to it? You do seem a little older than the other men. I'd hate for you to get hurt."

He scoffed at her words, but Abby could see the laughter in his eyes. "Ye worry is for naught. Come on," he said, gesturing for her to join him at the door.

Abby took in his muscular shoulders, large hands that were strong and able. You'd be an idiot, indeed, to dismiss the might of a Scotsman with a steel blade in his hands. It made her feel a little sorry for the men going up against him today, as it was obvious Aedan had a lot of pent up tension he needed to expel. But still, she hoped he would listen to her thoughts about the war. Even if only a little bit.

•••

Aedan had fought through two opponents already, but the third, the eldest son of Clan Scot, was as large as a bear and strong. Sweat dripped off his forehead, his muscles burned blocking strike after brutal strike. He was supposed to lose this battle of his own accord, and yet the way he was faring, he'd lose, anyway.

The crowd swore and yelled for both of them, and Aedan knew the only way he'd win would be to keep moving, make the larger man exert more energy, and hopefully, make him more vulnerable.

But as the bout went on, it became apparent the warrior was desperate for the purse of money the event would wield.

Aedan thought of the sweet lass Mae, who didn't deserve to be married off to the brute, Rory Kirk. He shuddered at the thought of anyone being handfasted to such a man, who liked to use his fists more than his mouth.

Distracted by his thoughts, he didn't see the strike that slipped along his sword and struck his arm. He tried to avoid the blade, but knew it was too late when he looked down and noted his arm gushing with blood.

He held up his hand to stop the bout. "Enough," he said, clapping Alec on the shoulder and congratulating him. "You've won this day. Congratulations."

Aedan smiled as the young man's clan surrounded him, offering ale and congratulations of their own. He caught the worried attention of Abigail and watched as she stood as if to come to him.

He clasped the cut on his arm and headed toward the tents, needing it tended to. He sat on a wooden stool, pulled back his bloodied shirtsleeve, and cringed at the mess. He needed to concentrate more. Being distracted would kill him and he couldn't let it happen again. Foolish mistake.

"Oh my God, look at your arm!"

He looked up as Abigail joined him, her brow puckered in worry. She swiped up a tunic that was lying on a nearby table, ripped it in two, and wrapped it about his wound.

"'Tis nothing a little stitching will not fix."

"Your sister is coming." She clasped his hand, stroking it in comfort. "What?" she asked when he chuckled at her ministrations.

"I'm fine, lass. Stop worrying so." She frowned, and he had the overwhelming urge to kiss her scowl away, to make her forget his blasted wound, and to look after him in other ways. More pleasurable ways they'd both enjoy.

"It's already bleeding through the bandage." She looked outside, searching for Gwen.

"Abigail, I will not die from this cut."

"Where is Gwen? She saw what happened to you. She should be here by now."

Aedan grabbed her as she paced by and pulled her down to sit beside him. Not caring where they were, he slid a flyaway curl behind her ear. "Ye look beautiful when you're worried. Did ye know that?"

She relaxed a little and threw him a lopsided grin. "I didn't, no." She applied pressure to his wound, the worry lines still marking her beautiful features. "If I had a cut like that I'd be flat on my back out cold."

"Do ye mean ye would've fainted?"

"Absolutely."

At that moment, Gwen strode in and busied herself preparing the bandages and stitching equipment. Aedan spied a bottle of whisky and asked Abigail to fetch it for him. She did, grabbing it quickly before seating herself next to him again.

Gwen grinned and he inwardly groaned. The last thing he needed was his sister starting to meddle in his private affairs. She'd meddled enough already.

"Do you think it's a bad cut?" Abigail looked to Gwen, gasping as the makeshift bandage was removed.

"Nay. Aedan's had worse and no doubt will again."

He downed a large sip of whisky and prepared himself for the sting of the needle.

"You know, Gwen, if you pour alcohol over the wound it can help clean it and sterilize it at the same time," Abigail said, while hovering over him like a worried wife. His sweet lass was a welcome distraction. She looked beautiful today, her gown of green velvet against her perfect creamy flesh made him want to slide it from her body and bask in the glory hidden beneath.

He swore when Gwen took Abigail's advice. "For the

love of all things Scottish, why did ye do that, woman?"

Gwen shushed him. "I trust what Abigail says, now do keep still."

He met Abigail's gaze. There was something innocently sweet about her. A kind soul, who although she had faced her own troubles and heartbreak, still remained true to herself. Only when they were alone did the sinful siren that lurked beneath her charm come out of hibernation.

The thought of her kiss, of how she pulled him against her, took her pleasure from his body, made him burn to taste her once more. To be alone and in private.

Black Ben stormed into the tent, sweat covered his brow and his hand sat atop his sword. The hairs on the back of Aedan's neck rose. "What is it?" he asked.

"The men on the southern lookout have spotted Clan Kirk."

"On their way to Druiminn? Why would they come here?" Aedan stood and his sister swore, pulling him back down. "Are ye nearly done, lass?"

"Nearly," she said. "Just one more stitch."

"The men have ye horse ready to ride out."

"What about the ladies archery contest? Do ye still want to hold it today with ye leaving?" Gwen asked.

"Nay. We'll postpone." Aedan nodded toward his arm, hurrying Gwen as she quickly tied a bandage around his wound. He grabbed a tunic lying on the ground and threw it on before following Ben. Unable to help himself, he looked back at Abigail and saw the worry etched on her face. He hoped it wouldn't be the last time he'd see the lass. Clan Kirk were as bad as the O'Cains, perhaps worse, because you never knew if the knife would be forward facing or in your back.

Chapter Fourteen

Abby paced the great hall, tonight's meal a somber affair as Aedan and Black Ben, along with Braxton, hadn't yet returned, which made Gwen quiet and withdrawn. They had taken approximately twenty armed clansmen with them. Surely, with such precautions, they would return to the castle without injury.

From what Abby could gather, the clan and laird coming from the south were the very epitome of cruel. To think the even-tempered Mae might be handfasted to such a man, made dread churn in her gut. Why her family thought it was a good idea to marry her off to a man who'd mysteriously lost his last fiancée was beyond her. They obviously had bats in their heads.

The castle doors flew open and slammed against the stone wall. The sounds of men bombarded the hall and everyone turned to see who'd entered. Aedan strode in, Black Ben beside him. They looked relaxed and happy and yet, something in Aedan's eyes gave her pause.

It was an act.

The clansmen had long since eaten, and so she was warming herself in front of the fire when Aedan joined them behind the dais. He bowed and turned to introduce her to their newest guests.

"This is Rory Kirk, laird of Clan Kirk from the Lowlands," he said, before stating her name.

Abby nodded in greeting. "It's nice to meet you, my lord."

Rory Kirk stared at her with an intensity that left her cold, and she shifted closer to Aedan.

"Is that what yer calling yourself these days, lass?" Laird Kirk laughed and some of his men joined in with his mirth.

Abby swallowed, unsure what he meant by that. "I beg your pardon. I don't understand."

"I hadn't thought the rumors could be true, but it seems they are. Come, Coira, do not play me the fool. How is it you're here?" The underlying tremble of anger she could hear in his voice told her he was angry, no matter how benign he was speaking outwardly.

But surely he didn't think… "I'm not Coira. I'm Abigail Cross, as Aedan said."

"I would've thought better of ye, Aedan. To house the very woman who dishonored a fellow Scotsman is treachery."

"Ye mistaken, Rory. This woman is not your missing betrothed."

Whispered gasps sounded and in Abigail's peripheral vision she noted Aedan place his hand on his sword hilt.

"I'm sorry for your loss, but you've mistaken me for someone else. I'm not this Coira you speak of," she said, not liking the tension that radiated around them.

"How can ye not be when you're the very image of the lass who went missing from my lands six months past? Mayhap ye hair is different, and ye skin seems to have improved, but ye certainly look like her to me." He too clasped his sword and fear spiked through her gut.

"I don't know what else to say, sir, other than you're wrong." Silence ensued and Abby wondered how she could get herself into so much trouble with very little effort. She wracked her brain, trying to think of an ancestor who could possibly be this woman Coira, but having lost her parents at a young age, and then fostered out, her study of her family had been minimal.

"She isn't who ye say, Rory, and I'd suggest ye stop stating such tales, less I take offense."

Aedan pulled her behind him, and she went willingly. The other laird seemed to think about Aedan's words and stepped back, laughing. "An honest mistake then." He bowed toward her. "Please accept my apologies, Mistress Cross."

She nodded, not willing to speak to the man again. He was well-built, with arms the circumference of both of hers put together. His face had a large, deep cut that had healed across his cheek, the corner of one eye a little droopy, probably resulting from nerve damage. The thought of anyone betrothed or married to this man left her chilled. There was nothing comforting about him. He was all hard angles, menace, and strength.

Brutal strength that she imagined had been one blow too many for his bride-to-be and he'd killed her. Making a scene tonight in front of all these people could well be a way to take care of the murder rumors that were following him all over Scotland.

And after meeting him, seeing him even now, glaring at her while speaking politely to those around him, as if nothing untoward had happened, she had no doubt his fiancée was dead.

"If you'll excuse me, my lords. I'm off to bed," she said, as evenly as she could. Not wanting Rory to hear the fear in her voice.

Aedan nodded and let her go. Gwen joined her at the

stairs and they headed to their rooms together. Abby had an overwhelming urge to run, but she didn't. If she was to survive the dreadful Rory Kirk then she must look as unflustered as possible.

Easier said than done.

•••

The next day Abby sat in the great hall, Gwen having headed upstairs to gather more wool for a shawl she was teaching her to knit. Sunlight filtered through the tall windows facing west, the afternoon warm and welcoming.

Most of the guests had dispersed down toward the games to watch the events, but Gwen, not feeling the best today, had decided to stay at the castle. Abby leaned down and grabbed another ball of wool, tying it to the knitting needle as Gwen had shown her.

Footsteps sounded on the flagstone floor, and Rory Kirk strode into the room. He looked about, and spotting her near the fire, walked over and sat in the chair opposite to her.

Abby tentatively smiled, and continued on with her knitting. "Lovely day today. Are you enjoying your stay at Druiminn?"

He leaned back in the chair, his hands tapping the side in manic rhythm. "I'm finding my stay most opportune, as you're fully aware. As I said last eve, I'd heard ye were here, but I hadn't expected it to be true. Although yer way of speaking is new, it does nay fool me, lass."

She took a fortifying breath, sick and tired of hearing she was someone she was not. "I'm very sorry your betrothed has gone missing. I'm sure you miss her very much, but it's not I who you seek."

"Is it not?" He stared at her a moment, before beckoning a passing servant to fetch him some ale. His coarse speech and demeaning manner toward the staff irked her, and Abby glared at him.

"No, it's not." She thanked the servant for the cup of ale that was passed to him. "As I said, last night was the first time I've had the pleasure of meeting you. I do not doubt that I may look familiar to the woman you loved, but that's where the similarities stop."

"So you're not Coira Travis, the woman who, the night before our handfasting, disappeared into the night like a ghost?" His attempt at a smile turned into a scowl. "'Tis been a tiresome few months, and I think you owe me an explanation as to how you came to be here."

She sighed, inwardly cursing the idiotic man who refused to believe who she was. Perhaps she ought to tell him of the time she really was from, that might shut him up for a while. Go and get her cell phone and take a photo of him and scare him shitless. But as he stared at her mockingly, waiting to hear her lie, or so he thought, Abby took a calming breath instead.

"I came here at the invitation of Gwendolyn. I'm not Scottish or English, and traveled from France to be here. I'm sorry if that's not the answer you want, but it's all I have to give. I don't want any trouble, my lord. I swear on my soul I'm not who you're looking for."

He made a growling noise, standing and walking over to the windows. "Ye see, I think you're saying these things to cause me angst. For months, I've wondered where ye were, if you were safe, who ye were with? And now I know. I must admit I'm a little disappointed in ye. I thought you would've traveled to your family in England rather than stay in the wilds of Scotland ye so detested."

"Again, my lord, I must state that I am not the Coira you seek and to be honest, I'm getting sick of you singling me out over it. Perhaps you should ask yourself why it is that she decided to leave you in the first place." His eyes burned with hatred and pinned her to the spot. Never had she seen such menace swirling about in soulless eyes. She shivered.

"Why don't you tell me, then?"

"Because I am not her!" she yelled, standing and storming over to where he stood. "I'm going to say this once, and only once. I'm not her, so if it's Coira you seek, perhaps you ought to visit her family and start your search there."

A servant walked past and cast them a curious look.

"I know you're a lying wench, and I'll prove it before I leave. Don't cross me any more than you already have, my sweet little bride-to-be. It wouldn't be in your best interest."

"Are you threatening me? Really?" Abby went nose to nose with him, well, nose to chest anyway, and glared. A muscle worked in his jaw, and for a moment she regretted getting so close to him. "I won't hesitate to tell Laird MacLeod of your continual annoyance over this matter. I've never met you in my life and from what I've seen of you since last night, I'm thankful for that. Now if you don't mind, I have things to do. Have a pleasant day."

Abby took a step and gasped when he clasped her arm and wrenched her back up against his chest.

"I don't like being made a fool of, lass. Keep up your inability to remember me, and my patience will expire."

His voice, devoid of emotion or feeling, left her colder than the stone of the castle walls. Abby wrenched herself free, absently rubbing her flesh. "Don't ever touch me again. Ever." Abby walked toward the stairs as Gwen came down. "I'm tired, Gwen, I'm going to head up to my room for a little while, if that's okay."

Gwen nodded. "Of course. Will you be down for dinner?"

"Yes, but not before." Abby smiled to hide her unease. The heat of Rory Kirk's glare on her back followed her upstairs until she was out of sight.

...

Later that night she rolled over and cuddled up to Aedan who slept beside her. A cold weather front had come through during late afternoon, and the games had finished early. Aedan had sought her out, and finding her asleep, had awakened her in the most delicious way possible, allowing her, for a time, to forget the vile Rory Kirk.

"Aedan, are you asleep?" He murmured something unintelligible and she smiled. "Wake up, I need to tell you something."

"*Hmm*," he said, stroking her back with his arm, making her skin prickle. "What is it, lass?"

"I need to tell you what Rory Kirk keeps doing to me."

She felt him come full awake, his muscles tightening at her words. "He better nay be doing anything with ye."

His tone was deadly and she leaned up, kissing him on the cheek. "Nothing like that, I promise you." Eww, the thought of being intimate with the man was enough to make her vomit. "He keeps harassing me about being this Coira woman he's lost. Every chance he gets to corner me alone, he tries to make me admit it."

"Why did ye not tell me when this happened, lass? I would've put a stop to it immediately."

All day Abby had debated telling him of the man's persistence, but then thought better of it before changing her mind yet again. She'd hoped that if maybe she continued to deny his claims, he'd soon look past her similarities to this Coira woman and move on. But his glower during this evening's meals had made her uneasy. Abby had to tell Aedan what was going on. "Worried, I suppose. I didn't want to make any more trouble for you, considering everything that was happening here already. I'm sorry."

"Nay, lass, don't be sorry. I'll talk to him in the morn, and threaten to pull his head out of his ass. Ye no need to worry about him any further, in any case, for I believe that no matter ye desire for ye friend Mae to marry for love, her brother is determined to have her settled before he returns home."

"What do you mean?" she asked, dread like a hard ball in her belly.

"Rory Kirk mentioned today that he's spoken to Alec, Mae's brother and said that they may possibly align their families and marry."

Abby sat up with a start. Imagining the sweet Mae married to Rory was more abhorrent than his fetid breath. "What did you say? I hope you persuaded him otherwise. I know for a fact Mae doesn't wish to marry him, and is actually in love with someone."

Aedan sat up and leaned against the headboard. Abby's attention momentarily turned to his chest and the line of muscle that it housed, before meeting his eyes.

"How do you know this?"

"I told you all this the day I asked you to lose the sword event. The day I was testing Mae to see if she'd be a good match for you, she spoke of it." Abby shook her head, not liking the small seed of worry that had settled in her belly. "She said herself her brother believes an association with Rory Kirk would be beneficial to her family, but it wouldn't, Aedan. There's something wrong with that man. He's obsessed with this Coira woman. Obviously, he's missing a few screws, if you know what I mean."

"Aye, I understand." He sighed. "I'll talk to Alec on the morn and see if he's serious about making his sister marry into Rory's clan and try and persuade him otherwise."

Abby knelt beside him, unable to stop herself from touching his toned abdomen, liking the way his smooth skin felt against her palm. "And will you try and dissuade him of the notion? Rory Kirk is dangerous. I don't like him at all."

He grabbed her hand, stilling her administrations when it dipped lower on his stomach. "He hasn't hurt ye, has he?"

"No. Of course not," she lied, remembering his harsh grip on her arm. She shouldn't protect a man whom she believed was fairly free with his fists when around women he boasted to love, but then she didn't want Aedan to declare war on his clan, either. It was bad enough he was looking for retribution toward the O'Cains. "I'm sure he's hurt his betrothed. I don't know if the girl is dead or alive, or run back to her family in England, but she's better off away from that man. I don't want Mae to suffer the same fate. She deserves so much better."

"Understandable." He pulled her down to lay beside him, his hand idly stroking her bare arm. "Promise me you'll tell me if anyone, Rory Kirk, or even a member of my clan, threatens or causes ye distress."

She smiled up at him, counting her blessings that she was in the bed with a sweet, loving medieval Highlander. "I promise. I'll not keep anything from you."

"Thank ye," he said, kissing her temple quickly before attempting sleep once more.

She watched him for a while before sleep, too, took her worries away.

...

The games continued as normal, but no longer were they carefree and fun—an underlying vein of tension thrummed around everyone. Aedan hadn't visited her bedchamber for the last two nights, and she was starting to wonder if he believed the ridiculous declaration from Laird Kirk.

But she dismissed the notion as soon as she thought it. Aedan knew where she'd come from and how, but it didn't explain why he'd taken to his own bed instead of hers.

She stood under a large tree, watching the stone put only

a few yards away, a test of a man's skill when throwing a large boulder the farthest. And some of those stones were boulders that Abby would struggle to even pick up. A hand clasped tight about her arm and pulled her behind a large shrub.

"How did ye get here, ye whore of an English bitch?"

She cringed at Rory Kirk's tight hold and remembering her self-defense course, she lifted her elbow and wrenched free of his painful grip. "Do not touch me." She thanked God her voice sounded strong and didn't wobble with the paralyzing fear welling up inside.

"Tell me how ye came to be in the Highlands and staying at the bastard MacLeod's keep."

"I said before, I'm not who you think I am. Although after meeting you, I can understand why your fiancée left. You're a brute who probably hit her a little too hard and made her disappearance permanent."

He snarled. "Ye still have a mouth on ye that needs to be shut. Perhaps I ought to put ye on your knees and make ye mute by other means."

She gasped. "Go ahead, but don't expect your dick to be on your person afterward, you bastard."

He punched her in the stomach, and she dropped to her knees. She gasped for breath, unable to get enough air into her lungs. A cold sweat broke out on her skin, and she clasped at the grass beneath her hands while trying to calm herself.

"Ye will be my wife and you'll keep your mouth shut, less something dreadful happens to ye precious laird's sister. I'd hate for the bonny lass Gwen to break her neck while out riding her horse. Do ye understand, Coira?"

She met his gaze and stood, her legs far from steady. "You touch one hair on Gwen's head, and you'll be dead before you cross the castle's threshold."

"You hold the laird's abilities against mine too high, lass. Do you not remember ye life back at Gladdis Castle? I'll have to ensure when you return with me that you're reacquainted with dizzying speed."

"I will never go there with you." She finally took a full breath, the action making her queasy. "If you weren't so blind with anger, you'd see I'm not who you seek."

"'Tis you, and I'll not be leaving here without ye. I'll also ensure the Laird MacLeod will feel my full wrath by taking in and hiding one of my own."

"I will not stay quiet about your treatment of me today. I suggest you leave before you cannot."

He crossed his arms, his manner one of mocking confidence. "I'm not known for my kindness. If ye want to keep those who've given ye shelter safe from impaling themselves on my sword, I'd keep your mouth shut." He pulled her close, his putrid breath turning her stomach. "Do ye understand now, lass? Or do I need to show you in other ways to secure your belief."

She nodded, the burn of tears threatening behind her lids. Damn bastard. Never had she been handled in such a way. "I understand. Now let me go."

He did, and staggering to stand, she walked back toward where Gwen sat watching the event. She checked her gown, making sure there were no signs of the struggle she'd been in. Her arm ached, and she rubbed it without giving away what had occurred.

Taking a deep breath, she struggled to calm her rapid heartbeat. Gwen smiled in welcome and patted the bench beside her to sit. Aedan walked past and caught her eye, throwing her one of his wicked smiles and she grinned back, not wishing to alert him to the trouble she now found herself. Why the laird of Kirk would think she was his ex-fiancée was too bizarre to even contemplate, but contemplate she should. This could turn into a very bad situation.

"Gwen, when do you think I can go home?" Gwen looked

at her in alarm and she read the hurt her question caused, but what other option did she have? Rory Kirk wasn't of sound mind, and the awful threats he'd promised her didn't bear thinking about.

"I've been meaning to speak to you about that." Gwen looked about, ensuring their privacy. "For the last few days I've not been able to see the aura that accompanied the magic around ye. I think it'd be safe for ye to return home whenever you like."

"Really?" Hope welled up within her, followed by despair. She wasn't ready to go home yet, but that choice now seemed out of her hands. To keep Gwen safe and Aedan from fighting with the barbaric Rory Kirk, she'd have to go. Or she could tell them what he'd threatened. At least toward them. "So I could leave today if I liked."

Gwen frowned, but nodded. "Aye. Today, if it pleases ye."

It didn't please her. Not at all. Just the thought of leaving made her heart ache. Rory walked past, his salacious smirk leaving her cold, no matter that the warm sun beat down on her back. "I think it's time I leave. As much as I've come to love you all, I can't stay any longer, not when I can return to my own time and leave you in peace."

"You're no trouble, Abigail. We love having ye here with us, my brother especially."

Abby swallowed the lump in her throat, having never felt more welcome or loved in a long time. The word love bounced around in her brain, and she frowned. Had she come to feel more than mere "like" toward Aedan MacLeod? The memory of his touch, his kiss, and sweet words whispered to her when alone told her more than anything that she had indeed left those feelings well behind.

"I will miss you both terribly. I know we didn't start the best of friends, but I certainly do class you as one now." Gwen pulled her into a hug and Abby returned the gesture. Tears welled in her eyes and she laughed as they pulled away, Gwen, too, wiping her cheeks.

"There aren't any games tomorrow, will that be soon enough for ye?"

She nodded. "More than soon enough."

...

Ben shook his head at the third sigh he'd counted coming from Gwen, seated beside him as they watched the last of the day's games, a footrace between the clans. He cast her a curious glance and caught her eye. "Something troubling ye, lass? You seem to be sighing a lot." She sighed again and he fought not to roll his eyes. "Out with it."

"Abigail has asked to go home."

"What?" Ben looked out to where Aedan stood talking to the delightful Abigail. She was a pretty lass, tall, nice shape, pleasing breasts…and by the way his friend gazed down on her, his carefree laugh ringing out across the field, Ben had the odd notion his friend had fallen in love.

Which wasn't a bad thing. Far from it. The lad had to marry someone, and the women parading around in front of him only saw the man as someone to give them a privileged life, a comfortable home. Not a man who could be loved or give love. "Then I'm sorry for your brother. He'll not take it well."

"No, he won't." Gwen sniffed, and he noted her eyes had grown glassy.

"Are ye crying?" Ben shifted in his seat, hating to see a woman who had held his own heart for many years, become upset. Not that they would ever be anything but friends, though not for want of trying on his behalf. He'd tried and failed and now she was destined for another. "Can ye not talk her out of it? Do you know why she's so determined to leave?

I thought the lass was happy here."

"So did I." Gwen met his gaze, her lips pulled into a thin line. "I'm going to try and talk her out of it, but I doubt I'll be successful. It's like a twig has snapped in her mind and she no longer wants to be here."

Ben nodded, frowning. "Aye, but why? That is something we should find out." He looked about the many clans that were at Druiminn Castle. Well, he looked at one clan in particular. Kirk. They stood to the side of the field, their salacious gazes raking the women present, the men showing no concern as to the offense they caused.

"I'm sure if she was concerned about anything, she would've told me. I had hoped Aedan would make her his wife. They seem so well suited."

"Aye, I canna disagree with ye there, lass, and we have until the morn to change Abigail's mind. If I come across her in my travels, I'll make sure to have a word or two."

Gwen clasped his arm, smiling. Ben's heart thumped loud behind his ribs. "You'd do that?"

"I'll always be here for you and your clan, Gwen. And try not to worry, we'll change Abigail's mind."

"Thank you, Ben. You're too good to us."

Chapter Fifteen

Aedan cast another look toward his sister and Abigail and again, the two women were somber, both lost in their meals, not full of chatter like they usually were.

Something was wrong.

He took a sip of mead and leaned toward Abigail seated next to him; she smiled up at him, but the gesture didn't fill her eyes. "What's troubling ye, lass?"

She fidgeted with the sleeve of her gown. "Nothing. Why would anything be wrong?"

He raised his brows. "Tonight, something seems amiss."

She laughed, the sound hollow and a spike of fear entered his gut. "Nothing. I assure you."

"Abigail, I want the truth. Now." She paled a little, meeting Gwen's gaze before slumping back in her chair. "I think it is time that I return home. I found out today that it's possible."

The impact to his gut felt like a sword had sliced through his innards. "What?" He glared at Gwen, wanting to reach across and murder her.

"The residual magic has worn off," Abigail whispered,

the breath of her words tickling his ear and making him miss her already. "Gwen thinks it'll be safe for me to return to my time."

He didn't want her going anywhere. "And if you end up in some other time, alone, vulnerable, what then? I'll never know if ye made it home safely or not." He paused, fisting his hands to stop their shaking. "Ye cannot go. I forbid it."

Abigail gaped at him, and he looked away. Perhaps if he ignored her, this whole nightmare of her leaving would disappear, too.

"I beg your pardon. You don't have the right to forbid me from this. It isn't your choice, Aedan."

"'Tis my choice, and I forbid my sister to allow ye to leave." His voice sounded high, not the even-tempered tone he usually spoke with. He cleared his throat. "For the time being, at least."

"No."

"No?" He narrowed his eyes, not liking the determination in her tone. She was stubborn, probably more stubborn than he was. It wasn't a good mix.

"No," she repeated, lifting her chin. "I have to go sooner or later and tomorrow is no different than any other day."

Her words cut him to the quick. He couldn't let her go. Just the thought of her no longer within his castle walls, warming his bed, smiling at him whenever their paths crossed, left a hollow crevice in his soul.

"Aedan," she said, placing her hand on his arm. "You knew I'd go eventually."

He stared straight ahead, not focusing on anything at all. "I don't want ye to leave." And that was the truth. Hell, he never wanted her to leave. Over the last two weeks that she'd graced his halls he'd come to admire her inner strength, marvel at her courage, and love her heart, when she wasn't annoying him, of course.

Tears welled in her eyes, and his panic increased. "Abigail, lass, is there something more yer not telling me? Surely, by now, ye know ye can trust me."

She bit her bottom lip and sniffed. She looked out toward the trestle tables, her face paling. Aedan followed her line of vision and locked gazes with Rory Kirk, the bastard playing with a dirk in his hand, his face one of pure hate.

A chill swept across his spine, and he swore. "Abigail, look at me. Did something happen today that yer scared to tell me? Do not try and protect me by staying silent. Ye best explain now and not later when it's too late for me to help ye."

She shook her head and stood. "Truly Aedan I'm fine, just tired. I'm retiring for the night. I'll see you tomorrow."

He watched her leave and then looked to make sure Rory Kirk stayed where he was seated. The bastard followed Abigail's progress, but didn't rise. He turned to his right and said to Ben, "I think Rory Kirk has threatened Abigail in some way. She's afraid of him."

His friend leaned forward on the table with a relaxed air that was anything but. Beneath his benign visage, Aedan knew the man was on full alert, as was he.

"And you think this is why she's wanting to return home?"

"You know?"

Ben shrugged, meeting his gaze. "Gwen told me this afternoon that Abigail had asked to return home."

"Well, that explains why they're quiet tonight." He paused. "Why did ye not tell me? I've been wondering what's wrong." Aedan finished his drink, slamming the goblet down on the wooden table.

"When I spoke to her today, she said not to. That she'd find the right time to tell ye."

"It doesn't make sense. And it seems too coincidental that the moment Clan Kirk arrives, Abigail wishes to leave. Especially with how Rory thinks she's his lost betrothed."

"Aye, ye have the right of it. I was watching the clan today. They're trouble, Aedan. I wouldn't turn my back on them while they're here. Rory Kirk is as slippery as an eel."

Aedan swore. "I'm certain he's threatened Abigail, scared her enough that's she's running."

"Perhaps the Laird of MacLeod is also worn out and needs an early night."

"Mayhap you're correct." He stood. "Watch him and don't let him out of yer sight. Also, tell Braxton to sleep outside Gwen's door tonight. I want her safety ensured as well."

"Consider it done," Ben replied, leaning back in his chair, as if nothing was amiss.

Aedan walked from the room and headed upstairs to where he could keep Abigail in his sight, where she was safe.

•••

He entered her room via the tapestry, heading for the door to ensure she'd locked it.

"What are you doing here?" She sat up in bed, her hands clutching the sheet to her chest.

He came to stand at the end of the bed, leaning against one wooden post. She looked so vulnerable and scared. He wanted to pull her into his arms, hold her, revel in her for as long as he could. Her hair was unbound and tumbled about her shoulders, pulling his gaze to her slender, beautiful neck. "What did Rory Kirk say to ye, lass? I know he's threatened ye in some way, and I need to know how."

"I can't. He said if I said anything, he'd hurt Gwen. I can't put her safety at risk."

"Gwen is being watched by the man who loves her. She'll be safe, I promise ye. Now tell me, please."

Tears slid down her cheek, and his resolve not to touch her until she'd explained what was going on crumbled. He walked around the bed and sat beside her, pulling her into his embrace. Her hands came about his back and held him.

Nothing in his life felt as right as this, Abigail beside him, trusting him.

"Are you sure Gwen's safety can be ensured? I couldn't live with myself if anything happened to her."

"I promise. She's well cared for." He remained silent, knowing she'd tell him when she was ready.

"Rory Kirk did threaten me. He found me alone today and continued to hound me, insisted I am his missing fiancée. He's steadfast that I'm his betrothed. It's ludicrous. He wouldn't listen when I explained, again, I'm not who he thinks I am."

"What was his threat?" Rage boiled up in his blood, and Aedan kept his focus on the mantle across the room, the flames licking the wood as hot and wild as his temper. He'd spoken to the troublesome laird after breaking his fast. Warned him to cease his insistence that Abigail was his missing Coira lass. That the man had stood before him, lying to him that he'd already let the similarities between the two women go, made his temper soar.

"There were two," she muffled against his chest. "The first one was to rape me. The second was against Gwen. He said she'd have an 'accident' while out riding. He mentioned her falling and breaking her neck."

Aedan swallowed, unsure if speech was possible. His grip tightened around Abigail. Clan Kirk would pay for such threats, as the O'Cains would. He thought back to today's games, having thought all his guests were enjoying his home and hospitality.

How wrong had he been? All the while, the vile Rory Kirk had been threatening his woman. Had abused her peace of mind.

I'll kill him.

"Did he hurt ye? And dinna lie. I want to know everything."

Abigail looked up at Aedan. "It doesn't matter now. I'm

more concerned about what you're thinking."

He leaned down and kissed her, the touch soft and far too quick. This would be their last night together. The last thing he wanted to do was spend it worrying about a man not worthy of the name.

"Tell me, lass."

...

Abby ground her teeth, hating the fact he could read her so well. But what good would it do to tell him what Rory had done? Nothing. Aedan certainly couldn't change the events of the day, no matter how much she may wish it.

"I know what you'll do if I tell you, and so I won't. I'll be gone soon enough. No need to cause you or your people any more trouble."

He raked a hand through his hair. "Damn it, Abigail. Tell me. That bastard cannot treat anyone under my protection in such a way. I'll not have it."

She sighed, her stomach knotting. "Aedan, please."

"Tell me. Now." His voice brooked no argument.

"He hit me, okay? Is that what you wanted to hear? Does it make this situation any better? No. It doesn't." When Aedan didn't say anything, she glanced up at him and stilled at the murderous rage she could read in his eyes. "What are you thinking?"

"He'll not harm you or anyone else from this night on. I promise ye that." He stood and walked to the door, pushing a large chest in front of it. "Leave it locked and with the chest there. I'll be back before dawn."

Abby jumped from the bed, following him toward the tapestry. "Where are you going?"

"I'm going to gut the bastard, make him bleed, and possibly kill him before his men."

"You cannot do that! Aedan, surely there's another way." He stared at her, seemingly not hearing anything she was saying.

"Not in this time there is not."

His words plummeted her heart into her stomach. The thought that Aedan could be injured, or worse, killed by the unhinged Rory Kirk was too much to comprehend. "Please, you can't. I didn't tell you so you would go off and seek revenge."

"But I will and there's nothing ye can do or say that'll stop me." He paused at the tapestry, turning slightly to meet her gaze. "Should anything happen, hide in the secret passage until help arrives. No one will find ye there. If ye manage it without assistance, the passage leads out under the southern wall where ye can escape or seek help."

Abby swallowed her gnawing panic. "Aedan, please. Don't go."

He didn't say anything, merely turned and left, the tapestry falling back into place as if he never was. Abby slumped onto the stool beside the fire, her stomach churning with what tonight would bring.

Again her mind replayed the events of the day. Of Rory Kirk's threats, his laughing, sadistic gaze. What's more, a niggling thought plagued her that the bastard laird had threatened her in the hopes that she would tell Aedan. Had she unwittingly led Aedan into a trap?

Noises sounded outside, and she crossed the room and looked out the window. From here she could make out the land that the games were used for. Torches burned bright in the night sky, the sounds of clansmen enjoying drink and good company whispered on the wind.

The moon caught her eye and she cringed seeing it was full. A bad omen? Or the sign of new beginnings? That she wouldn't know for some hours. The longest she'd ever lived in her life.

•••

She jumped at the loud bang against her door. She sat up in the window seat, touching her cold cheek that had been leaning against the stone wall. The banging sounded again and she stayed where she was, frozen and unable to decide if she should speak or run for her life.

"Who is it?" Her voice sounded timid, pathetic. She cleared her throat. "Who is it?" she said, loud enough for whoever was on the other side to hear.

"It's me, mistress. Your chamber servant. Laird MacLeod sent me up to check on ye, and ensure you were settled for the night."

Relief poured through her as she crossed the room, sliding the trunk to the side. "Yes, I'm fine, Betsy." She opened the door and gasped, trying to shut it as Rory Kirk stood on the other side, knife to her servant's throat. He was too strong and pushed his way into the room, throwing the woman to the floor with enough force that she didn't get back up again.

"Foolish woman, Abigail, if that's what yer calling yourself these days." He laughed, shutting the door and bolting the lock across. "I thought it'd be much harder gaining entrance into ye room. Seems ye still as daft as ye ever was."

"What do you want?" She backed toward the fire, the closest place in the room that had some sort of weapon, the fire poker. If only she could reach her bed and grab the small knife she'd stashed under her pillow. The fire poker could only do so much, and against this brute she doubted it'd give him a bruise.

"Don't fight me on this, lass. You're comin' with me."

"I'm not going anywhere with you." Her hand clasped the cold metal and she held it behind her back, hiding it in the skirts of her gown. He advanced on her, a menacing beast she knew she'd never win against. "Where's Aedan?"

"Taken care of." He smiled, showing off his rotten front teeth. "He'll not be looking for ye tonight."

Despair washed over her, nearly crippling her limbs. "Is he dead?" Her breathing came in quick succession and she clasped her throat, finding it hard to catch her breath.

"Not yet. But one day, and hopefully, one day soon. Now come." He stepped toward her, but stopped when she backed away.

She sidled around him, trying to get closer to the door. Knowing it was now or never to make her move, she threw the poker at his face and bolted toward escape. He swiped at the projectile like it was an annoying moth and flung it to the floor. Unharmed, he caught her at the door, pushed her up against the wood and undulated against her bottom, the strength of him hurting her, her hipbones grinding against the wood sent pain ricocheting up her abdomen. She cried out as the air in her lungs was squeezed out.

His hand slid about her throat, and she stilled. "Do not run again, lass. I don't take nicely to be treated with so little respect."

"Screw you."

He laughed, squeezing her neck until blackness flickered before her eyes. "Later yes, but right now, I need ye to shut up so I apologize for what I'm about to do. It pains me more than it'll pain you, I assure ye."

"Bullshit." Abby tried to push him off before something hard slammed into her skull. That it did hurt was the last thought she had before blackness consumed her.

• • •

The cold wind pierced her face, her head feeling like it would split in two from the pounding headache. Slumped over a horse, her hands fastened behind her back and her ankles tied, left her feeling unbalanced and vulnerable. Her skin burned where they were latched together, and with every clop of the horses' hooves, the bones on her ankles rubbed.

Dawn was breaking in the morning sky as they galloped to a destination she'd never seen before. Mountains rose on either side of them, and it looked like a dry riverbed, if the amount of stones the horse tripped over was any indication. On either side of the bank, heather rose up across the lower hills, its purple flowers the only ornament on an otherwise barren landscape.

The man holding her on the horse shouted out orders in quick succession, his voice loud enough to send pain spiking through her skull. She cringed.

"Awake are ye?" He patted her bottom, his hand squeezing painfully against her flesh. "'Tis about time. There is nothing more boring than having a woman when she isn't conscious."

"You're a vile pig." Abby tried to wiggle off the horse, death by a brain injury would be better than having to stay one more moment with this vile being.

His hand held her fast, and he made an awful noise of displeasure. "Try that again and I'll slit ye throat and bleed ye over me horse's neck."

Abby remained silent as something told her he'd do exactly that, should she push him too far. Aedan would come for her, of that she was sure. She needed to keep this man's hands and sword off her until he did.

Easier said than done.

"Where are we going?"

He laughed, the sound tinged with mockery. "That's the brilliance of my plan. I've sent half my men with a woman from Clan MacLeod headed toward the eastern borders. Last reports have your stupid laird following them instead of us. We're headed for O'Cain land, where me and my men will all have a turn of ye, before I kill ye stone dead."

"I'm not the woman you seek. I have never met you before our introductions at Castle Druiminn. I don't know why you won't believe me." Her voice rose in panic. The thought of being passed around, a play toy to these men made her stomach lurch. She'd never survive it. And what did it matter if she did, they were going to kill her, anyway. "If you have any moral fiber in your body you'll let me go."

"You are who I seek, no matter what you say. You've proven yourself a lying wench, and I'll have my revenge."

They stopped, and he clasped the back of her gown, wrenching her backward and throwing her off the horse. She landed with a thump, sprawled on her ass.. The muscles in her back screamed in pain as she tensed to stop her head from hitting the ground.

"Maybe I'll have ye now." He jumped from the horse and came around to stand over her, nudging one of her legs with his boot.

"Look at me," she screamed. "I mean, really look at me. I'm not this Coira you seek. Surely in the months she lived with you, you noticed some sort of mark, a scar even, that will prove my innocence."

He seemed to think on this a moment, before disdain covered his features. "Ye are who I say ye are."

"How fortunate." Abby looked around the location, searching for anyone to come and get her out of the dire situation. She noted a rough stone cottage farther down the hill, a thatch roof and no door, just a space to enter the building. The windows had no glass panels. It didn't look like anyone had lived in the dwelling for years.

He slashed the rope at her ankles, the knife slicing into her skin. Abby gasped, but didn't have time to see how much damage he'd done, as he hauled her up and pushed her toward the cottage.

"Inside."

She did as she was told, entering the building and noting it was empty save for an unlit fire and an old cot to one side of the room. The floor was dirt, the air smelling of damp and mold. "Why have we stopped here?"

He looked out the door, ignoring her question.

"Why have we stopped?" Abby raised her voice the second time she asked, the fear over the unknown making her bolder.

He called out to one of his men to come to the cottage. He still didn't answer her, but instead spoke to his clansman. "Watch the lass and don't let her leave. If she tries, kill her, I don't care how."

Abby gasped in shock as he left her with a man that looked at her as if she were a tasty morsel of food, not a prisoner of his laird. She tore her gaze away as his attention lowered to her bosom, not wanting to see the salacious smirk that covered his god-awful visage.

She was a sitting duck, a target for anyone who wanted to hurt her, and tied up as she was, there was nothing she could do about it.

After a few hours of being held, Abby started to doze. It was dangerous to sleep, she knew that, and yet the pounding headache and lack of sleep the night before were catching up with her. The guard hadn't moved, and even if he seemed to be thinking of taking her for his own pleasure, he hadn't ventured from his post.

Famous last thoughts. No sooner had she thought it, than the sound of boots stomping across the floor woke her. She gasped as the guard grabbed her legs and pulled her down into a laying position. Abby screamed, kicking out as he tried to grab her legs and spread them apart.

Images of the horror that was about to come filled her mind. With her hands tied, she fisted them together and struck his jaw, snapping his head back. He laughed at her attack attempt, seemingly unfazed, before he slapped her hard. Abby blinked, wondering where she was for a moment, before absolute terror crashed her into reality.

He slid between her legs, the slimy tip of his jutting penis touching her thigh. Abby wrenched herself to the side, making him lose his balance. She used the moment to get up and run for the door. He caught her, pushing her forward, making her face plant into the ground. Dirt and moss entered her mouth as adrenalin flew through her veins.

Cool air touched her legs as he threw her gown up over her back. His hand pushed hard on her nape, pinning her against a rock. "Try that again, and I'll slit yer throat. Now hold still, or it'll be more than my cock you'll feel back here."

...

Aedan pushed hard through the night, his tracking hounds not taking long to find a scent of Clan Kirk and the bastard who dared to take Abigail. When he'd left her, he'd rounded up his clansmen, some less than helpful after a night of revelling, and gone looking for the soon-to-be-dead laird.

And found him missing.

That their camp was deserted wasn't a surprise, but it made him wonder what the man was up to. He'd sent men off to try and see which direction they'd traveled, as he headed back toward the castle, wanting to ensure Abigail and Gwen were safe.

He'd found Braxton leaning up against his sister's door, the man confirming all was well in that part of the castle. He'd then headed to Abigail's room and found her servant with a broken neck on the floor, and no sign of his lass.

A chilling rage enveloped him and he'd bolted for the stables, calling to his men to take arms against Clan Kirk.

They'd caught up with some of the other laird's men within the hour who notified him the Kirks were headed toward O'Cain lands. No doubt hoping they'd find sanctuary within their treacherous walls. Rory Kirk would never reach O'Cain land, and he'd find no safety by the end of this night. Aedan would make sure of that.

Hours later, the light of day pierced the sky and he could see the fleeing clan in the gully beyond. He stopped his men, looking to see if he could recognize Abigail among the many men. Not seeing her, a paralysing fear that he was too late gripped him.

He looked farther up the ridge and spotted an old crofter's cottage, movement near the door said there was a man there, but he couldn't make out much more than that. Aedan urged his mount on, knowing that if they didn't act soon, Abigail's life would be in danger should they cross into O'Cain ground.

If Rory had hurt Abigail, he'd ensure his death was long and painful. Nothing would stop him from having his revenge on a man who was a blight on Scottish soil.

He yelled to his men as they barrelled into the enemy's camp. "No prisoners. Kill them all." His men shouted their agreement as they surrounded Clan Kirk. Aedan pulled his sword and sliced into a man as he rode past with no thought or care that the man's last hours on earth would be long or painful. All that mattered was Abigail. Her safety.

The battle was bloody, swords clashed, and horses screamed. Aedan fell from his mount and fought with his clansmen to avenge their honor and home. The fight seemed to last forever, each stroke jarring his already injured arm, blood oozed from his wounds.

He looked up to the cottage and realized that from here, whoever was up there with Abigail, should she even be there, wouldn't know the clan had been attacked. He headed in that direction. Sweat poured down his face, and he rubbed his eyes to clear his vision. He stopped, halting his men as Rory stood, surrounded by a few remaining clansmen, the snarl on his face making the blood in his veins turn cold. The bastard would pay for this, no matter what came out of his mouth in the next few minutes.

"You'll lose this battle, Aedan. The woman isn't yours, and she'll do to you what she's done to me, no matter what promises she makes. I'm only taking back what is mine and making her repent."

Anger thrummed through Aedan, and he clenched his jaw. The urge to gut the man, spill his body parts, and let the dogs eat him alive, was tempting. "She's not who you seek. Wherever your betrothed went was not to my keep. Your actions this past day have brought nothing but dishonor to your family and yourself. It ends here. Now."

"You're too late, in any case. I've already taken your sweet woman's body." He laughed. "She liked it, too. Begged for more, scraped her nails down me back." Rory's men joined in with his mirth and Aedan's temper snapped.

He charged the man, his sword raised to chop off his head, anything, as long as the man died. Abigail would never have gone willingly to this traitor's bed, and it left him enraged that she'd been raped.

Shock registered on Rory's face, but it wasn't from Aedan's strike. The spike of a silver arrow protruded through the man's chest, and he looked down on it for a moment in awe, before his eyes glazed over in death and he fell forward. MacLeod clansmen took care of the last remaining Kirk men as Aedan looked around for who it was that had shot the arrow.

"Are ye alright?"

His attention flicked up the ridge to a copse of trees, and he met his sister's gaze. He swore. "What are ye doing here, Gwen? How did ye get out of yer room with Braxton at ye door?"

"You forget my room also has a hidden passageway. Braxton didn't let me out; in fact, he's no doubt snoring against my door right at this very moment, none the wiser."

"We'll be having words about this when we return home, I can assure ye." He stood. "Now, what are ye doing here? Explain yourself."

His sister smiled and gestured to the trees a little way away. "I was behind the tapestry in Abigail's room when he took off with her. I followed him and knew you'd catch up, eventually. But when I saw you were going to fight him after he goaded you, I had to shoot. Your sword skills have never been the very best when you're angry. And he angered ye on purpose."

Shocked mute for a moment, he stared at Gwen, not believing what she was saying. "You push me this day, sister, but I'm glad of it. It seems your aim is true."

Gwen smiled. "Are ye proud of me then?"

He nodded, starting for the cottage. "More than ye know. But ye still shouldn't have put yourself in so much danger. These men are not the sort I want my sister around."

"I know," Gwen said, frowning slightly.

"Give me yer arrows. I may need them."

She shrugged off her gear and handed them to him. Accompanied with two of his men, he ran for the cottage, the sound of a scream and swearing echoing over the ridge.

If they'd touched one hair on her body… Aedan crawled up the last of the rise and looked over a small ridge of stone and saw Abigail run from the cottage, a haggard, nasty-looking man close on her heels, before he pushed her over, sending her spiralling forward.

"Stay here. I'm going to move around and see if I can get closer without being seen."

His men and Gwen agreed and he left, never taking his

eyes off the woman he loved.

•••

Abigail gasped, her eyes wide with fear as he released the arrow, watching with satisfaction as it thumped into the bastard's back and popped out where his heart would sit. The man cried out, before falling over.

His lass rolled away from the dead man, scurrying farther still as blood pumped onto the soil and toward her foot.

"It's alright, lass. I've got ye. You're safe now."

And thank God he did…

Aedan scooped Abigail into his arms and cradled her against him. Her body shook. He pushed a lock of hair away from her face, hoping she'd say something. Look at him, anything, but only blankness stared back at him from her normally beautiful, vibrant eyes.

She was as pale as a new moon, and as cold as the loch in winter. He felt her skull and noted the large bump protruding from the back. No doubt how Rory Kirk had removed her from his keep with little fuss. He swore, glad the bastard who'd done this was dead.

She sniffed, seemingly trying to pull herself back together. Relief poured through him that she'd not been silenced mute by her suffering.

"How did you find me? Rory said you'd headed in the opposite direction to where he was taking me."

"We let him think we were headed away from his direction, but we weren't. Or, at least, I wasn't. My men informed me he'd headed for our enemy's land. 'Tis closer than his own." He cut the ties free from her wrists and cringed at the bloody rub marks. Picking her up, he walked over to his horse. "I need to get you and Gwen out of here. Do ye think ye can ride?"

"I think so."

"I'm so relieved Aedan got to ye in time." Gwen gave her a quick hug before Aedan ushered her toward a horse.

He helped her mount and pointed toward the gully to the south of them. "Ye need to ride hard in that direction, Gwen will show ye the way. You'll come to where the river splits in two. Turn right and cross there. It isn't deep. Ride for a few miles and then stop when you come to a clearing in the woods. We'll catch up to ye before nightfall, I promise."

"I'm scared, Aedan. What if something happens to you?"

He wiped a tear away from her cheek, smiling a little. "I promise ye I'll be there. We have to end this skirmish, bury our dead."

"Okay, I'll see you tonight, then."

"Aye. Nightfall," he said, slapping her horse's rump while watching her ride off with his sister.

Chapter Sixteen

Abby cringed and opened her eyes, shutting them just as quickly. Her brain pounded with a migraine unlike any she'd ever had before. And damn it, there was no Tylenol.

Memories of the ordeal bombarded her in quick succession. Of Rory Kirk, her chamber servant, of being hit over the head with something like a hammer. A cottage, a filthy Kirk clansman looking at her with degrading, horrifying intentions, of the man's putrid breath, rotting teeth, and a mouth salivating with lust.

Panic rose and she took a calming breath, relaxing a little when she recognized the room she occupied was the one back at Druiminn. She was home. Back within the safety of Aedan's keep. Back with Aedan.

A cool cloth pressed against her forehead, and she welcomed its calming effect. The bed dipped and a finger glided over her cheek, a soft caress from a person she recognized without even looking.

"Should you be in my room, Aedan MacLeod?" She smiled as she heard him chuckle, his lips pressing gently against her temple.

"Aye. The rules change when one's been injured."

She did look at him then, reaching up to touch his handsome face, kind and affectionate. He hadn't shaved, and the rasp of his stubble scratched her palm. "Isn't there enough women in this castle to do that?"

He shrugged, rinsing out the cloth and placing it back on her head. "Nay. You're my responsibility, and one I take very seriously. And I wanted to be here when ye woke, in case ye couldn't remember what happened and panicked."

"I remember most of the night. I think the knock to my head has jumbled the order in which they're running through my mind, but I haven't lost my memory. What I do know is I owe you a huge thank you for saving me from a fate worse than death. If you hadn't come to that cottage when you did, I don't want to imagine what would've happened."

"None of them will ever threaten ye again." Aedan's voice was hard and cold. A shiver stole down her spine at his vehemence.

"I don't remember you meeting me at the clearing." She tried to sit up, but the pain increased, stabbing down her neck, and she flopped back onto the pillows, rubbing her temples.

"You need to rest, Abigail. You've had a nasty hit and from the bruises on your body, you took a few beatings as well." He frowned. "You were unconscious by the time we met up with ye and Gwen at the clearing. You've been asleep for the past two days. I was startin' to worry, especially when Gwen thought the strike to ye skull could've killed ye."

She nodded, knowing that was probably very true, considering Rory's cruel nature and strength. "I'm glad it didn't."

Aedan nodded, chuckling at her attempt at a joke. "So am I."

Her heart swelled at his words. He looked worried and

anxious and she wanted nothing more than to kiss him, to show him how much she'd come to like him. Adore him, even. "Are you really?"

"Aye, lass. I don't know what I'd do if I lost ye. I've grown quite fond of ye."

His heartfelt words reminded her of her plan to return home. The thought of leaving him now turned her stomach. She couldn't do it. Not yet. And if what Aedan said was true about Rory Kirk not being a problem anymore, why couldn't she stay a little longer?

He poured her a cup of water and handed it to her. "Do ye still plan on leaving me?"

She shook her head, eliciting another thump behind her eyes. "No. I don't want to go." And she didn't. She didn't ever want to leave him. The thought of living a life without this man left a hollow crevice the size of the Grand Canyon inside where her heart would sit. She'd already lost one man she loved. She couldn't do it again. And maybe with her knowledge of future technology, she could make Castle Druiminn a little more modern and less harsh to live in. More homely. Maybe… "I don't ever want to go, but I know that's not possible. I don't fit in here. I'm not at all what your family needs. I'd bring nothing to a marriage. No fortune or army. Nothing."

He gathered her into his arms, and she went willingly into his embrace. His strong arms encircled her back, the support and safety she felt when wrapped against him unlike anything she'd ever experienced before. He kissed the top of her head, rocking her a little.

"Stay with me. Make my time yours."

She took a deep breath, having wanted to hear such an offer from him for some days now, but too scared to even think of the consequences should she choose this time to live in.

It would mean a lot to give up the twenty-first century. All of life's luxuries would be a thing of the past. Her life would be harder, dangerous even. Not to mention, the small amount of friends she did possess would never know what happened to her. All her years of schooling, trying to make something of herself so she may give her children, if blessed with any, a better childhood, would be for nothing. There was no need for museum curators here. Not to mention Abby wasn't cut out for seventeenth century life. This time was hard and volatile. What if she became ill with a disease and needed twenty-first century medicine? She could die in pain.

They were all points to consider, but then, when leveled against having Aedan as the man she would build a life with, support and love…there was really no question at all.

She pulled back and looked up at him. "Do you really mean that?"

"I do." He paused, his face deadly serious. "I want ye to be my wife. I don't want any of the women who're here."

"But Aedan," she said, not fully convinced, "I have some ancestry of Scots in my blood, but I'm not Scottish born, nor do I come with a powerful clan or army. You are giving up a lot to marry me."

"I want you. No one else, no matter how much power they may wield. Damn my previous stance of who would make the correct wife for Laird MacLeod. I want ye to be mine. Always. I love ye, lass."

His tone was serious and she bit her lip, loving his declaration. "So, you don't want me to help you find a wife anymore?" Abby grinned, liking the idea more and more. Not that she'd been helping much in that regard, since she'd been sleeping with and keeping Aedan to herself these past weeks.

"Well, if I remember correctly, ye haven't exactly been doin' what I asked ye to do. I've not had a report from ye in a week or more. And do ye not want to say something back to me?"

"I must confess I'd pretty much forgotten to do it, but I'm not sad that I did. Not if it means you're only looking at me." And right now he was looking at her with so much affection that had she been standing, her legs would've given out. Her first impression of him had been so wrong. Aedan was as far from a Neanderthal as one could get. "I love you, too." Emotion welled up inside and forgetting her headache, she clasped his stubbled jaw and pulled him down for a kiss.

Their lips touched and the slow, intoxicating seduction soon blazed to a wildfire between them, their tongues sliding, tasting, teasing the other. He nipped her lip, and she gasped when he pulled her up to straddle his legs, her wet, needy core against his cock.

He was long and hard, and Abby undulated against him. She needed release, to feel alive and joined with him, to remove the awful memory of what others had tried to do to her. It'd been too long since they'd been together this way.

A light knock sounded at the door and neither of them were quick enough to pull away. Gwen walked in and stopped, her mouth agape with shock. Abby didn't move from Aedan's lap, and instead she smiled tentatively to hide her embarrassment. "Hi Gwen." Heat rushed to her cheeks.

"Good morn, yourself," Gwen said, shutting the door quickly.

Aedan sighed and placed her back on the bedding, pulling the blankets up to her waist, and quickly meeting her gaze. He looked pained, and no doubt frustrated as hell after what they'd not been able to finish. Her own body burned with unsated need, and she clasped his hand, squeezing it a little. He turned and faced his sister.

"Are ye after something, Gwen?" he asked, his voice calm, a touch of boredom even.

"Me?" his sister said, pointing to herself. "I'm not after

anything, but I can see you are. I wanted to check on my friend, whom, by the way, ye seem to have forgotten, took a nasty hit to her head."

"I've not forgotten." His voice rang out with disdain. Abby bit her lip to stop the silly, loved-up grin that threatened. He didn't like his sister's accusation that he didn't care for her, and would take advantage of her in such a state.

Abby sighed. He'd not taken advantage of her, he could have her anytime and anyplace. It was official; she had it bad for the Scot.

"Perhaps you ought to tell your sister the news."

Aedan looked at her and frowned. "What news?"

Abby rolled her eyes. "The news about us." She rubbed her temple, shaking her head at his aloofness.

"What news?" Gwen asked, looking back and forth at them.

Aedan continued to stare at her, a small smile spreading across his lips. "So you're agreeing to my question then, lass?"

She grabbed his hand and kissed his palm. "Aye, I am, lad."

"What is going on here?"

Abby laughed at the annoyance in Gwen's tone and took pity on the poor woman. "Aedan and I are going to be married. He's asked for my hand, and I've said yes."

Gwen smiled, clapping her hands together in joy. "I'm so glad. This is the best of news."

"I think so, too," Abby said, meaning every word. Living in this time would be hard, she had no illusions, and Aedan thinking of war against the O'Cains was certainly something to take into consideration, but maybe she could change his mind. And a life in the future without him seemed bleak and lonely. Only half complete, no matter how pampered people lived in her time, the technology, travel. It all paled when compared to him.

She couldn't go back. Aedan was her life now. The man she wanted to make a future with.

"A servant will be bringing up some food to break Abigail's fast." Gwen walked over to the chair beside her bed and sat. "I suggest ye not be caught in such a predicament again, betrothed or not. As Abigail's to be the laird's wife, you need to think of her reputation, brother."

"It'll not happen again." A muscle worked in his jaw, pulling Abby's gaze to his lips. As much as she loved Gwen, she really had chosen the worst time to come and see her. Just then, a woman Abigail had seen downstairs a few times walked into the room with a wooden tray, an assortment of food spread out for her to choose from.

Abby thanked her, looking down at the stew-like soup and mead. If it wasn't for her headache, she'd feel almost normal, but still her stomach rumbled, not in the least fazed by her head trauma.

"How is Betsy? I hope she's being cared for after what Rory Kirk did to her. The bastard."

Both Gwen and Aedan looked at each other and dread pooled in her gut. "Is Betsy okay?" She thought over what happened in her room, of how Betsy had been thrown to the floor. She hadn't hit anything going down, but her memory was hazy at best… "Tell me what's going on."

"I was hiding in the secret passage, Abigail, and I saw everything that happened in the room with Rory. I remained quiet as I knew he'd try and flee with ye, and when he knocked you out, I checked on Betsy. She was dead. He'd broken her neck before throwing her to the floor. I'm so sorry."

Abby shut her eyes, the burn of tears making them sting. Betsy had been a sweet woman. A mother with little children. And now, because she'd traveled back in time and had reminded a crazed man of his missing betrothed, the woman was dead. "It's my fault. I can't believe he killed her.

She didn't do anything to him other than being my maid."

Aedan came and sat beside her, pulling her against him again. "Nay, lass. 'Tis not your fault. Rory Kirk was a bastard, has always been an uncharitable, cruel lord. Had it not been you, he would've chosen someone else to cause trouble for. It was his nature, as it's in Scotland's nature to be wild and untamed."

She sniffed against the crook of his neck, pulling him close. "She has little children, Aedan. We have to make sure they're looked after. Never hungry or without clothes. Promise me this."

He nodded. "Aye. I promise. They'll never be without."

She relaxed a little and weariness swamped her. "I think I'll rest a little while," she said, lying against the pillows. "Would that be okay? I'll eat later. I don't feel like anything now."

Gwen stood. "Of course, my dear. I'll check in on you later." She took the tray and set it on the bedside table, raised her brows at Aedan when he didn't venture to leave. "Are ye coming, brother?"

He kissed her quickly and strode from the room. Abby watched them go and sighed when the door shut. Rolling over, she hugged her bedding, the tears flowing freely for what had transpired in the last three days. An innocent, beautiful life lost for no reason. Life could be cruel. She knew that as well as anyone else, but it still didn't make it any easier to bear.

•••

A few days later, Aedan strode across the courtyard and stopped when he saw Abigail talking to one of his clansmen. He started toward them and then stopped when she hugged the man before pulling away and heading for the castle.

The clansman walked off to continue with his business,

none the wiser that he was under the scrutiny of his laird.

A cold knot of jealousy spiked in his soul, and he yelled out to Abigail to stop. "Replacing me already, lass?" He was sure what she'd done was wholly innocent, but he needed to hear it from her. He was merely curious, not a jealous, love-sick lout.

"That's Betsy's husband. He came up to the castle to thank me for the food hamper and linen for new clothes for his children. I told him they'll never be in need. I feel so bad, Aedan. It's like her blood's on my hands."

"Nay, lass. 'Tis not." He wanted to hold her, give her comfort, no matter where they were, but Aline emerging from the castle halted his impulse.

"Good morning, Aline. I hope you're finding yer time here well worth the visit," Aedan said.

Aline looked at Abigail with disdain, and he frowned. The woman was as sharp as his dirk.

"It is a beautiful day, is it not," she said, not bothering to include Abigail in their conversation. "Would ye walk me down to the games, Aedan? I want to watch every event, being it is the last day."

Abigail smiled. "Yes, what a shame we'll not have you here to grace our presence anymore, Aline. You've been such wonderful company to be around. You'll be sorely missed."

Abigail leaned up and kissed Aedan's cheek. "I'm going to lie down for a while. I'll see you at lunch." Aedan stared at Abigail's retreating back, smiling at her candor. She was as refreshing as chilled water. Aline made a strangled sound that resembled a wild animal caught in a trap, and he fought to not laugh.

"What vulgar friends your sister has. I'm sure you should never invite her again to yer home."

He shook his head, knowing how wrong the woman before him was. Abigail was the best of people. Granted, she came from the future, her life easier in many ways, and yet not. She had no parents, had been given to people as a child who really did not care to know her. Had lived through the death of her partner, and yet still had room for him in her heart.

Aye, she was outspoken, fiery, too, but so was he. She was perfect for him in every way, unlike the woman standing before him. Aline was the veriest she-devil if ever there was one. "Abigail Cross will always be welcome in my home. We're to announce our betrothal tonight."

A tinge of guilt stabbed his gut at the girl's crestfallen visage, but at her next words his moment of weakness disappeared.

"Ye cannot marry her. She's not even Scottish, no matter what she says her ancestry is."

He shrugged, walking toward the games that were about to commence. "I care not." He slowed his steps to allow the girl to keep up. "She could be a thatcher's daughter and I'd still marry her. She's the best woman I know."

Aline scoffed. "I must admit, since we're speaking so candidly, that I'm shocked by this turn of events. Father will be disappointed to hear this."

Aedan stopped before the viewing platform the women and older clansmen were using to observe the games. "He may discuss the matter with me after dinner tonight, although I fail to see how this concerns him."

"I would think a man who's about to do battle with Clan O'Cain would be securing as many alliances as he could."

"Are ye suggesting that because I haven't asked for your hand in marriage I'll lose the support of your father's clan?" Aedan knew marrying Abigail could possibly sever the ties he'd formed over the years, but Scotland was full of clans, some helpful, some not. And he had many fighting men, more than enough to keep his home and people safe. Aline's threat was weak and showed a spitefulness that he'd only had glimpses of until now.

"Talk to Father yourself and see. And best wishes for your future, I fear ye may need as much luck as ye can get."

Aedan bowed. "Thank you. You're acceptance and generosity in my future happiness shows how much breeding and ladylike temperament you possess." His voice dripped sarcasm before he turned and headed for the weight-over-the-bar event, leaving Aline gaping after him.

...

Later that night a servant ushered Aline's father, the Laird of Grant, into his anteroom. He stood, beckoning him to sit, before he, too, took his seat.

The large clansmen looked flushed in the face, his hair ruffled and sticking up. Aedan waited for him to speak, not the least interested in the forthcoming conversation. His mind was set, he would marry Abigail and be damned anyone who dared to step in his way.

"After Aline told me of ye plans today I thought that you were bluffing, but after the meal tonight and your announcement, I see that you're not."

Aedan smiled, remembering the roar from his clansmen at the announcement of his betrothal. That he had the support of his people was enough for him. His closest ally, Black Ben's clan, when joined with his in battle, was a force to be reckoned with, and he certainly didn't need the support of Clan Grant to secure his future.

War with the O'Cains withstanding or not.

"I'm deadly serious with my offer of marriage to Abigail Cross. I believe she'll suit me well." He kept the smile off his lips at the memory of her and their time together. Now that he'd announced his intention, he would ensure they had even more time alone…and undisturbed.

"To say I'm not disappointed would be a lie. I had hopes you'd offer for Aline, but 'tis what it is."

Aedan poured the man a whisky, slid it across the desk, and leaned back in his chair. "I must admit to assuming a different reaction from you."

The older man chuckled, downing his whisky in one swallow. "Nay, as much as me daughter is disappointed, I'll not stand in the way of yer happiness. I'm happy for you and the lass. And of course, I will still support ye should ye declare war on the O'Cains. The bastards are always stealing me cattle."

Aedan nodded, knowing only too well what the O'Cains were like. "Tomorrow the clans will be leaving MacLeod land, and then the celebrations for Lammas and my sister's forthcoming handfasting will commence. Of course, you'll be invited."

"Aye, two unions within months of each other. Yer father would be proud of ye, boy."

Aedan nodded, hoping this was true, and yet his father, a hard man, not one to show any emotion other than at the end of a sword, would probably disagree. "Are ye all set for your journey in the morn?"

"Aye." The older man rose, stretching. "We are. Just make sure ye send word when ye need our help, and we'll be here as soon as we can."

"Thank you, I appreciate yer support. Likewise, send word if you're ever in need."

Aedan watched the older man leave. Walking over to a window, he stared out at his lands. In the outer courtyard, lanterns burned and the muffled sounds of men could be heard. The meeting with Laird Grant had gone better than he'd hoped. Aline would be disappointed to hear it. He smiled and thought of Abigail, who at this very moment waited for him upstairs…

It had been too many nights since he'd lain with her. He turned to go and stopped as the very woman haunting his every thought walked into the room, sliding the bolt across the door and locking them in.

"Abigail," he said, watching the sway of her hips as she made her way across the room.

"Aedan," she replied, running her hands up his chest as she came to stand before him. "I was lonely. I thought I might come and keep you company."

...

Aedan chuckled as she started to untie his sporran. "Ye can keep me company whenever ye like. You'll never have an argument from me on that score."

"I'm glad." She pulled him over to his desk, sliding up to sit before him. His hands moved up her legs, bringing her gown to pool about her waist. The pull for him to touch her, to make her come apart in his arms, made her wet between her legs. He cupped her sex and she moaned, biting her lip as he teased her flesh. His heavy lidded gaze pinned her in place as one finger slid between her folds.

"You're so beautiful," he said, his eyes cloudy with desire. "I'm in awe of you."

She smiled, pulling him down for a kiss. His lips took hers, his tongue stroking against hers in a tantalizing rhythm. Using her legs, she wrapped herself about his hips, pulling him where she craved him most.

He growled, letting her go a moment as he fought with the belt on his kilt. It hit the floor with a *swoosh*. He stood before her, his chest rising and falling in quick succession, his chiselled body all for her and no one else. Desire ran hot in her blood and threatened to make her go up in flames.

Each time they were together like this, it was like opening

a naughty Christmas present. He was magnificent, and that his heart was true, beat only for her, made him impossible to deny. She was absolutely, without question, in love with him.

His penis jutted against his stomach, and she clasped it, sliding her hand against its velvety smoothness, teasing him, stroking him, using the little droplet of come that pooled at the end to give her lubricant.

Aedan looked up at the ceiling, his hands a vice-like grip against her thighs.

"Would you like me to use my mouth on you?"

He met her gaze, the wicked tilt to his lips telling her that he would.

"I will not force myself on ye for such favors."

"You don't need to force me. I want to do it." Abby pushed him back and slid off the table, pulling him around to sit where she'd vacated. He lay down and placed his arms beneath his head, his attention wholly on her ministrations.

He shivered beneath her at her first taste of him, and she revelled in his moan of pleasure. Heavy in her hand and as soft as silk, she touched him, falling into a rhythm as his cock strained rigid, his breathing hard and labored.

Abby kissed along the toned muscles of his stomach, biting her way up his chest until she was laying over him, looking down into the greenest orbs she'd forever adore. She grabbed his hands, grinning. "I want you to place your hands above your head. Keep them there until I tell you to move."

He nodded, but didn't reply, just wickedly grinned at her. Abby straddled him, rubbing her hands across his body, feeling the light sheen of sweat on his skin. The essence of him filled her senses, that of a man, lavender soap, and something that was wholly Aedan.

She flicked her tongue across his nipple, savoring every groove and muscle indentation he had, before kissing his jaw, the lobe of his ear.

"You're killing me, lass."

He tried to kiss her but she sat up, wagging her finger at him. His penis jutted against her core and she slid over it, enjoying the friction it created against her aching flesh. Taking him in her hand, she guided him inside, sighing as he filled her.

Aedan swore, the sheen of sweat across his brow growing with every moment she made him wait. Slowly, she rose, only to lower herself again in agonizing strokes. Abby braced her hands on his chest, her fingers playing with his nipples as she started to ride him in earnest.

Her body sang, his body the instrument. He was large, with a thickness that left her full, aching, hot. Each thrust hit that special spot deep inside and she couldn't get enough.

Abby found her groove, her breathing rapid, and she soon let go of any inhibitions she might feel. Instead, she set out to enjoy him, to allow his body to bring her to ecstasy.

She moaned, leaning back as an orgasm teased her. With her eyes closed, she felt Aedan's hands come around to clasp her ass as he sat up. With his hands behind her, he grabbed her shoulders and pulled her down hard on his cock. It was enough to spike her over the edge and she came, her body convulsing, draining him of his seed as he joined her.

Her orgasm seemed to go on deliciously long, and she stayed fused with him as the last tremor subsided from her body. She sighed, contentment making her bones weightless in his arms. "That never gets old," she said, kissing his shoulder.

He nuzzled her neck, kissing her softly beneath her ear. "Not when it's with the right person."

Abby hugged him to her, the raw emotion of love that filled her at his words threatening to make her cry. "Why is it you always seem to know exactly what to say?"

"Are they the right words, lass?"

She smiled even though he couldn't see it. "They so are. Every one."

Chapter Seventeen

Over the next few weeks, Aedan showed Abby the rest of his estate, his land and tenant farms. Scotland in this time, its raw beauty, was like nothing she'd ever experienced, and she was in love with it as much as she was in love with Aedan.

Sleeping under the stars, with only a few of his guards, gave them plenty of time to enjoy the quiet and solitude the weeks afforded them. Having left Black Ben and Braxton, along with Gwen, in charge of Druiminn, Aedan had taken her away to recover from her injuries, both physical and mental, from Rory Kirk.

With each passing day, the more time they spent in each other's company, Abby became more sure of her heart. She'd fallen for him, absolutely and without doubt.

To live in this time with the man she loved was a dream come true. Nothing had ever been so exciting in her life. Yes, it was hard, cold, and damp, but it was also wonderful and beautiful. Aedan warmed her soul, thawing any chill the Highland wind brought with it. He was caring, a loving lover, and adored his family. It was like he'd stepped out of a fairy tale.

She watched him as he beckoned her into the small pond that they'd found on their return home to Druiminn. It'd been a couple of days since they'd bathed, and the day was surprisingly warm, but as she dipped her toe into the water, she gasped as the chill seeped into her skin.

"It's so cold! I'm not getting in there with you." She stood at the edge, Aedan waist deep, grinning at her, a devilish light in his eyes.

"Yes, ye are, now dinna make me come out and get ye, lass. I'm naked."

She bit her lip, the thought of what was beneath the surface warming her enough to dive in, but she wasn't stupid. "Naked as a wee babe?"

He laughed at her teasing.

"Have I ever told ye how much I love it when ye talk to me in my accent." He walked toward her. "Come now. I'll keep ye warm."

Abby cringed as she pulled off her light shift and jumped in, pulling her legs up and cannon-balling Aedan. He may as well get as wet as she was.

"Minx." He went to grab her but she swam away.

The water bit into her flesh, and she shivered. "Oh my God, it's so cold. Please tell me that it does get warmer at some point during the year."

"Ye do know you're in Scotland, no?"

He pulled her against him, and she wrapped her legs about his hips, the hardness of him pressing against her core. Desire thrummed between them, Aedan's hot, hooded gaze making her pulse race.

"I'm pretty sure I know where I am." She slid against him, smiling wickedly. She wrapped her arms loosely about his neck, watching him watch her with an intentness that she'd forever remember. "In fact, I really like my current location."

"Really," he said, raising his brow. "Perhaps we ought to move ye south, north, and south again for the foreseeable future. Could be enjoyable."

Abby clasped the hair at the back of his nape and pulled it a little. "You're so naughty. Whatever will I do with you?"

"I could think of a lot of things."

"Why don't you tell me, then?" Abby raised herself and slid slowly down his shaft. His member filled her completely, causing her need for him to flame with a fire that was never extinguished.

His jaw clenched. "I want ye like this. I want ye on my bed, in my private chambers, on top of the heather on a grassy hill. I want to taste every inch of your body, to love, learn, and worship all there is to love about ye. I want to feel your mouth wrapped around me, loving me to completion. In fact, I want you to do that while I do the same to you."

Abby shut her eyes, as she continued to love him with her body. His dirty talk, the low timbre of his voice, the delicious accent was almost too much. She tightened her core about him, and he swore. "What else?" she asked.

He swallowed. His Adam's apple bobbing against his throat. "I want to bend ye over, lift ye skirts, and take ye wherever we are and whenever I see ye. I want to touch ye, hear your sweet voice, and smell your beautiful scent, whenever I can."

Tears pooled in her eyes, and she kissed him. His soft lips meshed with hers with a ferocity that scared her. The emotions he pulled forth in her, what he made her feel, were terrifying yet liberating. He jerked her hard against him, one hand helping her ride his cock, while the other guided her mouth. The kiss deepened, turned hot, demanding.

She broke the kiss, held on as he pushed her to orgasm quickly, taking her repeatedly. She loved it. When Aedan was like this, she glimpsed the hardened Highlander who made her quiver with need.

Rough sex, raw and hard, was too addictive by far. With a growl, he too followed her to orgasm, her body clenching in exquisite aftershocks.

His forehead was against hers, and he watched her as they both tried to calm their rapid breathing. "I mean every word I say, lass. What is the term you would use for a man in love with a woman? A modern expression, say?"

She pushed some hair off his face, running her hands over his jaw as he placed her back on her feet. "That you've fallen for her. We still use the word love." She laughed.

He sobered, all mirth wiped from his visage. "Well then, I've fallen for ye, lass. I love ye. What say you?"

"You have no idea how hot you are when you talk in my type of language." She bit her lip. How lucky could one girl be? "I love you, too. Utterly besotted with you, actually. Aren't we blessed?"

"Very blessed," he said, taking her lips again and showing her how blessed he was—in water and out.

Chapter Eighteen

The castle and the surrounding lands were a hive of activity. Abby strolled with Aedan toward a field at the northern side of the estate. The land this side of the castle was relatively flat and went for some miles uninterrupted by woodland.

They walked side-by-side, the odd bumping of hands followed by heavy-lidded gazes that made her stomach clench. Somehow, in the last few weeks, Abby had started to call this land, this time, her home, and the future seemed so very far away—an impossibility that she'd no longer have to concern herself with.

She smiled, contentment warming her soul. "It's so beautiful here. I don't think I'll ever get used to Scotland's majestic splendor."

Aedan put an arm about her shoulder and pulled her against his side. "Aye. It has a way of needling into yer heart."

They stopped at the side of a wheat field, the tenant farmers hard at work with the start of the reaping. "Explain to me again how Lammas works?" A young boy ran past, giggling as an older lad chased him as if the hounds of hell were on their tails. Abby laughed and watched them disappear toward a small, shallow river.

"It's the first harvest festival for the year. All my tenant farmers will bring a loaf made from their new crops harvested during Lammastide."

The wind picked up, and the wheat made a dry rustling sound, its golden yellow color all but shouting it was ready for cutting. Abby caught the faint smell of Wheat Chex cereal and smiled, as it reminded her of home. "And what happens then?"

"It's blessed and broken into four bits and placed at each corner of our barn, to protect the garnered grain."

Abby looked up at Aedan and took in his features. They were relaxed, a slight smile tweaking his lips, completely serious. "And do you believe that the blessing actually works?"

"Of course." He pulled back a little affronted. "Don't ye?"

"Not at all." She chuckled at his shocked expression. "Somehow, I can't see how saying a prayer over wheat will stop it from going moldy, or sprouting, or whatever wheat does once it's harvested. I think the elements or rodents are more likely the cause for any trouble you have with the crop and no wishing it away will change that."

"Perhaps you'd like to tell me what you really think."

Abby laughed at his teasing, wrapping her arms about his waist. "Just because I don't believe the prayer will work doesn't mean I won't be standing beside you, hoping it does."

He leaned down, taking her lips in a kiss. Abby leaned into him, pulling him close. The continued sound of sickles chopping through wheat stems sounded around them. She ran her hand over his shirt, the smoothness at odds to his woolen kilt. "Do you think it'll be a good harvest?"

Aedan nodded, turning them toward the castle. "I do. There was plenty of rain in the season followed by good growth periods. The harvest should be enough to keep all of those involved happy."

They walked for a little while in silence, before something that had been bothering her for the past few days niggled to the point she had to ask. "I have a question that's not related to farming, but I don't want to alert you to anything, as I'm not sure if you've noticed like I have." They continued toward the large grey edifice of Druiminn Castle, but Abby could feel his curious gaze.

"Out with it, lass."

She placed a stray strand of hair behind her ear, the wind coming straight at them in this direction. "Well, I wanted to know if there was anything ever between Gwen and Ben. Sometimes, the way he looks at her…"

"How does he look at her?" Aedan pulled them to a stop, his easy-going manner now replaced with that of a protective brother.

"You are not going to declare war on your friend. So behave yourself. Gwen is a grown woman, well and truly old enough to make decisions for herself." A muscle in his jaw worked, and Abby ran her finger over it. He glared, and she smiled.

"He looks at her sometimes how you look at me, and it made me wonder if they'd had a past."

Aedan seemed to think on it, a slight frown between his brows. "'Tis possible, I suppose. We have known each other since childhood, but Ben's never mentioned anything, and Gwen is in love with Braxton."

"I know she is, I'm not disputing that, but I wondered." Abby stopped them beside a slow flowing river, watching as the water trickled over stones, green moss swaying beneath the surface. "We should set him up with someone. Maybe's he's lonely now that all of his friends are marrying, finding the person they want to be with forever, he's becoming nostalgic."

He lifted her chin with one finger, smiling down at her.

"You're too kind-hearted, and I love ye for it. As for Ben, and whether he wishes to be saddled with a woman, I'm not certain. I'm sure whatever ye picked up on between Gwen and him was affection that stemmed from familiarity and duty. Nothing more."

"Perhaps." Abby shrugged, not buying that for a moment. There was history there, but for whatever reason, Gwen wasn't as enamoured of Ben as he was of her. It didn't mean that Ben couldn't find love elsewhere. He had to meet the right woman. "I was just curious… I promise I'll leave him alone."

"Trust me when I tell ye, he's more than busy with the lasses. He doesn't need any help." Aedan smiled. "Behave, wench, or I'll be forced into actions that ye may not approve of."

Abby leaned into him, sliding her hand over the front of his kilt. Whenever they were together like this, all she wanted to do was consume him. Touch him, bathe in his love, wonder that he doted on her. He was becoming a very addictive man to be around.

She stroked his manhood. His eyes darkened with desire, his hand coming around her back and holding her against him. "There aren't many things I wouldn't approve from you, Aedan MacLeod. Do your worst."

"You try my resolve." His breathing hitched when she covered him with her hand, pulling, teasing his hardened flesh that she craved.

"Do not threaten me with things that I'd enjoy. And certainly do not tease me where we cannot act on our desire."

"There is no one about." Abby looked up at the castle walls and didn't spy any men on the battlements, nor were there any loitering on the outside of the castle walls.

He nipped her earlobe, kissing his way down her neck. Taking her hand away from him, he lifted her slightly against his chest, undulating against her sex. Abby gasped, fire replacing the blood running through her veins.

"Behave, lass."

Abby laughed and stepped away, pulling him toward the castle. "You know, you shouldn't—" her words trailed off when she saw Ben and Gwen down by the river, seemingly in some sort of argument.

"What's wrong?" Aedan came to stand beside her, and she pointed out what had caught her attention.

"What do you think they're talking about?"

"With those two? It could be anything and nothing at all."

Abby didn't think it was, but then why would they be arguing if they didn't have anything to discuss. "It's a little odd. You should ask them. Gwen could be up to something like bringing someone else through time for someone else she wants to matchmake."

Aedan laughed. "They've argued for as long as I can remember. If one said the grass was green, the other would say it was blue. 'Tis how they are. Come, I need ye."

The deep sound of his voice and his words, which could only mean one thing, sent her body into overdrive. She was turning into a horny, insatiable woman and she loved it. "What for?" she teased, grinning up at him.

He raised one rakish eyebrow, and her legs turned to jelly. As usual. "What do ye think?"

"Well, I don't know. It could be anything…" He kissed her, putting a stop to her prattle, and all thoughts of Gwen and what she was doing with Ben flew out of her mind. In fact, Aedan kept her occupied for the remainder of the day with little thought other than themselves.

•••

Lammas came and went and so, too, did the day of Gwen's wedding. Scotland had pulled out all the stops to ensure the day dawned without a cloud in the sky, and no sign of forthcoming weather. Abigail was certain her future sister-in-law's life would follow a clear and sunny disposition, as well.

The morning had passed in a rush of bathing, eating, laughing, and joy over her friend's forthcoming nuptials with Braxton. Gwen's chamber servant had fixed the bride's hair in plaits with an assortment of ribbons and flowers threaded throughout.

The gown was tartan in the family colors of red and blue. With long sleeves and a low square neckline, the dress reminded Abby of the sort she'd seen in princess books, but without the silk. There was no veil, only a train that fell from the lower back and made from one solid color of emerald green. Gwen looked beautiful and from the smile she offered to Braxton when she came to stand beside him for the ceremony, she was a woman in love, filled with hope for the future.

The wedding took place in the castle church. It was a simple building made of stone, with slate tiles covered with green moss. Graves sat scattered about its exterior in a chaotic order, not lined up in an orderly fashion, as they were in her time. Abby looked about, trying to see if she could spot where Aedan's parents lay, but couldn't find them. Inside the building was a simple room with a large stained glass window at one end and an altar made of stone, not marble.

Abby sat in the front pew. The coarse wooden seat could use a cushion or two and Abby shifted about, trying to find a comfortable position. She gave up when the church started to fill with guests and the groom himself.

Light sprinkled in through the stained glass window, casting colored shadows on the aisle. The church doors opened and Gwen, on the arm of her brother, walked toward Braxton. Abby took in Aedan and could clearly read his face. He was like an open book that screamed pride and love. Abby smiled at them, her eyes welling up with tears and she quickly searched for a handkerchief.

The service was to-the-point and quick, the priest not taking the opportunity for a lengthy scripture because the church was full of congregants. It seemed no sooner were promises made and the exchange of rings performed, along with the handfasting, that it was over.

Abby took Aedan's hand and smiled up at him as the priest announced the husband may kiss his bride. He squeezed hers in return and lifted it to his lips, placing a kiss against her palm. Abby's heart beat out a fluttering tattoo at the heavy lidded gaze he assailed upon her. Just a look or touch and she was lost.

Swallowing the lump in her throat, Abby looked back toward the happy couple. Weddings had always made her emotional, even if she'd been a plus one and hadn't even known the couple, she'd never failed to cry, and it seemed that today was no different.

Gwen and Braxton kissed and the guests cheered, standing and clapping to mark the end of the ceremony. A piper, standing to the side of the church, started a lively tune and led the newly married couple outside. Aedan stood, pulling her beside him to follow them. "That was so beautiful. I'm so glad I was here to see it." She stood on the steps of the church and watched as the newly handfasted couple made their way toward the castle, the tenant farmers, clansmen, servants alike, shouting out congratulations as they made their way along the grassy path.

"Aye, it was. Gwen will be happy, which in turn makes me so. I'm glad for her."

Abby nodded. "Braxton loves her dearly, but I'm sure you'll miss her. How far is his estate?"

Aedan frowned in thought. "His land borders mine to the south. Two days by horseback. I'm sure we'll see her often."

"So not too far then." Abby didn't know if she should bring up the fact that his other sister was not present, but her absence was odd. "Why isn't Jinny here today? Gwen mentioned it a few weeks ago that you'd sent word for her to return."

He made a growling sound, and Abby thought maybe she should've kept her mouth shut. "Jinny never wants to return. She feels she's a burden and embarrassment for the family. Utter nonsense, of course, but she's as stubborn as Gwen. I'll not change her mind."

"So she's to stay at the convent for the rest of her life? Doesn't she wish for marriage or a family? I thought being handfasted, even though it was with the wrong man, didn't mean the end of the world for a woman of her standing. Life goes on. She could find love and marry again, I'm sure of it."

Aedan smiled, shaking his head. "Ye modern mind dismisses the deep scar that the O'Cains inflicted on Jinny. She feels humiliated and unworthy. Thinks all men would view her as disabled and barren. She was married into the clan for a year and no bairn came of it. Perhaps 'tis better she stays where she is. At least she's happy and safe."

Abby pulled back and tried to understand Aedan's words. "I think that's all the more reason for you to bring her home and make her see sense. To make her see that there is a future to be had after such a disappointment. That there are good men out there waiting to be plucked like a petal." Annoyance tinged her tone, and she narrowed her eyes when Aedan grinned.

"'Plucked like a petal?' Do I even want to know what ye mean by that?"

She shrugged, losing a little of her anger at his teasing. "Probably not. My mind wasn't being totally proper." She laughed. "But really, Aedan, you should think about it. She can have a future, even if it isn't what she first thought it would be."

"I'll think on the idea," he said, placing her hand back into the crook of his arm.

When they made the castle, Abby was pleased with what they'd managed to create for the wedding party. Every available surface in the great hall was decorated with wildflowers. Multiple candles sat on every table, their soft light casing the room with an air of romance and beauty. Gwen looked eagerly about, the smile on her face giving her joy away.

"Congratulations," Abby said, kissing Gwen and Braxton on the cheek and hugging Gwen. "I wish you all the very best for the future."

"Thank you, Abigail." Gwen beamed up at her husband. "I'm sure we will be very happy."

Abby left them to talk with the other well-wishers and sat down at the dais with Aedan. Servants bustled about with mugs of ale and wine, before the first dishes were brought out.

The first course was a vegetable soup that looked as delicious as it smelled and Abby remembered having a similar meal at a wedding in the twenty-first century. She looked out over the guests, each one enjoying the night, partaking in the celebration, getting obscenely drunk, and she smiled. Being here, living here, dressing in the fashions of the time, following rules appropriate to her status, resembled what she thought it might be like to make a period movie.

Except, the man who graced the seat beside her was no actor playing a part. He was real, with true emotions and reactions. No acting at all, just honest, genuine feelings and thoughts, and with all of it combined, it made the night more than she imagined.

Never had she felt more at home, or more welcome than she did around the present company. This was her home now. Aedan was her future, and she couldn't wait to take the vows that would join them in marriage and make him hers for all time.

"Did I tell you that you're looking very handsome in your newly made kilt and freshly pressed shirt?" She placed her hand on his leg and stroked the linen high enough that her palm touched the flesh of his thigh. The hairs on his leg tickled her palm, and she smiled up into eyes that would rival the darkest emerald.

"As do you," he said, halting her hand when she slipped it a little higher.

His intense gaze sent her stomach into knots. "Thank you for making me feel so special, Aedan MacLeod."

"I've been meaning to apologize for my treatment of ye when you first arrived. I acted appallingly, and I'm not proud of it. Please understand it was out of fear for Gwen that I blamed you and made ye pay for her interference. I'm truly sorry."

She blinked back tears, never expecting the great Laird MacLeod to right a wrong, especially to a woman, but then he wasn't like most men. Not of her own time or his. "Thank you. And I hope you, too, can forgive my mouth, which at times has a tendency to blurt out words before they've been properly thought through."

He laughed and gestured to the servants to commence the second course. "Your mouth is one of the things I love best about ye. I'd never wish to silence it. Always speak the truth to me, lass. Promise me you'll never lie."

"I promise." Forgetting where they were, Abby leaned up and kissed him. He didn't shy away. In fact, he clasped the nape of her neck and deepened the kiss.

Gasps, clapping, and laugher sounded around them, but she didn't care. As long as he continued to kiss her as he was now, like there was no ending in sight, that forever and a day this was all he wished to do, she'd be one content woman.

Like all their kisses, this one sent a fiery need burning through her soul. And by the demanding, hungry touch from

Aedan, he, too, didn't seem to care where they were or who they were in front of.

"Are ye trying to outshine your sister's day of days, brother? Very bad taste, if I do say so myself."

Aedan laughed as he pulled away, swiping his thumb over Abby's bottom lip. Every inch of her skin responded, craved for his touch. Her well-kissed lips were swollen, and she grinned.

"I would never try to do so, Gwen," Aedan said, winking.

Abby flopped back into her chair, marveling at how, while her body was going crazy with unsated need, Aedan went back to eating his meal, as if nothing was amiss. The thought of dragging him up to her room and having her wicked way with him crossed her mind more than once as his strong arms reached out for his mug of ale, or to place more food on his plate. He was so devilishly handsome, so sweet, that her teeth ached.

His lips quirked into a grin.

"What are you thinking?" she asked, wanting to know what was going on in his mind.

He leaned back in his chair, eyeing her over the top of his cup. "That you're the most interesting, consuming, beautiful woman I've ever had the pleasure of meeting, and how thankful I am that Gwen found ye and brought you back."

Warmth flowed through her, making her a big pile of love. "Really?" she asked, not sure she'd heard right. He clasped her hand and kissed it, nodding.

Gwen leaned over to them, smirking. "And yet I'm still waiting for my apology from ye, brother. Calling me an interfering so-and-so all those weeks ago. As far as I can see, you'll never be able to repay such a boon."

"Apologies, Gwendolyn. I hope you'll forgive my extreme reaction to ye meddling with the Abigail lass."

His sister snorted. "Aye, that'll do. It's probably the best I'll get from ye, in any case. Now, dear brother, signal the minstrels. I want to dance with my husband."

Aedan looked up at the minstrel's gallery and gestured for the music to commence. The guests helped the servants push the tables to the side of the room, making plenty of space for the dancing. Gwen and Braxton started off with a reel that soon had everyone joining in.

The bagpipes sounded clear and strong, and mixed with drums, harps, and flutes made the music come to life. The haunting sound washed over Abby and she sat there for a moment and watched this medieval life at play. Within the castle this night, there was nothing but enjoyment, high spirits, and merriment. Gwen couldn't have had a better wedding reception no matter what century she was in.

"Do ye want to dance, lass?"

She took Aedan's hand and held it in her lap. "No. I want to sit here with you." And she did. Just being near Aedan left her feeling a contentment she hadn't known before. Even in the twenty-first century something had never sat quite right within her, like a part of her was missing, or she was missing something from her life. Now she knew what that was.

Her soul mate.

"Do ye miss your home?"

Abby looked out over the wedding celebrations, the clan that had welcomed her as one of their own, of the man beside her who loved her beyond any doubt. "No, I don't. Not really."

"Not really?"

She laughed, knowing she missed one thing at least. "I suppose I miss toilet paper. I can't quite get used to the leaves and linen rags that you use here." She sighed. "And I'll miss my cell phone, the technology. Oh, and my studies. I guess you'd call me a scholar in this time."

"Well, now ye must explain what a toilet is? And once you've answered that, what the hell is toilet paper?"

Abby pushed her plate away, not able to eat another

bite. Grabbing the wine flask she filled up her cup. "A toilet is a garderobe or privy. Toilet paper is what you use to…you know, to wipe yourself."

Aedan watched as she took a sip of her drink, his gaze darkening with intent. "I'm not sure if I want to know any more about ye time." He laughed, pushing a lock of hair from her shoulder. "I'm glad you're here."

"So am I." Abby stood and pulled him up to follow. "Let's go outside for a walk. I think there's a full moon and it'll be nice to have you all to myself."

"Are ye trying to lure me to an indiscretion with ye? I'm a gentleman, I'll have ye know, lass."

"I don't believe that for a moment," she said, clasping him about the waist, the corded muscles of his lower abdomen distracting her for a moment. He was so hard and toned. A real, live fighting machine. "I think you'd love for me to lead you into temptation…"

"Aye, you know me well." They walked toward the outer courtyard, climbing up a staircase that ran on the outer kitchen wall, leading up to the roof. Aedan dismissed the guard who greeted them at the top and told him to wait until their return.

Aedan leaned against the battlement, pulling her against his chest. She loved the feel of his arms about her waist, the thump of his heart strong against her back. They stood in silence, both lost in thoughts as they looked out onto the Isle of Skye glistening in the moonlight beyond. The few cottages that lay scattered within the forests and along the shoreline had small lights burning in their windows.

Abby looked up into the sky and sighed at the millions of stars that twinkled in the heavens. In Salem where she lived, such a sight was marred by city lights, and with the clear air here in Scotland and not a cloud in the sky, every star shone as bright as the sun.

"I think I could look at this view forever."

Aedan kissed the skin beneath her ear, nibbling his way down to her shoulder. "Just as I'd wish for ye to see this view forever."

His kisses made her shiver, and she tilted her head to give him easier access. "Are you certain it doesn't matter if you marry a woman who isn't a clan member or a woman of importance from the surrounding clans?"

"Nay. My wife. My choice, as I said, lass." He kissed across her shoulder, slipping her gown partly off her shoulder. "And I choose you."

Abby turned in his arms and met his gaze. "I don't want to be the cause of any trouble for you, Aedan. This time is hard enough already."

"Ye are not. Trust me when I tell ye, you're never a burden to me."

Slowly, he leaned down and kissed her, the slightest touch, a flittering of lips. "I want ye to stay. You know that. And I wouldn't say I want ye as my wife, unless I was sure of the fact."

Abby nodded, swallowing the lump that formed in her throat. "I don't want you to regret your decision. You know I'll not always agree with you on everything. I'm opinionated, stubborn, very much like you, actually." She smiled.

"Minx." He tickled her, and she squealed. As she tried to squirm away, it only made him more determined to torture her, and she ended up more entwined in his arms. "Aye, that mouth needs to shut for a moment."

She gasped, and he grabbed the opportunity to distract her. His lips took hers, and she was lost. The embrace turned hot, wet, and demanding. Abby lifted herself to be against his chest, wrapping her arms about his neck. Their bodies fit perfectly. Like they were meant to be. Her breasts, pushed hard against his chest, felt full, and she moaned when his hand came up and cupped one, his finger finding her pebbled nipple and rolling it between his fingers.

Her tongue touched his, a melding of mouths and souls. His deep growl caused her body to flush hot, and she willed him to do whatever he wanted with her.

"Should we sneak off to my room where I can have my wicked way with you?"

He nipped her bottom lip, kissing his way down her chin and neck, eliciting a shiver down her spine. She was so ready for him, was in fact, too impatient to take them back to the room to finish what they'd started.

"Don't tease me, Aedan."

"I like teasing ye." His hand slipped over her bottom, clasping her through her dress.

Two could play at this game and she slid her hands down the front of his kilt, over the coarse wool to clasp his erect cock. Her hand struggled to circle his length. "You know, in my time, there is such a thing as the internet, with social media platforms that people use to keep in touch. I know none of this is making sense, but on the internet there are funny sayings and such that people use to explain what they're feeling or thinking at times. You and me, here, now reminds me of a funny saying I read once."

He pulled back and watched her, his hand still firmly against her ass. "What was the saying?"

"What does a real man wear under his kilt?"

"Ye know what I wear under me kilt." Aedan grinned, kissing her quickly.

She laughed. "Do you want to know?"

"Aye."

"Lipstick, if he's lucky," she told him, running her hand over his balls.

"I know not what lipstick is, but I can guess." He gasped as she continued to tease him. "You're a wicked lass. And here I was thinking ye were sweet and honorable."

"What can I say? You bring out my special talents." She

stepped closer, running her hand over his ass, running her hand inside his kilt to have flesh against flesh.

"Seems like I bring out your special talent as well," she said as he dipped his head to kiss the tops of her breasts, his hand kneading her senseless.

"You do, and quite often."

She smiled, loving that she could bring this Highlander to his knees. Aedan closed his eyes, and groaned. It was one of the hottest things she'd ever seen or done to a man and she loved it. The way Aedan stood, even if someone came up to them they'd not notice her hands beneath his kilt. But the sound of ongoing revelry inside masked their pleasure and the sentries knew better than to follow their laird to see what was going on around the corner.

She flicked her thumb over the head of his penis and met his gaze, his eyes burning with unsated lust.

"That feels good, lass. So good."

Abby tightened her hold and stroked his full length, squeezing a little. Aedan's breathing became heavy, and she touched his chest, loved the feel of its sudden rise and fall, could picture in her mind the hardened contours that made up his muscular abdomen flexing with each breath.

"I want to taste you," she said, watching as he slowly opened his eyes and comprehension dawned.

"As much as I'd adore allowing ye to do that to me, we cannot. We could be found at any moment."

"Adds to the excitement, though, doesn't it?" She kneeled before him and lifted his kilt, bunching it at his waist.

"Abigail, nay. Not here."

His hold loosened a little and she licked her lips, liking that his gaze snapped to her mouth and stayed there. "Let me. I'll make it quick. We'll not get caught."

He looked around, torn between his desire to let her have him this way, and that of a laird who should probably show more decorum than what they were. "No, lass."

Abby pouted, but did as he bid. She slipped her hand up to his chest and felt the corded stomach flex at her touch. "Very well, I'll behave."

Aedan stood and settled his kilt back about his legs. "You'll behave? Don't ever become too tame, lass. I love the fire within ye."

Her heart did a little flutter at the word love. Abby wrapped her arms about his neck and hugged him, paying homage to his earlobe. "You say the sweetest things."

"And I'm going to do the dirtiest things to ye upstairs. In private."

He lifted her and she squealed, having not expected to be thrown over his shoulder. "Aedan, put me down. You can't carry me across the castle and through the hall like this. What will people think?"

"That I'm going to have my wicked way with ye, which I am." He slapped her ass, squeezing her a little.

"Ouch. That hurt," she said, grinning.

"It was meant to, but don't worry, I'll kiss it better in a few short minutes."

She ran her hands down his back and clasped as much of his backside as she could from this position. "You better kiss me in more than that spot, my liege. You owe me after denying me what I wanted."

"Minx!" he said, as he casually strolled through the hall.

Abby waved to everyone who stopped to watch the laird carry her upstairs and out of sight.

"I plan on using my mouth on a lot of your person, so prepare yourself for much pleasure."

She bit her lip, only managing to hold back a moan at what delights he'd bestow on her in the next few hours. "Hurry it up then. Your minx is impatient."

Chapter Nineteen

Abigail sat up with a gasp at the sound of a wrenching scream from outside. With it came the tinkling sounds of metal hitting metal. She reached over to wake Aedan and found the bed cold, only the indentation of his head remained on the pillow, highlighted by the moonlight that streamed through the window.

She started at the sound of more yelling, crying, and the unmistakable sound of someone coming through the secret passage that joined her and Aedan's room.

"Quick, lass. We're being attacked by the O'Cain Clan. Ye have to get dressed quickly and follow me. Do what I say when I say it. Do ye understand?"

Abby nodded at Gwen's harried tone and did as she was asked, pulling on the shift Aedan had stripped from her only hours before. "I didn't think Aedan was going to fight with them. At least, there's been talk of war, but nothing confirmed. How is it they're here?" She quickly grabbed a dark-colored gown from her dresser and turned to Gwen to help her tie the lacings.

"Somehow or another they've found out we were to attack. To hit us when we're at our most vulnerable, in the dark depths of night, shows you what a callous, cowardly clan they are."

Abigail grabbed a woolen shawl and slipped on the sturdiest boots she had. She thought back to what she'd learned about the clan battles between the MacLeods and O'Cains and one prominent fact stood out more than the rest. This battle that was to take place in 1601 hadn't occurred at the MacLeod's castle, but elsewhere. So why had history changed its course? Had her coming back in time, the delaying of Aedan's attack due to her presence, changed the past?

And what did that mean for the family? Did the O'Cains attacking Druiminn mean Aedan would die this night along with the laird of the O'Cains? History told of many deaths, but a battle that was won by neither side. Would that change as well?

"Hurry, Abigail. They're coming."

Dread pooled in her stomach, and a cold chill ran through her blood. "Where's Aedan?"

"Fighting in the courtyard. He only had enough time to warn the villagers to get their women and children into the hills, where they'd be safe, for the time being. But we must go. Get away from the castle, in case it falls to the O'Cains. Our outcome, should we stay here, isn't certain."

Abigail followed Gwen into the musty, dark passage and clasped the back of her friend's woolen skirt. Not knowing where the hidden corridors went, the last thing she wanted was to get lost in some dank, scary, unknown tunnel. As they ran through the narrow space, down stairs and winding passages, the overwhelming urge to scream every time a spider web brushed her cheek was almost impossible to suppress.

She could hear the sounds of men ransacking the rooms as they broke off from the main fight outside, the bastards searching for possessions and women, no doubt, to take in any way they could.

"Where are we going?"

Gwen kept up her quickened pace, not slowing, even when Abby's lungs burned.

"My cottage. The one where we first met. There's a secret room beneath the floor. We'll hide there until Aedan comes to get us."

"And if he doesn't?" Abby didn't even want to think of such a possibility. To lose Aedan now. The man she loved more than life itself was an unbearable torture she couldn't face. He was everything to her. Was her future and her past wrapped up in one? "What if they lose?" Even Abby could hear the horror in her voice.

"They won't. They cannot," Gwen said.

Abby bit her lip as tears threatened what little vision she had in the dark space. Even to her ears, the resonance of uncertainty tinged Gwen's tone. "But what is your plan should this happen? You can't stay here."

Gwen stopped and she nearly ran into her. "And neither can you."

"What do you mean?"

A rustle of leaves sounded as Gwen pulled back an ivy vine that hid the opening to the outside. The moon was bright, casting light across the land and the sound of the battle seemed to be coming from behind them. There was a severe drop that led down toward a small inlet, and the tinkling sound of water was at odds to the sound of the battle that echoed in the night.

"This isn't the easiest climb down, but it'll be unlikely we'll be seen leaving from here. Step where I step."

It took some minutes to climb their way down, some of the rocks and moss made their feet slip. Once they made flat ground they bolted across the grass. Abby looked back at the castle and realized the direction they'd come from was beneath Aedan's anteroom. Lights blazed from the room, and she wondered what would be left of his home after the O'Cains were gone.

The terrain was uneven, and more than once Abby stumbled. Fear assailed her. The thought that at any moment an arrow could pierce her back, or a lone horseman could knife them, his only goal to kill anyone in his path, threatened a panic attack. She was a twenty-first century woman. She wasn't used to this type of horror.

They stopped near a tree and hid behind its large trunk, taking a moment to look around to see where the majority of the fighting was taking place. Near the castle gates, men fought vigorously, the twang of metal as sword hit sword, the sudden cry of someone when they fell.

Abby's stomach turned at the thought of what was happening before her eyes. Shadows shifted not far from them and she tried to meld, become one almost with the tree. Adrenalin coursed through her blood, and as much as she loved this time, being with Aedan, she'd do anything to be back in her own time, safe in her apartment where no medieval clan war could kill her.

Abby thought she saw Aedan in the thick of the battle, but she couldn't be sure. She did, however, see Gwen's husband Braxton who seemed to be holding his own, thank God.

"Do you think it's safe to continue," Abby asked, hating that her voice sounded as petrified as she felt.

"Aye." Gwen must have said a silent prayer and, grabbing her hand, pulled her in the direction of the cottage. "'Tis not far now. We'll be safe there, for a time."

They came to the road that led in and out of Castle Druiminn and they paused to see if anyone was about. Seeing no one, they crossed it as the sound of thumping horse's hooves sounded from the direction of the castle.

"Quickly," Gwen urged.

Abby made the mistake of looking to see whom it was and froze when she noted the large, blood covered Scotsman with death and revenge masking his visage. "We're in really big trouble, Gwen."

Gwen swore, pulling her into a run. "'Tis Laird O'Cain."

They made the cottage as the man and a large portion of his men surrounded the small building. Their laughter and filthy jibes about what they were going to do to them, and how often, made her skin crawl. They bolted the door and slid Gwen's working table in front of it, before sliding a large cabinet to cover the only window in the room.

"Gwen, lass. Come out and introduce me to yer visitor. We'll not harm ye, we'll be right pleasant. Won't we, lads?"

Laughter rang out and Abby looked to Gwen whose visage paled to a person who'd never seen sunshine before in their life. "They're going to kill us, aren't they? And they're going to enjoy doing it." Abby swallowed the bile that rose in her throat at Gwen's nod. They both stood in the middle of the room, frozen with fear and unsure what to do next. Through the haze of what was happening, the smell of smoke flittered across her senses. "Do you smell that?"

Gwen swore, her gaze snapping to the ceiling. "They've set the thatch alight."

"What!" For the first time in her life, Abby didn't know what to do. She'd never had to prepare herself for situations like these. Her life, boring as it was in the future, had never been so threatening or scary. Who set buildings on fire with people in them?

"You better come out. I'd hate for two beautiful women like yourselves to go to waste."

Gwen yelled something at them in Gaelic. Abby assumed, by their enthusiastic laughter, that is was some sort of warning or swear word.

"We can't go outside. We're dead either way." Abby

coughed as the air started to thicken with smoke. She tried to think of a way out and could've cursed herself when nothing came to mind. All she could think about was the awful way in which Laird O'Cain would seek his revenge against Aedan for a war that hadn't had anything to do with her or Gwen, but Jinny. This was absurd.

Neither of them deserved what the men outside had in store for them. Hell, no one on earth deserved such a horrific death. "We'd be better to stay here. The smoke will kill us long before the flames. He'll torture us if we go out there." Gwen took her hand and rubbed it in silent consolation.

A loud roaring sound, followed by shouts from the threatening clan sounded as another sword battle started outside. Hope fleetingly filled her heart as the sound of Aedan's voice, his battle cry, permeated the air. He was here. He'd save them. Of course he would.

He'd never let them die in such a way.

"Help me with the floor, Abigail. We'll go down in the secret room. It may buy us some time. If the roof caves in, it'll crush us."

Abby nodded, pushing a small table full of bowls and glass containers to the side, seeing the square stone slab that covered the stairs leading to the underground room.

"The room has a stone roof, so even if the building goes up in flames, we may survive, depending on the smoke."

Abby didn't think they'd have much chance of survival should they go down there, but then, their options were limited. She started when a small wooden trap door near the fireplace pushed in and Aedan's head popped through.

She went to him quickly, pulling him inside, feeling his body to make sure he was in one piece. "Is it safe to leave with you? Is the battle over?"

"Nay, lass," he said, pushing her hair out of her face, his brow furrowed in deep worry lines. "My men are holding them at present, enough for me to see ye. I couldn't let ye go without saying good-bye."

"What do you mean?" His gaze moved to the corner of the roof, which was now well alight, small embers dropping onto the floor below. "We don't have time to discuss the matter, but know, Abigail, that I've never loved anyone as much as I love ye."

She nodded, tears welling in her eyes. "I know you do. I've never doubted your affections, Aedan." She hugged him quickly, pulling him tight against her, worried that should tonight be the last time she saw him alive, at least he never doubted how she felt about him as well.

"Send her back, Gwen. Get Abigail out of here."

Abby's gaze widened and she frowned. "What do you mean?" As the truth of his words slammed into her, she reeled back on her heels as if slapped. "You cannot mean to send me back to my own time? I don't want to leave, Aedan. You know that."

"Aye, I do, lass. I know what ye feel, and I know you're true, but I can't assure your safety this night. There are more O'Cain clansmen headed our way, and it'll be a miracle if anyone is left standing at the end. I can't lose ye to them. I can't let them take ye in the way they would. I want to know you're safe, happy, and home in your own time, than be selfish and keep ye here and risk ye life. Please, go into the cellar and do as I ask."

Shouts from outside called out to Aedan and his body tensed. Abby kissed him, threw her arms about his neck, and took one last taste, one last touch of the man she doubted she'd ever see again. He deepened the kiss—its raw intensity making her body ache with longing that would forever be her curse.

He pulled back, staring at her with such pain she physically hurt. "Gwendolyn, you'll send Abigail home. That's an order from your laird."

His tone brooked no argument. Abby looked around to see Gwen nod. "You know what you ask, brother. Are ye sure?"

"Aye, I know what I ask." He pulled her against him once more, his strong arms encircling her back. "I'm glad I met ye, Abigail Cross," he whispered against her ear, kissing her lobe quickly. "Time may separate us, but you're my soul mate without doubt, and I'll love ye forever and we will meet again. Maybe not in this time, but another."

A sob broke free, and she swiped at her cheek. "As you are mine." Abby pulled away to meet his gaze. "I love you, Aedan MacLeod. I think the moment I ran into you at this very cottage, my heart was lost."

He grinned. "It warms my heart to know that what we had was true."

"It's as true as I'm standing here." She paused, knowing he had to go and her as well. "Please be safe. Please don't die this night."

"I'll do my best not to displease ye. I promise ye that."

As the roof creaked, Abby stood, strode quickly toward the trap door, and looked one last time at the love of her life. "Bye."

"Bye, lass," he said, leaving the same way he came.

Gwen grabbed her hand and pulled her down the stairs. They slid the stone trapdoor back in place and went to stand away from the opening. Abby looked about the empty room as a loud crash sounded upstairs. "Hold my hand, Abigail. 'Tis time we left."

Abby met her gaze and frowned. "We? What do you mean?"

Gwen shrugged. "I'm coming with ye. I doubt I'd survive tonight should I stay, and I refuse to give up my future with Braxton because of the bastard O'Cain. I'm going to have bairns with my man, maybe not in the near future, but one day."

Tears pooled in Gwen's eyes, and Abby pulled her into a hug. "I think that's a fantastic idea and one I want to see happen. Let's go."

Gwen started chanting words that sounded Gaelic, or perhaps Latin, she wasn't sure. The room didn't change, just became quiet, before Gwen swore, stopping the chant.

"What's the matter?"

Gwen ran a hand through her hair, her gaze darting back to the trapdoor where a slither of smoke started to filter through. "It's not working. I have enough power to send you home, but I can't accompany ye, Abigail. You'll have to go without me."

"But what will happen if you stay? There's smoke coming in already." Abby wanted to vomit at the thought of going home and never knowing if her friend survived or not. "I'm not going without you. If you have to stay then so do I. I'd rather die with you, than live knowing I left you to die alone."

"I won't die, lass. Like I said, I have plans with Braxton that I'll not allow even a measly fire to get in the way of. Now ye will go, and that'll be the end of it. My brother would never forgive me if ye stayed."

Abby coughed. "I refuse to go." She crossed her arms over her chest and glared.

Gwen shrugged. "I didn't want to have to do this, but ye leave me no choice."

Again strange and ancient chants started and Abby swore. Gwen was going to send her anyway. "No. Please don't send me away. How will I return? How can I live knowing you may die?" Her voice rose in panic and she hugged Gwen to her, and yet her friend continued, unheeded by her touch, the words continuing on without a stutter.

Shit.

The sounds from outside dimmed until there was no

sound at all but the pitter-patter of a passing shower. Abby shut her eyes as her stomach churned before everything went black. When she opened them and looked about, the room was empty, devoid of Gwen and smoke, and the stone trapdoor was open, allowing her to leave with ease.

Abby walked up the stairs and climbed out. The cottage was as she'd found it that day before she'd been pulled back in time. It was daylight as well, and the war that had been battling on outside was forever lost in the sands of time.

Abby walked outside and noted some people walking toward Druiminn Castle, smart phones in full use, taking images of the medieval estate, people posing in front of the great castle in the distance, taking selfies to tweet to their friends. "So, I'm back." Saying the words out loud left an ache in her chest. Abby bent down and scooped up the soil at her feet, letting it drift through her fingers.

It floated off into the wind, and she bit back a hysterical sob. Aedan was gone, perhaps forever. She didn't know if he survived the war, had kept his title and land, nothing. The clan battle having taken place at the castle and not Coire na Creiche as history had dictated, had maybe changed the victor? Before her landing in seventeenth century Scotland, the clan battle hadn't had a winner on either side.

But things had a way of changing and not always for the better.

Abby started toward town, hoping the hotel had at least kept her luggage, since she was dressed in a gown that stood out like a sore thumb in this time. Perhaps she'd been gone so long she was now classed as a missing person. Were her friends, the few she had, looking for her? Or had time slowed to the point where she hadn't even been missed?

Taking one last look at the castle and the surrounding grounds, she headed back into town. She supposed her questions would be answered soon enough.

Chapter Twenty

Despair crashed over Aedan as he watched the building that housed Abigail and Gwen go up in flames. The roof, now well alight, crackled and creaked as the fire engulfed anything it could. Anyone who remained trapped inside would surely die. He prayed his sister could get Abigail safely back to the twenty-first century without mishap, and that Gwen herself had found refuge inside. His sister was a clever lass. Surely, she'd be well.

The clink of swords sounded behind him and he re-joined the battle, determined to finish this war once and for all, and to make it the last battle his people would ever have to suffer against Clan O'Cain. Over the many weeks he'd spent with Abigail, her knowledge and outlook on life had changed him.

No longer was he the Scottish laird who thought first with his sword and second with his mind. They would stay in the dark ages, if the country continued on in this vein. Abigail had allowed him to see things from a different perspective…a modern one. Life didn't have to be filled with war, feasting, and war once again. It could hold so much more, be so much more. And from this day forward, should he survive the night, he silently promised Abigail that he'd try and live that way as much as possible.

Perhaps King James VI was right in bringing forth ideals that would ensure Scotland became a peaceful, more stable society. His people couldn't remain as hired arms, they should be able to choose their future, be it farming or iron works, whatever they wished. The time of clan battles had to end. And for Clan MacLeod, tonight would be his men's last.

The fighting went on relentlessly, the screams of men, the clink of metal hitting metal were like a razor against his soul. Aedan fought with his men, too many already fallen at his feet, along with O'Cain men. All their deaths nothing but a waste and his soul screamed at the senselessness of it all. Did these men even know what they were fighting each other for anymore? He doubted it.

The wind picked up and with it came large droplets of rain. Aedan noted some of the opposing clan stopped, pulling back and dispersing into the night as fast as they'd appeared. Embers from the cottage turned night into day as they scattered across the ground, before the heavens opened up in earnest, the ground soon becoming a pit of mud and blood.

With the last of the O'Cains pulling back, Aedan called his men to stop. He sent a scout up to the castle to fetch the elderly healer who'd taught Gwen all she knew, to come and tend his men. The young lad took off at great speed, as if the devil himself was at his heels.

Aedan looked over to the small cottage that his sister and Abigail had hidden within. The thick thatch and a few pillars holding up the roof were now a smoldering mess on the floor. He helped tend the few men that he could on his way over to it, when a woman's yell sounded from the cottage.

"Braxton," he shouted, catching the attention of his closest ally who was tying a bandage around a young man's arm. "'Tis Gwen. She's alive in the cottage."

The two men ran and smashed out what was left of the window, climbing into the shell of the building as rain continued to pour down. Forgetting the few injuries he'd sustained, Aedan made his way to the cellar.

Large charred pillars lay across the floor. The thatch, still burning, burned the bottom of his legs. He ignored the pain shooting across his skin, and cleared what they could, as quickly as possible.

Time ticked by agonizingly slow, and still he could hear the muffled female voice. Had Abigail stayed? Was it both his lass and Gwen? Were they injured, one of them dead? Panic clawed at his gut when they finally made the stone floor slab, lifting it and pushing it over.

Smoke puffed out, the cellar unrecognizable to what it was. He reached down, hearing her choking cough, and lifted Gwen from the room.

Braxton kneeled beside them, pushing Aedan out of the way to lift her up. He frowned down into the room, not hearing or seeing anyone else. "Is Abigail with ye, lass? Can ye tell me that at least?"

His sister coughed again, the sound retching and raw. "No. I sent her home as ye asked." She coughed again, trying to take a deep breath. "I didn't have enough power to send us both through and so I stayed. She's safe."

Aedan nodded, frowning. "Take her up to the house and don't leave her side. The smoke she's inhaled can't possibly be good for her. Have cook bring up a broth for her and water. I'll bring the healer back to see her once we're done here."

"Aye." Braxton left, clutching Gwen to his chest. Aedan set out to clean up the mess the clan war had wreaked on his people. He looked up at the sky, and the sky was as beautiful as the woman he'd farewelled only hours before. How could such heavens look down on such hell?

He said a silent prayer that his lass was well and safe.

Men cried out around him and he set to work, helping those he could, or notifying his able clansmen to take others up to the barracks and have them housed.

Perhaps it was for the best that Abigail had returned to her time. This period of Scottish history wasn't for the faint of heart, and although she wasn't a whimpering miss, she didn't deserve such a hard life.

A future that was uncertain, and the times were unsafe, as she well knew.

He would miss her, more than the very stars looking down on them would miss the night, but knowing she was alive, a young modern woman in her right time, lessened the blow. Or at least dulled it to a bearable ache.

Chapter Twenty-One

Time, it seemed, had almost stalled. Arriving back at the hotel, Abby learned that it was, in fact, only later the same afternoon that she'd traveled back in time. No missing person's file had been opened for her. None of her friends were missing her.

If that wasn't enough to make her depressed, the one person who had cared about her, loved her for the last month or so, was still in seventeenth century Scotland. She flicked on the television, listened to the news with little interest. Same shit, different day.

How would she live without him?

A knock at the door sounded and she opened it quickly, the hope that Aedan stood on the opposite side dashed as a silver trolley, laden with her room service order, was wheeled in. She tipped the waiter, the smell of hot chips making her mouth water, even as her heart dropped to the floor.

She ate alone but she missed the clan meals, the laughter and chatter among Aedan's men as they sat at the table, socializing and gossiping, telling tales during their nightly dinner.

The thought was followed by another, even more disheartening. Would she ever see him again? Would Gwen be able to pull her through time once more? That was, if her dearest friend had lived to do so? In the rush to say good-bye, her panic of leaving without Gwen, she'd not told her to bring her back when she could. Stupid mistake, and one she'd live to regret forever, should she live her entire life in the twenty-first century.

She finished her meal quickly, deposited the tray in the corridor, and headed for the shower. It felt like forever since she'd washed her hair properly, and she took longer than usual under the spray.

Aedan would love showers. He'd certainly look mighty fine with water running over his delicious figure, soap bubbles running down his spine and between his perfect ass cheeks.

Tears flowed as easily as the water, and Abby gave in to her emotions and sobbed. She missed him, would do anything to be with him again, and yet, the choice wasn't in her hands, and possibly wouldn't be in his or Gwen's, either.

•••

Later that night, Abby started when her phone rang, the caller ID stating it was her roommate in the States. She flicked her phone screen and hit the speaker button. "Hi Sophie. How are you?" Benign conversation seemed the safest course.

"Hi Abby. I'm calling to see how your vacation is going. Nothing new here, other than studying."

"Sounds like fun." She sighed. "What's the weather like?" Could she have any more boring conversation? It was any wonder no one liked to hang out with her.

Sophie laughed, sounding like she was eating something on the other end of the phone. "I just wanted to let you know that I'm moving out. I'm moving in with John. He asked me to, and I thought it was about time we took the relationship one step further."

Abby nodded, knowing only too well how it felt to find someone you wanted to take the next step with. "That's great." Even if it would hurt her budget to come up with double the rent until she could find someone to take the room. "Can you advertise the room for me? I won't be home for some weeks yet. I'm going to stay here a little longer."

"Of course. Actually, I may have someone already. She's really nice." Abby half-listened as Sophie rattled on about nothing important. She said, yes, no, and oh wow, where appropriate while she Googled information about clan MacLeod that only turned up information that she already knew. The library, however, had archives and there would be a more detailed account of any skirmishes and history of the area. Abby looked up the local library's address and opening time.

"Anyway, I wanted to touch base with you. I'll see you when you get back. We'll go for coffee."

"Sounds great. I look forward to it." Abby hung up with a sense of relief. Only months ago she would've jumped at going out with Sophie and her friends, but now, the concept of kissing other people's asses just to have friends irked. If anything, Abby had learned from the past there was a strength in her she hadn't known existed. A confidence that it was okay not to be the best at everything, that winning wasn't everything. That she was okay as she was, even if it was alone.

"Gwen, if you can hear me, as soon as you can, I want to return to Aedan. There's nothing here for me any longer. Please bring me home." If she expected Gwen to magically appear, she didn't. Just the rambling of the television broke the silence that divided her from the man she loved.

She was restless and rolled over in bed, unable to find a comfortable position to sleep, she was so impatient to return.

The hardened body, smooth and strong, that she was used to snuggling up against, was no longer beside her, his even breathing lulling her worries away.

As much as she loved this time, the standard of living most of all, she missed Aedan more, and it hadn't yet been twenty-four hours. How would she survive if being back here turned permanent? She could never love another. The thought of learning to love again left her stomach in sickening dread.

She stared up at the white ceiling, the flashes from passing cars the only light penetrating the room. It had been a comfortable space before she'd traveled back in time, but now she felt out of place. She'd become so used to the water lapping against the shore, the odd birdcall late at night, or the sound of the servants dousing the sconces, that now, this time no longer felt normal.

Abby may have been born in the twenty-first century, but she wanted to die in another, as an old woman, warm in her bed, surrounded by the family she'd create with Aedan.

She hugged her pillow, wondering what Aedan was doing, only to realize that his time had passed. He wouldn't be doing anything. Was that how it worked? The difficulty of the situation made her head hurt and she closed her eyes, wishing that come morning, something, anything would give her hope that she'd see him again.

It was a fanciful dream, but it didn't stop her from yearning.

Chapter Twenty-Two

Eight weeks later and Abby was still in twenty-first century Scotland. Each day her mood deteriorated, to the point where she pondered doing physical harm to anyone who looked or spoke to her.

Having gone down to the library the day after she'd returned, Abby had found out that Aedan did in fact survive the war and so, too, did the laird of Clan O'Cain. History noted that the O'Cains had scurried back to their lands, and the battle was known as the last clan battle between the two foes in Scotland.

There was no mention of Gwen—if she'd survived or passed away from the fire. Perhaps, Gwen had died. That her only link to the past was gone. Both thoughts were horrific. Her friend was dead and Aedan was lost to her forever.

King James VI had made an amendment to the law to stop such wars from happening again. Had, in fact, made the Scottish lairds make use of their men, by farming and a trade, such as blacksmiths or bakers. The start of a new era that still resonated today.

Abby hadn't been game enough to look any further into Aedan's future, for fear of reading he'd married someone. Had fathered children to a woman who he had fallen deeply, madly in love with. The thought was a little imaginary, but desperation, want, and need, were playing tricks on her mind, and sometimes Abby actually thought she was losing it. Literally.

She sat on a park bench that looked out over the Highlands. Little children played on swings and slippery-dips in the park beyond, dogs chased Frisbees and tennis balls. Not a breath of wind tainted the day. It was a warm, beautiful Highland day, and she hated it.

The thought was soon followed with another. That she'd have to accept her situation in life. She wasn't going back to the seventeenth century. That her dearest friend Gwen had perished in the fire. Her heart crumbled at the thought. And Gwen had had such grand plans for her future with Braxton. Of a long and happy marriage filled with children. That Gwen hadn't pulled her back through time told her more than anything, that her summarization was true.

She looked toward Druiminn Castle, standing high and foreboding over the town and Abby stood, walking toward it. If she was going to return home to America, to her old life and try and wrangle some sort of future in this time, then she'd say one last good-bye to Aedan. Up until now, she'd not been able to bring herself to visit the castle again. But now, it was time.

It took her half an hour to reach the base of the grounds. The grey stone looked forlorn and sad, like her. She walked around, not that much different from Aedan's time. The small inlet of water still flowed with the tide, but trees had grown where once there had been only barren fields.

Abby walked around to where she thought the exit was that she and Gwen had used to flee. A wall of rock had been built in the hidden doorway, preventing the use of the tunnel.

Her gaze lifted to the window that was Aedan's anteroom.

No handsome, wickedly sinful laird looked out at her, just the countryside reflected on the glass. The front entrance to the castle hadn't changed, either. In fact, Abby was sure the doors were the same ones, weathered and creaking their only sign of old age. She stared at the brass plaque that was screwed onto the wood that stated opening times.

She walked into the small foyer and paid her money to the lady sitting behind a little desk, waiting while she handed her a layout of the building for her to use. It was strange being here again, seeing it the same but so very different.

The family still owned the estate, but were not in residence. It was probably a good thing, she'd hate to run into descendants of Aedan and his wife.

Despondent, she walked into the hall and looked toward the dais. It was the strangest sensation being here, seeing pieces of furniture she'd used that were now accompanied with an array of others that spanned the four-hundred years of history that had taken place.

She headed up the stairs, smiling at the memory of her first kiss with Aedan in that very spot. She'd miss him, would never forget those piercing green eyes that had a way of melting her limbs on the spot.

The rooms upstairs were completely changed, and where she'd slept was inaccessible on the do-it-yourself tour. The sound of footsteps behind her made her turn, and she smiled at the young woman who looked at her in some shock.

"Abigail Cross?"

Abby stopped, turning back to the woman whose voice resonated with one she knew well. Of Gwen's. "Yes. That's me."

"Wow, I had no idea that an image I've looked at since I was a child would be something that would actually be standing in the flesh before me." She shook herself, holding out her hand. "I'm sorry, where are my manners? I'm Kenzie, great, great, so many greats I forget, granddaughter of Gwendolyn MacLeod. Does that name sound familiar to you, by any chance?"

The girl's eyes twinkled with the same laughing gaze as Gwen had and Abby laughed. "It's a pleasure to meet you, Kenzie. You look like Gwendolyn. Did you know that?"

"Aye. I do. Her features have been most prominent in all her descendants. Must be the magic."

Abby raised her brows. "You seem to know quite a lot about Gwen." Did the woman know what had happened to her? Kenzie's presence told her she had, in fact, survived the fire, so why hadn't she brought her back? Did they not think her suitable for Aedan after all…

"I know what ye thinking, and I think we need to go downstairs to a private room and have a chat. Would ye mind?"

"No. Of course not." Abby followed her downstairs and they walked into a small room off the main hall.

They sat in plush sofas, the walls surrounded by bookshelves and large carpet squares. It felt very homey and comfortable. Instantly, Abby felt at ease.

"I suppose I should begin with telling ye that Gwen survived the night ye left, did in fact go on to have a family with Braxton and a long life. The tale of your arrival in her time is known in the family as a folktale now, but I always knew you'd arrive one day. I just didn't know when."

"If you know of Gwen's abilities, why hasn't she brought me back to their time? I don't understand."

"She couldn't." Sadness tinged Kenzie's tone. "After the fire, something changed within her. It wasn't until her own daughter started showing signs of the 'gift' that she realized the only way to have you return was through her descendants. She made a vow and it was passed down through the female line, each child brought up to know of yer story and Gwen's wish to bring ye back. I so happen to be the granddaughter who is fortunate enough to be born in the same era as you. And so, I'm to help ye."

Tears blurred Abby's vision, along with the flicker of hope. Did this mean… "So, you're going to help me go back to the seventeenth century?"

Kenzie smiled, sitting back in the chair with an air of excitement. "I am. I'll help you as soon as you're ready."

Abby's heart leaped to her throat, hearing the words she'd longed to hear. To think that in a few short hours she could be back in Aedan's arms, talking to him, loving him as she desperately wanted, was a relief that poured through her like wine.

"I'm ready. There is nothing left for me here."

Kenzie raised her brows, a little shocked. "Wow. You must really love Laird MacLeod."

Abby's heart thundered and she touched her chest, needing it to calm down before it jumped out onto her lap. "I do love him. Very much."

Kenzie smiled at her admission. "I know ye do, but there was two stipulations Gwen wanted ye to know of. I'm to return ye twelve months after the clan battle against the O'Cains—after ye left. The first reason being ye cannot travel into the past if you've already been there at that time. 'Tis an unwritten time travel law. Secondly, things change fast in the Highlands, and in the hard time in which they lived, she wanted ye to know that no matter what ye see on your return, that ye trust in Aedan's love. Can you do that?"

Abby nodded but wondered what that meant. Was Gwen trying to warn her of something? Had Aedan found another? Had been badly injured perhaps? "I can." She swallowed, hoping what she'd said was true. "Twelve months later seems like a long time. Did Gwen say why she'd marked this date and not any other?"

"There was a lot of conflict in the area, uncertainty with the clans. I think she thought this would be the best and safest time for you to go back."

Nerves pooled in Abby's belly, and she wondered what she would find on her return. Had Aedan missed her as desperately as she missed him? Or had he thought her missing in time, never to return to his? The fact he would've known that Gwen couldn't bring her through time changed things. Had he moved on? Did he marry? Would she find him married already? And could she take that risk, should she return, and he was with another?

She met Kenzie's concerned gaze and frowned. Going back was a gamble, a big one that involved her heart. She shut her eyes and thought for a moment. Could she do it? The image of Aedan, looking down at her, laughing, his eyes sparkling with mirth, twisted her stomach.

Of course she should go back and if she found him with another, she'd fight to get him back. "When did you want to do it?"

"We can do it now, if ye like. I'll make sure ye land in the healer's cottage, twelve months after ye left. I'd hate for ye to arrive right in front of a servant, I'm not sure how ye'd explain that away."

Abby nodded, standing as Kenzie did. The young woman clasped her hands. "It was lovely meeting ye, Abigail Cross. I hope ye enjoy yer life."

"So do I," Abby said, laughing a little at both the illogical situation but also, with the knowledge that she would soon see Aedan. "Perhaps you could visit us, Kenzie. You'd be most welcome."

Kenzie smiled, and it was like looking at Gwen again. "I may. Time will tell."

The ancient language Abby didn't understand wrapped

about her, pulling her into their meaning and pushing her back in time. The room went quiet and Abby shut her eyes as Kenzie started to disappear, the room distorting and making her dizzy.

And then there was nothing but the sound of horses outside, and the damp dirt floor beneath her bottom. Abby opened her eyes, and the unmistakable cottage of Gwen's—although rebuilt and modernized a little—greeted her. Medicines, seeds, and dried plants were scattered about and she laughed. She was back, and now it was time to find her laird.

She walked over to a closet where Gwen had spare gowns—should the one she was wearing become sullied after tending to a patient—and changed her dress. She threw her jeans and T-shirt on top of the small fire and set them alight, watching to make sure they burned to ash before heading up to the castle.

She was only minutes from Aedan. Minutes from being in his arms. Her blood pumped through her veins and made her dizzy with joy. The sun had dipped in the west by the time she made the castle proper. Some of the clansmen greeted her warmly, although surprised, while others looked at her strangely, no doubt wondering what a woman was doing out this late in the day.

Sconces hung about the castle walls, giving those who walked the battlements enough light to see. Not a lot had changed since she was here last. Abby noted a few familiar faces, and some she'd not seen before.

Abby nodded to the guard at the door and walked toward the great hall. The sound of raised voices and laugher met her ears, and she realized everyone had congregated for the nightly meal. She entered the hall and stopped when her eyes took in what was happening up on the dais. Silence as quiet as the grave settled over the gathered clan, and she swallowed the revulsion that rose up in her throat.

Aedan sat beside Aline, their heads bent in private conversation, a delicate, perfect flush making Aline look prettier than Abby had ever thought possible.

She waited for Aedan to see her, lifted her chin in unvoiced defiance when their gazes met. Held. The shock that registered on his visage followed by hope gave her some of the sentiment herself. But when Aedan went to stand, Aline clasped his arm and halted his progress. Abby didn't know what was worse, that Aline was beside him, or the fact he listened to her silent command and sat back down.

Gwen stood, a small babe clasped against her chest as she ran toward her, pulling her into a one armed hug. Tears threatened and hearing the welcome for her friend, the joy in being back overrode the concern she felt over Aedan's feelings for her.

"You're here. Tell me how it is so?" Gwen stood back, smiling.

"Well, it was your plan, actually. Your great—too many greats to count—granddaughter has your gift and sent me back. There is a promise passed down through the family that should I turn up at Castle Druiminn in the twenty-first century, I'm to be returned to this time. It was a promise that was passed down because of you."

Gwen nodded, tears pooling in her eyes. "I'm so proud of her, and I'm so happy to see you again. This is very timely, as we ourselves have only just arrived to visit Aedan." Gwen looked down at the sleeping bairn in her arms. "I had a daughter. Her name is Mairi."

Abby ran a hand over the fine red-haired baby's head. "She's so beautiful. Congratulations. I'm so happy for you and Braxton. Your descendant Kenzie, who sent me back, is an exact replica of you, absolutely lovely." Abby paused and looked about the room. "But I fear my arrival may have come too late." Her attention snapped to the dais where Aedan remained seated, his gaze steadfast on her. Despair washed over Abby, and had Gwen not been holding her hand, she was sure she would've crumbled to the floor. "I couldn't face seeing what happened to Aedan after the clan battle with the O'Cains, other than finding out if he survived or not. I fear I should've looked further into his future. He seems to have settled at last."

"There have been discussions. I know she wishes to marry my brother, but their clan only arrived last week. There is still time, Abigail."

Abby cursed herself for not looking up his future. Had she done so, she could've saved herself a lot of embarrassment and heartache. "I suppose I should go and say something."

"I'll come with you, and then we'll go upstairs. We have a lot of catching up to do."

Smiling as much as she could, Abby walked toward the main table, though her heart threatened to dissolve into little pieces. The thought of Aedan courting someone else tore her soul in two. Had he kissed Aline? Did he now have feelings for her? She shut her eyes against the image of them sitting together, a laird and his lady. She shouldn't have come back.

She curtsied. "And so we meet again." Aedan's eyes stared at her with an intensity she'd never seen before. A muscle clenched in his jaw, his body stiff and unmoving.

"Ye didn't tell me, Aedan, that Abigail was coming. What a joker you are," Aline said, no mirth in her words.

Abby met the woman's toxic gaze and read the hatred behind her beautiful angelic features. She hid her venom well, but not well enough for another woman not to notice.

"Yes, what a joke it is." Aedan flinched at her words, and she hoped he understood what she meant. She was being cruel, but she couldn't help it. To her, she'd only been away from him for weeks, to see him with someone else after such a short time killed her inside. Jealousy clawed into her stomach and wouldn't let go, no matter that she tried to remind herself that a year had passed since the battle and she must now fight for him.

"I hadn't expected you to accept the invitation." His voice wrapped about her, a comforting elixir that she'd missed with every breath she'd taken since their parting.

"What can I say?" she said, smiling. "I loved my time here. I loved everything about the Highlands, and I wanted to see Gwen's new baby."

"Loved? Not love?" He took a sip of his mead, his gaze pinning her over the top of the mug.

"That's to be seen."

Aline looked at them, a confused frown on her perfect brow. Abby curtsied. "I shall see you in the morning. I've had a long day."

She joined Gwen just as her friend handed off the babe to a servant before heading upstairs. They walked toward her old room, and Abby was relieved and yet nervous about being placed in the same chamber. Aedan had full access to this room. Would he come to her tonight? Would he seek her out and explain what was going on between him and Aline?

The reunion with Gwen went on for some hours, and Abby was happy to have her friend back again. The thought of her being a mother filled her with excitement, and she was so pleased that something that Gwen had longed for had finally come true.

As the sound of the revelry downstairs quieted, she yawned, the comfortable bed calling her name.

"I'll let you have some rest and will see you tomorrow. And please, do give Aedan a chance to explain. The past twelve months have been very hard for him."

Abby rolled her eyes. "It looks like it." She wanted to pull the words back as soon as she'd said them, but every time her heart softened toward him, the image of Aline and Aedan, having a cozy tête-à-tête downstairs, soon pushed it away. "I'm sorry. Seeing him with her… I hate it."

"He loves ye, Abigail. Trust in that, no matter what."

"I'll try." She locked the door after Gwen left and changed into a shift. She looked through all the cupboards and was surprised to see all her old dresses and shawls were still there. In fact, when she looked about the room, nothing had changed at all. It was exactly as she'd left it.

A heavy wooden door in the adjacent room slammed shut and she jumped, knowing Aedan had retired. A moment later the tapestry pushed back and he stood at the threshold of her room, his breathing labored, his eyes wild with something she'd never seen before. Anger? Need? She couldn't be sure.

"Aedan." It was the only word she could manage as her tongue felt thick and heavy.

"Abigail?" His voice was low, even, but she heard the slight tremor that ran through it.

She shut her eyes, reveling in the sound of him. How she'd missed that deep baritone that wrapped about her heart and filled it with warmth.

"Your hair is longer." He continued to stare with an intensity that left her breathless. "Otherwise ye haven't changed."

He stepped into the room, letting the tapestry fall back into place. "How is it you're here? Gwen told me that after the fire her gifts were no longer as strong and that bringing ye back was impossible."

"Gwen's great-granddaughter sent me. Your sister is quite clever. She passed the tale about us down through her family, until the one born in my time knew of us. Her name was Kenzie, and she is the spitting image of your sister." Abby smiled, remembering the beautiful girl. "She sent me back by whatever magical gift your sister once had."

He nodded, but looked less than enthused by the explanation and she wondered why.

"It's been a year, Abigail."

Abby frowned. What did he mean by that? So? Did he mean things had changed? That *he'd* changed? Had he moved on? "I know. On the night you told Gwen you were getting betrothed to Aline, she promised that should her daughter have the gift, that she would bring me back to you. Gwen also stipulated that I return twelve months after I left, something about not being able to return to a time you'd already been in."

He ran a hand through his hair and cursed. "I canna marry ye, Abigail. I mean…" He paused, his face paling. "I want to marry ye. You're all I've thought about these past months, but I didn't think there was any hope."

A terrible feeling clutched her stomach, the type you get when something awful, an unimaginable horror, is about to be disclosed to you and you can't stop it. "What are you trying to say?"

"I've asked Aline Grant to be my wife and she's agreed. The betrothal was announced tonight, before your arrival."

The room spun, and vomit rose in Abby's throat. She stepped back, feeling for the bed for support. "What?"

He came toward her and Abby lifted her hand, halting his progress. "You're engaged?" She shut her mouth, feeling it gaping like a guppy fish. This wasn't happening. This couldn't be happening. "Why would you do that?"

"I dinna think you were coming back. Gwen never told me of her plans."

"Perhaps she did and you weren't listening, too busy thinking with your other head." Or, as Abby suspected, Gwen had to wait for her daughter to show signs of the gift required to pass down through her own daughters.

Anger flickered in his gaze. "Dinna be half-witted. Why

wouldn't she tell me such an important thing? I'll be sure to ask her come morn."

"What does it matter now?" Abby looked toward the windows, not wanting to see the man she no longer could have. Holy crap, this wasn't good. What a colossal mistake. "Your path is set, and you are to wed. What Gwen has to say isn't going to change that."

He swore again. "Tell me again what she had done?"

Abby sighed, but did as he asked. "She passed a message down through the women in her family about us and how to send me back."

"My meddling sister will never learn," he mumbled, glaring at something over her shoulder.

Had Abby been punched in the stomach it would've hurt less. "I must say, you didn't take long to get over me. Twelve months! Hell, Aedan, that's pathetic." Her voice trembled, but was tinged with acid, the toxic chemical threatening to eat her alive. What was she going to do? "Maybe she hoped if I returned before the wedding you'd rethink your decision."

"Even if I wanted to, I canna. I made a promise to Aline and her family." He came and stood before her and kneeled, taking her hands in his.

The pull between them was electric, and Abby wanted to say to hell with Aline and her nastiness, but she couldn't. "You should leave my room. When Gwen leaves for her own estate, which I'm assuming should be after your handfasting, I'll go with her. I'll think of some way to fix my colossal mistake."

"I can't let ye go. Och, Abigail. I'm sorry."

Tears pooled in her eyes and she blinked them away, refusing to cry in front of him. The last thing she needed was for him to pull her against him, touch her more than he was already. That wouldn't be good at all. She'd likely turn into an adulterous woman hell-bent on breaking up an engagement. "It's not your fault. I should have known that in this time things move quicker than my own. I'll be fine with Gwen and maybe, when her daughter is old enough, I'll have her send me back to the twenty-first century."

Aedan cupped her cheek, swiping a thumb across her jaw. "You're so beautiful. I've missed ye."

She bit her lip, nodding. "I've missed you, too." Abby's breathing increased as he pinned her with his determined, hungry gaze.

"I dinna know how I'll go on, knowing you're only a few miles away. It'll be the veriest torture."

He leaned closer, their lips but a whisper apart. "But one we'll have to endure," she said. "You can take comfort in the fact you'll have a wife to warm your bed here and give you heirs." He pulled back, and she was thankful for it. She didn't need him close, touching her, looking at her with so much love and pain that her heart yearned and broke at the same time.

She needed him to go. "Leave, Aedan, and don't come back in here again. I should've looked up what your future held. I should have realized that since Druiminn is still within your family that you'd had heirs. Had I pushed past my own fear of what I would find, I would've saved us both a lot of heartache."

"Ye never studied to see what became of me and my clan?" He stood.

"I looked up the battle and found out you'd survived the night, but I never looked beyond that. I thought Gwen would bring me back, but when she didn't, I assumed she'd perished in the fire but I couldn't find anything to confirm that."

"If I could change my circumstances I would, ye must know that. But I canna do that to Aline. I've given her and her family my word. I cannot dishonor her or myself by breaking my oath."

Abby took a deep breath, the tightness in her chest as painful as the knowledge that he'd never be hers. "Of course."

She shrugged. "I'll try and stay out of your way as much as possible and please tell Aline that I'm sorry if my appearance here makes her uncomfortable."

"Ye don't need to do that, Abigail. I'm sure we're mature enough adults not to succumb to our emotions."

You may be. "Of course," she said. "Good night, Aedan."

"Good night, lass."

As soon as the tapestry settled, Abby let go of the emotions she'd been holding at bay. What a mess of things she'd made. And now she was stuck in a time for who knew how long, and around the one man she loved, who she could no longer have.

She crawled into bed, not bothering to pull the blankets up. What could she do? Knowing all the while, there was nothing she could do. Aedan was lost to her, would never wake up next to her, nuzzling her neck and whispering the sweetest Gaelic words in her ear, not that she ever knew what they meant in the first place, but still…it had been sweet.

The thought of becoming the scarlet woman flickered through her mind, but she pushed it aside. She could never do that to Aline, or any woman, no matter how much she may want to, or thought Aline deserved such treatment.

That option wasn't a path she wanted to go down. She'd bide her time and wait for Gwen's daughter to send her home. She'd be older when she went back to her time, but that's what happened when mistakes were made.

Foolish, foolish mistakes that resembled a living nightmare.

•••

Aedan stood on the opposite side of the tapestry and listened to the sobs that wracked Abigail's body. He cursed himself to Hades for wanting to go to her. Wrap her in his arms and comfort her. To kiss the sweet lips that had haunted his mind for the past twelve months.

She hiccupped and he swore. To be the cause of her pain wasn't something he'd ever thought to be. He loved her. Loved her so much that the severing pain was likely to rip him in two.

He couldn't listen to her crying so he strode out of his room, heading toward his sister's quarters. He knocked loud on their door, pushing past Braxton when he finally opened it.

"Do ye have any idea what you've done, lass? Abigail is now, right at this moment, sobbing, and there's nothing I can do to help her. Why would ye bring her back to see what I've done?"

"Because what you've done is a mistake." Gwen swung out of bed and pulled a shawl about her shoulders. "Aline is poison for ye soul, while Abigail is the antidote. Do not marry her, Aedan. You'll regret it."

"If ye planned on bringing Abigail back why didn't ye tell me? I would've waited for her. You knew how much I loved the lass."

"Loved? Does that mean you no longer do?" Gwen crossed her arms, one eyebrow raised.

"I love her still and I canna have her. How do ye think that makes me feel? Makes *us* feel?"

Gwen sighed. "When the announcement was made my decision was also. I swore on my daughter that should she have the gift, I'd pass down the story required for Abigail to return. I suppose by swearing that oath, I've also found out Mairi is gifted like her mama, for Abigail appeared like a ghost not long after."

Braxton went over and stood next to his wife, placing a comforting arm about her shoulders. "Are ye sure, Gwen?"

"Aye, I'm sure," Gwen said, kissing Braxton quickly before looking back at Aedan.

"Well, I'm very happy for ye both, but it doesn't change the mess you've made."

"I've never liked Aline and she knows this. She's aware that I'd do anything to keep ye from making such a huge mistake. As for the rest of your future, it's up to you, brother. Who will you choose?"

"Choose? I've already chosen. I can't go back on my word. The Grants are not a clan that we need to be at war with." No matter how much he wanted to say the hell with everything required of him. To hell with everyone who expected him to do the right thing all the time.

"Well, I suggest ye find another way, before it's too late."

Aedan rubbed his neck, a headache thumping behind his brow. "Abigail will return to your estate with ye. I can't have her here with me. It's not safe."

Gwen raised her brow, grinning. "And why's that? Don't ye think you'd be able to keep ye hands off the lass?"

He gritted his teeth. The urge to strangle his sister pulled at his soul. "I dinna wish to hurt Abigail any more than I already have." The memory of her tears, of her sobbing, tortured him. She'd only have to look at him, nod for him to follow her, and he'd go. He'd do anything to be with her again. To taste her, smell her, touch her one more time. He ran a hand through his hair and swore. "She leaves with you."

"I'm so glad ye came to see us, brother, as we've more news for you. We've decided to stay for a few months after your wedding. I hope you don't mind. Of course, anyone who's my guest is welcome to stay here for that length of time, as well."

"Dinna do this, Gwendolyn, or I'll be forced to remove ye both physically from Druiminn."

She laughed, the damn vexing woman. "Don't be foolish. You wouldn't dare throw me out. This is the home of my birth, and for as long as I wish, I can stay. 'Tis not my problem you'll have to tread carefully around your prickly fiancée and the woman you love more than life itself."

"We'll discuss this more in the morn." Aedan stormed from the room, not caring how much noise he made as he walked to his chamber. He wanted to hit something, hard, make it hurt as much as he did.

The thought of never being able to be with Abigail wasn't something he'd ever contemplated, not when she was here, in the flesh, only a corridor away…

He punched his door, the wood creaking, but little else. His hand was another matter. He looked down at it with little concern. Nor did the outburst of temper do anything to numb how he felt. He'd never survive with Abigail under his roof. Now, at this very moment, his body ached to be with her. To make her his once more and bring pleasure to them both.

Damn it. Damn it all to hell.

Chapter Twenty-Three

She was living in a perpetual state of hell. From the moment she'd stepped into medieval Scotland, each tick of the clock hurt every fiber of her being. The following day made it even worse. Aedan's gaze had followed her about, watching her, wanting her…

And today would take every strength she possessed not to crumble into a pile of lost hopes and dreams.

"Aline's chamber is this way, miss." A servant pointed to a room on the opposite side of the castle to Aedan's quarters. Abby didn't delve into the thought as to why she was housed in the room beside his and not his future wife.

She knocked and heard Aline beckon her to enter. The room was as spacious as hers, animal furs covered the bed and parts of the floor. Two chairs sat before the roaring fire, and although the room wasn't warm, it wasn't chilly like so many others.

"You wished to see me, Aline?" Abby shut the door, but didn't venture any farther into the room. She didn't want to be here in the first place. This woman was the sole reason why she'd never get what her heart wished for. Not that she could blame the woman entirely. Aedan had chosen her, had decided to move on and marry another. The thought brought tears to her eyes and she took a deep breath, less she start blubbering like a fool.

"Come and sit beside me, Abigail. I'm in need of your advice."

"Of course." Abby sat, folding her hands in her lap. Aline played with the long plait of hair that came over one shoulder. She smiled, and yet the gesture didn't meet her eyes.

"I wish to discuss something with ye that is of a personal nature. In fact, there are a couple of things I wanted to know, if you're willing to discuss them with me, of course."

Abby swallowed, not sure if she should agree or not. "I'll be as honest as I can. What is it you wish to know?"

"First, I'd like to know why you left Aedan after the battle. You were betrothed. Surely there was no reason to flee Scotland."

Abby thought back to the story she and Gwen had come up with. All lies, and yet, they would suit their needs and explain why she was back within their fold. "After the fire, I was called back to the estate where I came from. A sick family member, who eventually passed, God rest her soul, needed me. I couldn't refuse."

"I see." Aline sighed, the sound contrived. "But, I still don't see why you would call off your betrothal with Aedan."

"When apart, I realized we would not suit. I wrote to him and notified him that my feelings had changed. He was in agreement." Abby watched as the words pleased Aline, and she mentally cursed the woman for the bitch she was. How Aedan could endure a lifetime with this woman was anyone's guess. She doubted they'd last, but then, divorce wasn't an option so… "What is the advice you wish help with?"

"As to that—" Aline giggled and Abby wanted to scratch

her eyes out. "I'd like to know what your opinion is on pre-marital copulation? Aedan and I have known each other for a long time, and there are times when a mere kiss isn't enough. I know by the feel of him he wishes to do more, when he clasps me hard against his body my own wants nothing more than to be as near to him as I possibly can be. Do you think I should offer him more before our marriage? Would that be too forward? Whoreish even?"

Abby stared at her a long moment, unable to form words. Aline smiled, the laughter in her eyes telling Abby how much she knew the question hurt. "I think, if it's what you wish, then you should sleep together. In fact, as you're already betrothed, I see no harm in it. No one has to know, right?"

Aline grinned. "That's right. I'm so glad we're able to have these chats, Abigail. I feel we didn't get along when I last stayed, but I'm happy we can now be friends. Especially since you're such close friends with Gwen and she will soon be my family."

"I'm happy for you, Aline. I'm sure you will do well with Aedan. He's a good man." Abby stood. "I must change before dinner. I've been outdoors most of the day."

"Of course. And please, do sit at the dais tonight. I wish to speak to you some more."

"Thank you, that is very kind." Abby left quickly, but once outside the room, she held the wall to stop herself from falling. Years stretched ahead of her, of being near Aedan, of hearing about his marriage to Aline, their children, all the while being stuck here, unable to leave, or move forward with her own life until Gwen's daughter was able to help her.

"Are ye alright, lass?"

Her attention snapped up to Aedan who strolled toward her. He was in a kilt, his muscular legs tightened and flexed with each step. He wore no shirt, his torso damp from whatever exercise he'd come from. Her mouth dried and words became impossible.

"Abigail, lass. Are ye alright?"

She nodded, but feared her head shook the opposite way to what it was supposed to do. "Of course. I'm heading back to my room. Excuse me." She went to walk around him and he clasped her arm.

"Ye dinna look well. Has something happened?"

Other than your fiancée breaking my heart... "Nothing's happened. I'll see you at dinner."

He pulled her into an alcove, a long rectangular window at her back. Aedan stood before her, blocking her path of escape. She sighed and skittered back as far as the small space would allow. She didn't need to be close to him, to have his presence envelop her, consume her, as it always did.

"Please tell me what has troubled ye. You must know I still care for ye and do not wish to cause ye anymore distress than I already have."

The lump was back in her throat. "I know, but truly, let me pass, Aedan. There's nothing you can do or say that will make this situation any easier for me." She shrugged, fisting her hands at her side, lest she grab him and force him to kiss her.

Although by the dangerous look in his gaze, she doubted he'd be a difficult convert. He looked like he struggled with his words, and sighing, he stepped back, giving her the much needed space she craved.

She stepped past him and headed toward her room. Tears pooled in her eyes, and she again cursed her own stupidity at not looking up Aedan's history. But then, anger thrummed in her veins with the thought that he couldn't even wait a measly year for her. And why hadn't Gwen told him of her plan?

She changed direction and went to seek out Gwen instead. She had a lot of explaining to do.

•••

Gwen was sitting before the fire in her chamber.

"I was wondering when you'd come to talk to me." Gwen's lips lifted in a small smile and she beckoned Abby into the room.

Abby sat across from her, leaning forward to warm her chilled hands. At least they matched her chilled heart. "Why am I here? I mean, seriously, Gwen. Did you know that Aedan was courting Aline? Had in fact thought to make her his wife?"

"I knew he was courting her, and I told him that it was a mistake, but knowing my powers were weakened after the fire, he thought ye gone. Before your arrival, I hadn't thought I could bring you back. All I know is, the moment his betrothal announcement was made, I swore I had to do something to change the course of history. I made an oath that should my daughter have my gift, that I would ensure you were brought back. That my descendants would make it so…" Gwen paused. "And almost as soon as I made the vow, you returned."

"I'm stuck here now, Gwen. God knows for how long, probably years, if I have to wait for your daughter to be strong enough to send me back." Despair crashed over her, and she swiped the tears from her cheek. Damn it, she wasn't going to cry anymore. She'd cried enough to fill Loch Ness last night.

"You won't be going back. You're Aedan's soul mate, and ye have to take back what's yours."

The resolve behind Gwen's voice brooked no argument. "You cannot be serious. I'm not going to break his engagement. As much as I love the guy, I'm not going to sink to that level." She paused, hating the fact she'd actually thought of this idea herself, but didn't want to voice it out loud. She needed to keep some sort of moral compass. "And even if I wanted to, contracts have been signed between the clans. I'd probably cause another war, if Aedan chose me."

Gwen scoffed. "Aline is not for him. Ye must do something, though I can't tell you what. I will give you a home should ye wish to leave here, but I'll not let ye go back to your own time. Your future is here, Abigail. You may not think so now, but 'tis true. Trust in his love, that's all I ask."

"I know he loves me, but as he said, things change. Life sometimes gets in the way of what we wish. He has a duty, Gwen, and I'll not cause trouble for him, no matter how much I want him to be mine." She stood, needing air. "I'll see you later. I'm going for a quick walk before dinner."

"Do ye love my brother, Abigail?"

Abby stopped at the threshold and studied the knots in the oak door. "More than anything in the world."

"Then whether the path is right or wrong, you have one to walk. I have faith that people who're born for one another, will find each other…eventually."

Abby left, and hearing the sound of loud voices from the great hall, decided against a walk and went back to her room. She closed the door and leaned against it. The situation was heartbreakingly hopeless.

•••

The next day, Abby had Cook make up a small picnic for herself. She wandered about the kitchen while the food was prepared. Two large fires burned and meats rotated above one, while on the other pots with an assortment of fragrances wafted from them. Two tables, L-shaped in their set-out, were covered with plates, cooked pies, and biscuits and apples.

"Do you leave the food out once it's cooked or do you have a place to store it?"

The older woman wiped her hands on her apron, a little flushed from work. "We have a larder my lady, over there," she said, waving to the opposite side of the room.

Abby went over to it and peeked inside. It was as warm as the kitchen and probably not the best place for food that required refrigeration. "You should put in an ice room beneath the kitchens, to help keep your perishable food longer and stop it from going bad."

The staff in the kitchens stopped and looked at Abby with something akin to bewilderment. "What in all things holy is an ice room?"

"During the winter you'd collect ice, you could cut it from the top of a frozen loch. You would then place that ice into a stone room, away from heat and light. The ice will remain frozen for a very long time and you could store your meats and milks, things like that, within the ice room, and it'll keep for a much longer time. At present, you salt your meat quite a lot to preserve it, and that would no longer be necessary."

"And have ye seen such an ice room before, my lady? I know I never have."

How did Abigail tell them that the ancient Romans had used them for years, and that in archaeological digs, even possibly China. "I have seen them." Or what was left of such structures on old estates scattered about England. "When you store the ice, you insulate it with straw or sawdust to make it last longer. You should see if the laird would approve one. I think you'd find it a blessing, once you got used to using it."

The cook pursed her lips, nodding a little. "Mayhap I'll think on it and ask the laird when next I speak to him about the kitchens." She placed the last of her food into a small basket and handed it to Abby. "Here ye are. Enjoy yer day, my lady."

"Thank you," Abby said, heading out the door that led off to the side of the castle. Not too far from the estate she found a secluded tree and sat. Her view overlooked the flowing waterway that ran beside the castle. Picking at a bread roll, her thoughts were far from the beautiful view of the Highlands that stretched out before her. Aedan, always Aedan, consumed her mind.

"Gwen told me ye had returned. I had to see for myself what she said was true."

Abby turned at the sound of a friendly, familiar voice. "Black Ben." She laughed. "It's great to see you again. What brings you back to Castle Druiminn?"

"My friend and his forthcoming wedding." He sat and started to rummage through her small basket. "I dinna think to see ye again. I must declare, I'm happy that you're here."

"I wish I could say the same." Abby poured some wine into her goblet and handed it to him. He downed it in one swallow. How stupid to think she could make a life in this time. She should've reminded herself how brutal this time was and stayed in the twenty-first century where she belonged. Not in this time, where marriages between clans moved at lightning speed and people you would've trusted with your life let you down.

"Ye not happy to be back, then? I thought ye'd be right pleased."

"I thought I would be, too, but." She shrugged. It was hard to find words for what she actually felt. Perhaps, there were no words for the despair she found herself in. "I don't know what I'm doing here, actually. Everything's buggered up."

"I don't know what ye mean by buggered, but I'm assuming it's a derogatory term?"

Somehow, even in her depressed state, Ben managed to make her smile. "Yes, it is." Abby covered her eyes, hoping that he'd not notice her crying. "He's going to marry her." A sob tore free, and Ben placed a comforting arm about her shoulders. She went willingly against, him, seeking comfort for a situation that wasn't going to change, no matter how much she cried about it.

"Aye, mayhap he will." He rubbed her arm. "Dinna fret,

lass. All is not lost yet."

Abby looked up at Ben, a flicker of hope igniting in her stomach. "What do you mean? Do you know something that I don't?"

"Nay. But Aedan is as close as a brother to me, and I'll not let him make such a mistake without some input into the matter first. Let me talk to him, and we'll see."

Abby clutched at his shirt, unable to wipe the smile from her lips. "You'd really help me. Oh my gosh, thank you so much, Ben." She kissed his cheek and he chuckled.

"You missed, lass. My mouth is in the middle of my face."

"Enjoying yourself, I see."

Abby's laughter died on her lips at the sound of Aedan's deadly tone. She stood quickly and looked at Ben. He stood slowly, seemingly unfazed, and yet his eyes looked wary.

"We were eating some lunch. You're more than welcome to join us, if you like," she said.

Aedan pinned Ben with a lethal gaze, and she shivered.

"What is really going on here? Explain. Now." Aedan placed his hand on the hilt of his sword and fear crept up her spine.

"Nothing, Aedan. We were just eating."

"It looked like more than eating." He did look at her then and she shrugged, not knowing what else to do. "If you're accusing me and Ben of an illicit affair, you're being an ass."

"Ass? I watched ye kiss the man."

A muscle worked in his jaw and Abby wanted to go to him, reassure him, and yet the thought of Aline halted her steps. "And in only a week or so I'll watch you marry Aline. Seems like a fair trade off."

"I'll leave ye two alone." Ben went to leave and Aedan pushed him back toward her. Abby grabbed his arm to steady him, which she didn't do a very good job of when she stumbled instead.

"What the hell do you think you're doing, Aedan?" She righted herself, glaring at him.

Ben smiled before letting out a roar and charging Aedan. Shocked mute by the sight of Aedan and Ben pummelling each other, rolling all over the ground, it took Abby a couple of seconds to realize she should do something.

"Stop!" She attempted to pull Ben back, but only managed to fall over as Aedan rolled Ben under himself and started thumping him with sickening thuds.

"Aedan, stop!" But they didn't, just continued to brawl on the ground. Looking about for a container, she spotted the basket. It wasn't waterproof, but it would hold water for a little while. She ran the short distance to the river and filled it, coming back to the fighting men and dumping the full basket of water on their idiot heads.

They gasped, pulled apart, and glared at her.

"What did ye do that for?" Aedan's chest rose and fell with labored breaths, and she tore her attention away from the magnetic sight.

"Why do you think? You're acting like medieval morons."

"I think the Laird of Druiminn is jealous. Ye can't have all the women, boy."

"You'll not have her," Aedan roared, startling her.

Ben stood without saying a word, and left.

She glared at Aedan, wanting to throttle him herself. "Get up."

He did, clasping his stomach as he did so. "What," he asked at length when she didn't say anything.

"What are you doing? You can't fight your closest friend for something he's innocent of."

"It didn't look innocent to me, lass. Do ye want him now?"

Abby strode up to him and slapped his face. Hard. His eyes narrowed, but he didn't react. "If I wanted Ben, I'd have Ben. You have Aline, after all. But I want you, Aedan, and I can't have you. Is that what you want to hear? Because it's true. I think of you all the time. The thought of you while I was away, the hope that I would see you again, was all that kept me sane."

She paced, trying to calm down. "You know that I had a boyfriend, a lover in my time? I thought I'd marry him, have children with him, but I buried him, instead. He was a cop, a peacekeeper, and the job killed him. Just like one day, this job of yours, your position as laird, could kill you."

His eyes clouded with jealousy but also a flicker of compassion. "What are ye trying to say?"

"I didn't have to come back, you know. I could've kept my heart protected from the pain of losing someone I love by death, illness, whatever, but I didn't. Life is nothing without love." Tears welled in her eyes and she sniffed. "And, what do I come back to? You. Engaged to Aline, of all women."

"I dinna think ye could come back. What did ye want me to do? Stay a saint for the rest of my life? I have to have heirs."

"Why didn't you ask Gwen to do"—she waved her arms about—"something!" She growled, wanting to hit something. "I'm so pissed off with you right now; nothing you say can change the fact that you couldn't even wait a year to move on."

"I was told within weeks of ye leaving that ye couldn't be returned. What was I supposed to do?" He ran a hand through his long locks, cursing in a language she couldn't understand. "I died when I knew I'd never see ye again. What did it matter who I married after that?"

"That may be so, but twelve months! Probably sooner, since you had to court her."

He shook his head, stepping back. "I'm sorry, lass. I canna say any more than that."

"No, you can't." Abby swiped a tear from her cheek and looked out over the serene water, hoping it would help her calm down a little. "It's over, Aedan. Do what you want, marry whoever the hell you want. I can't allow myself to care anymore."

He clasped her arm, pulling her around to face him. "Ye can't allow yourself to care, or you don't care?"

His eyes burned into her soul, and she knew he'd gathered the answer before she spoke. "I can't."

"Lass…"

She placed her hand on his lips, stopping him from kissing her. "Don't you dare, Aedan."

"Why not?" Anguish tinged his voice.

"Why do you think? I don't trust myself around you." Abby pushed him away, gathered up what remained of her picnic, and held the basket before her in a pathetic attempt at a barrier. "I won't become the other woman, not even for you. Aline and I deserve better than that."

"What do ye plan on doing?"

"I'm leaving with Gwen, and maybe I'll marry eventually, or go back to my own time when I can." She shrugged. "Who knows?"

His eyes burned with hatred. At her or her words, she couldn't be sure.

Abby started back toward the castle, leaving Aedan under the tree. It was better this way. She couldn't be around him without wanting to give in to desires that she no longer had the right to feel.

He was as lost to her now as he had been when centuries separated them.

…

Aedan stormed into Black Ben's chamber, slamming the door behind him. Ben sat before the fire, one eyebrow raised in amusement. "Come in."

"You stay the hell away from Abigail. She's not for you."
His friend laughed, and a red haze dropped over his vision.
He'd kill him.

"And she's not for ye, either, since you've decided to
marry Aline." Ben took a sip of mead. "Sit."

Aedan slunk down in the opposite chair and swore,
running a hand over his face, wishing he could undo his
decisions of the past few months. "What am I going to do?"

"You'll marry Aline, of course. What else can you do?"

Nothing… He gritted his teeth, wondering how fate could
play such an unfair game with his life. "I didn't think I'd ever
see Abigail again. Had I even thought it was a possibility, I
would've never signed an agreement with Clan Grant."

"I sought out Gwen and she explained everything that's
happened here these last few weeks. I happened to run into
Abigail. I didn't seek her out, if ye were wondering." Ben
met his gaze square on. "She's a friend and nothing more. No
matter how bonny I think the lass, ye are my friend first and
foremost."

"Thank ye." Aedan reached over to the little table before
their feet and poured himself a cup of mead and took a sip.
"When I saw —"

"Abigail kissing me you went into a rage? How are ye
going to marry another when ye have such strong feelings
toward the lass? The marriage will be a disaster. You'll
eventually despise Aline for being herself, and she'll hate you
for ruining her life. Ye canna go through with it."

"To pull out now would cause another clan war, and I
can't do that to my people. We're still healing after the battle
with O'Cain." But damn it he wanted to. To hell with everyone
else's expectations, the alliances — everything. He would go to
war with everyone if it meant he could keep the woman he
loved.

Ben cleared his throat, grinning. "I may have a solution."

Aedan snapped his head up, willing to hear anything, if it meant he could possibly have Abigail back. "What is it?"

"I'll seduce your betrothed. One night in my bed and she'll not look in your direction again."

"I canna ask for ye to do such a thing." He ran a hand through his hair. "I cannot marry Aline. I will go to Laird Grant when he returns and declare my intentions. What will happen after that I do not know, but I'll be prepared for anything."

"My offer stands. You have saved my life more than once, 'tis time I repaid the debt. I'll seduce the lass and she'll never look in ye direction again."

Aedan laughed. "You're more ballsy than my male Highland heifers. What makes ye think she'll fall into your bed so easily?"

Ben looked sheepish. "Let's just say Aline Grant and I have some unfinished business from when we were staying here last."

Aedan sat up. "You've seduced her already?"

"Nay." Ben shook his head, frowning. "But after watching the woman and her viciousness, I was intrigued to know if she was always so vile. I found that she was not, not when kissed within an inch of her life, at least."

For a moment speech was impossible, followed by a grain of hope. "Do ye want my permission?"

"It wouldn't hurt. No one need know any of this, and think of it as a pre-wedding gift. Of course, ye know I'm speaking of your wedding with the delectable Abigail."

"Dinna push our friendship, Ben," Aedan said, only half joking. Delectable and Abigail were thoughts only he was allowed to have. To have the woman he loved more than life itself back in his arms, to feel her soft skin, smell her delicious scent, sent fire through his veins. "If ye seduce Aline, you'll have to marry the lass. Are ye willing to do that?"

Ben shrugged, seemingly unfazed. "I need a wife, and although Aline seems verbally potent with most people, on her own she's a different lass. I'll keep her so occupied that she'll never feel jaded with her life again."

"High praise for yourself." Aedan laughed. "I suppose I should apologize for earlier."

"Aye, and so should I."

Aedan stood. "Whether ye seduce the lass or not, I will be going to her father and telling him that the marriage will nay be going ahead. As much as I appreciate yer friendship and what ye are willing to do for me 'tis unnecessary. Do think on ye choice before ye take the lass as yer own."

"Aye, I'll think on ye words," Ben said, catching his gaze.

"Ye are a true friend, and a man I'll be forever indebted to, no matter what you do."

Ben smirked, raising his goblet in salute. "Dinna forget it, lad."

Aedan laughed as he left, closing the door behind him. *He never would.*

Chapter Twenty-Four

The next day something odd was happening. After the initial summons into Aline's room for the woman to rub the engagement in Abby's face, a distance had sprung up between the betrothed couple. Certainly, it didn't seem like Aline was seeking out Aedan for pre-marital sex. There was no flirting, hot glances. In fact, it looked like nothing could be further from their thoughts, if Aedan had ever thought along those lines in the first place.

And as Abby had asked, Aedan held up his end of the bargain and kept away from her. He spoke, of course, wished her good morning and good night, but other than that, they didn't spend any time together. It was what she wanted, or certainly, what she needed, but it didn't change the fact their separation, when being so close in a physical sense, hurt like hell.

She missed him…

Keeping away from him wasn't easy, either, especially when she caught him watching her, his dark hooded eyes that sparked sin and beckoned her to jump into the shoes of "the other" woman all but called her over.

And she so wanted to go…

No.

Abby bit into a chicken leg and listened to the idle talk between Gwen and Braxton. Tonight they were seated at the dais, Aedan and Aline quiet in the middle of the table, neither one venturing to speak to their clans or family seated beside them. Black Ben, seated out with the clansmen, seemed solemn as well.

Seated to one end, Abby knew she couldn't let what she suspected was going on between the once close friends continue. Aedan and Ben were friends. What had happened on the day of her picnic should not ruin a lifelong friendship.

Especially when nothing had happened. She liked Ben. He was a nice guy, but he'd never turned her head. Only one Highlander had managed that, even if he was no longer hers.

Music commenced up on the gallery overlooking the hall and Gwen stood, holding her babe. "I'm retiring for the night, Abigail. It's been a long day, and I'm not feeling up to dancing this eve."

"Are ye okay?" Aedan turned to his sister, noting her distress. Their eyes met briefly and butterflies took flight in her stomach.

"Aye. I'm fine. Just tired. I'll see you in the morn."

"Good night." Abby finished her wine, leaning back in her chair and watching as Braxton escorted his wife away. A smile lifted her lips at seeing how he doted on her. How lucky Gwen was to find love in a time when marriages were looked upon as a means for more power, land, or money.

Aedan's and Aline's a prime example.

Out of the corner of her eye, she heard Black Ben ask Aline to dance. They joined the other couples and for the first time, she noticed Aline letting her guard down and enjoying herself.

Aedan shifted to sit beside her and the pull of him, the need to turn and be wrapped up in his comforting embrace was a physical struggle to ignore.

She could feel the heat of his gaze on her face and she steadfastly refused to meet his eyes. He cleared his throat and leaned back in his chair.

"You're ignoring me." It wasn't a question.

"Not really," she said, flicking him a quick glance. "This will be easier if we stay away from each other."

His hand moved down between them and stroked the underside of her arm. Shivers skittered across her skin and warmth pooled at her core. Abby swallowed, gathering her wits. "Don't do that."

"I miss ye."

His deep, gravelly tone was almost enough to make her forget honor. "I miss you, as well, but missing each other doesn't change anything." Abby sat forward, pulling her arm out of his reach. She met his gaze and held it. "You made your choice. Now you must live with it."

"My choice would've been different had I known Gwen's alternative." He leaned over the table, their shoulders bumping. "I love ye."

"I know." Abby looked out to the dance floor and caught Ben's eye when he winked. *What is he up to?* "I'm retiring as well." She turned to face him. "Maybe you and I weren't meant to happen."

"Yer talking pish. Had the Laird of Grant not returned to his holdings for a few days, our lives would be different. I promise I will fix this so we can be together."

Abby stood, throwing her hands up in the air. "I don't know what you want, Aedan. You're betrothed to another. I'm not going to sleep with you. I'm not going to do anything with you, so leave me alone," she whispered as loudly as she could.

He made a low growling noise before standing, knocking his chair over. Some of the clan looked to see what was going on and she pasted on a pleasant smile to ease their concern. She swallowed at the wild, untamed look in Aedan's eyes as he pulled her to the side of the room. Large wooden pillars ran the length of the wall, giving them privacy.

He pinned her against the wall, the cold stone at her back firing her blood. "What the hell do you think you're doing?"

"I'm going to tell the Laird of Grant that I'll not marry his daughter, no matter if my words cause another clan battle. I'll not live without ye. Now damn well kiss me, lass, one last time, in case he puts a sword through my gullet after my declaration."

Abby placed her hand on his chest to stop him from advancing. She cursed her stupid body for wanting to do as he asked. The thought of his mouth on hers, to feel the delicious slide of his tongue against her own. She bit her lip, fighting the emotions he'd always sparked. Damn it. "Are you really going to break your betrothal with Aline?"

"Aye. There is no choice. I canna live without ye."

"You're the devil." *And Heaven all wrapped into one.*

A slight smile lifted his lips. "Then jump into Hell with me."

Her hand fisted about his shirt, pulling him against her. Their kiss wasn't a sweet, beckoning, tempting embrace, but an inferno that would make Lucifer proud.

He took her mouth hard, lips, teeth, tongue meshed, demanding, both trying to control the other. Abby moaned, her body after weeks of feeling lifeless, sparked to life with renewed energy. Her hand wrapped about his nape, the action pulling him fully against her.

His hardness pushed against her stomach, and her core thrummed with need. He pulled back, kissing her chin, her neck. "I choose you. I want you," he whispered.

The words acted like a cold bucket of water. Abby stilled, pushing him out of her arms. "I think that's a fair farewell kiss, until you do as you say."

Pain flickered through his gaze, but he nodded, allowing her to go. "I will do as I say." He bowed. "Good night, Abigail."

Abby walked from the room, looking to see if anyone had seen them in the darkened alcove. No one seemed to be looking their way, and she couldn't spot Ben or Aline. Guilt pierced her soul over her actions and tears pooled in her eyes. She'd promised not to touch him, but then he had said the most wonderful thing. He would be hers in only a matter of days. Or sooner, she hoped.

Chapter Twenty-Five

Abby woke with a start at the sound of loud knocking on her door. For a moment, panic clutched at her stomach, thinking the O'Cains had returned, but the sound of Gwen's excited voice on the other side of the door put all her fears to rest.

"Come in." Gwen stormed into the room, shutting the door quickly behind her. "What's going on?" Abby asked, rubbing her eyes.

"Ye will never guess what has occurred this morn. When the servant went in to wake Aline, all she found was a missive on her bed." Gwen paused. "Her unslept-in bed…"

Abby narrowed her eyes, wondering where this was going. In her time, this sort of thing was common, certainly not the drama it seemed to be here, which was a sign of the times, she supposed. "So what did the note say?"

Gwen sat on her bed, grinning. "She's run off with Black Ben. They're to be married. The letter to her father, who's expected to return today, explained her feelings had changed and that she no longer wanted to marry Aedan."

Abby shut her mouth with a snap and tried not to smile,

and with the thought of Aline out of the picture…she could have Aedan.

"Aline begged for forgiveness and wished everyone the very best in their life."

"Where's Aedan?"

"Breaking his fast downstairs."

"Is he upset that Black Ben has done this?"

Gwen shrugged, seemingly taken aback by the question. "He dinna look it. In fact, he seemed quite pleased about the whole situation."

I bet he did… Abby's chamber servant walked in, a deep purple gown in her arms.

"Louise, can you organize a bath for me this morning, please?" Her servant curtsied and went off on her chore.

"I must ask, Abigail. Will you marry my brother now?"

"I'll let you know after I've seen Aedan."

"Very well." Gwen kissed her cheek quickly, the woman almost hopping with excitement. "I'll be in the hall doing some mending when you're ready to come down."

Abby watched her go, the butterflies in her stomach at full flight. Aedan was no longer engaged. She grinned, unable to control the excitement that coursed through her veins.

What luck it was that Aline cried off, stopping the need for Aedan to break alliances with clan Grant.

The bath, although not the deepest, was refreshing. She lathered her skin with lavender soap, and thought about what the next few days would mean. Had what happened between Ben and Aline been what Ben had hinted at the other day when he joined her on the picnic? Had he planned this? Or had their attraction been an ongoing thing, and one he'd wanted to pursue, especially after finding out his best friend was about to marry the woman?

There was nothing like wanting something you couldn't have to make you realize how much you needed it.

"Abigail."

She gasped and turned to find Aedan walking into her room from the secret corridor. "I'm a little busy here. Perhaps you can come back later." Not that she meant a word of it. Aedan could intrude on her anytime he liked.

He strode quickly across the small distance, ripping off his shirt and dropping his kilt as he did so. Abby's mouth dried at the sight of him standing beside the tub, his bronzed form hers for the taking, if she wished.

And she so wished.

He climbed in, the water rising and threatening to swoosh over the side.

"Please, join me." He smiled at her sarcasm.

He sat at the opposite end to her, which wasn't all that far considering the size of the tub and stared, his dark emerald eyes beckoning her with untold delights. "Come here."

Abby bit her lip but did as he asked. Their bodies slid against one another, the feel of his muscular thighs under her bottom making her burn with need.

"What do you want, Aedan?" From the hardness that pushed against her core, she knew what he wanted, as did he. His hands clasped hard against her hips, his cock sliding, teasing her toward madness.

She moaned.

"Marry me."

She nodded, trying to form the word past the lump in her throat. "Yes."

He kissed her long and slow. Abby ran her hands across his unshaven jaw and up into his hair. His locks were longer than they'd been when she was here before, and she pulled them a little.

He lifted her and she took him in, his member filling her, making her feel secure and complete. Everything about him she adored—his strength, mind, ability as a man.

As he rocked into her, their need increased. Abby leaned back and watched as they made love to each other. His eyes darkened to a murky green with desire, sparking her enjoyment. She loved having control of a man in such a way, a man who'd normally control every facet of his life, including sex.

But not here. Here Abby had the upper hand and she made full use of her wiles.

• • •

Aedan ground his teeth as the woman in his arms, his future wife, tormented and pushed him within an inch of his ability to not come before she did. Having not had sex for the past twelve months, a man could only stand so much tupping, and after their kiss last night, his capacity to last was fraying faster than his well-worn kilt.

He ran his hands over her soft flesh, her skin as smooth as pummelled leather. Her breasts rocked before him as she rode them both toward ecstasy. He ran his palm across the pebbled flesh of her nipples. She gasped, laughing a little as he rolled the peaks between his fingers.

Her breasts were supple and all his. "I missed ye, lass. So much."

She kissed him again and he lost himself in the embrace. He clasped her hard against him, pushing her down on his cock, his body roaring to come.

"Yes. Keep doing that."

He bit down on her shoulder, helping her to ride him, wanting her to come with a need that matched his. She moaned his name, nibbled his earlobe.

"I'm going to come," she whispered, sighing against his ear.

He growled and held off his own release as she climaxed

in his arms. Tremor after tremor pulled on him and he came hard, following close on her heels in his own orgasm that shot pleasure to every extremity of his body. Their breathing labored, he stroked her back as they slowly gathered their breath.

"I love you." She kissed his shoulder, her lips leaving fire in their wake.

"I love ye, too. So much."

She pulled back and met his gaze, ran a finger over his bottom lip, and he clasped it between his teeth. "We should spend the entire day in here. Forget the world for twenty-four hours."

He stood, taking her with him as he stepped out of the tub. He clasped the linen cloth for drying and quickly wiped them both down before carrying her to the bed.

Abigail looked good enough to eat laid out on the furs. Her long, dark locks sat about her face and over her shoulders, partly hiding the most perfect breasts he'd ever beheld.

"Let me lock the door."

She sat up with a start. "Oh my God, I totally forgot that wasn't locked. Anyone could've walked in." A blush stole over her cheeks, making her more beautiful than he thought possible.

Aedan laughed. "I think they would've heard ye were otherwise occupied." His words only produced a darker shade of crimson on her face.

"I hope no one thought I was playing with myself in here. How embarrassing."

He slipped the bolt across the door and strolled back to the bed. "That's an interesting thought, and one I'd love to delve into later. But first, I'm going to make due on a promise."

"What promise?" She frowned, but laughter twinkled in her eyes.

"I said ye were good enough to eat, and now I'm going

to do so."

"Oh really?" She raised her brow, but lay down, placing her hands behind her head. "The thought of you doing that is such a turn on."

Aedan groaned and kneeled over her. He kissed her stomach, the top of her thigh, between her legs. "Then lay back and enjoy my mouth on yer delicious sex." He flicked his tongue against her and she moaned.

"Oh, I will." Her hands clasped his hair, kneading his locks. "Trust me."

•••

Later that night in a tangle of limbs, Abby rested her head on Aedan's chest, the sound of his beating heart lulling her to sleep. "We should have a bathroom made, just for us so we can bathe together whenever we want."

"And what will ye put in this bathroom?"

She smiled, thinking of all sorts of wonderful stuff. "We could have a larger bath made that would fit us both. Maybe tile the floor so it's cleaner when we've finished washing. And if you're clever, you could plumb pipework from downstairs so running water, both hot and cold, could fill this tub whenever we wished."

"If I made such a room for ye, I'd never get ye out of it."

Abby laughed. "If you were with me, why would we want to leave?"

"True," he said, and Abby could hear the smile in his voice. "You'll have to tell me more about it and mayhap we can plan something. Anything to please my woman."

"Thank you. You won't regret it."

They were quiet for a moment, before Aedan said, "When I saw ye in the hall after so long without ye, I thought you were an apparition. I'd been dreaming of you for months, I thought I'd started doing the same while awake."

Tears welled in her eyes and she sniffed. The last thing she wanted to do was turn into a blubbering mess in front of him. She looked up at him, resting her chin on his chest. "Yes, it's me."

"I'm sorry for putting ye through the last few weeks. Will you ever forgive me?"

"Aedan, it wasn't your fault. Not really. You're a product of your era. Marriage and heirs are expected of a laird and rightly so. I was crazy jealous that you'd moved on." She watched him digest her words, wondering what was going on behind that calculating visage.

"I should have demanded more of Gwen, but with the thought of losing ye, I suppose I fell into a hole I couldn't raise myself from." He cringed. "I know it's not fair, but I would've married anyone. I really didn't care who."

"Oh, Aedan, that's terrible, but I understand. I do. Please don't think that this will be an ongoing problem between us, because it won't." And surprisingly, Abby felt the truth in her words deep inside her heart. Aedan loved her. She certainly wouldn't hold anything against him for the choices he made.

"I dinna want it to be," he said, leaning down to whisper against her lips before kissing them quickly.

She wiggled over his chest, deepening the embrace. How amazing to have had such an opportunity to meet and fall in love with such a man. He wanted to marry her without a penny to her name, no grand family behind her, nothing other than her love. She was the luckiest woman on earth. "So when are you going to make an honest woman of me?"

He smirked and her stomach flipped. "Is tomorrow too soon? From this day forward, you'll never leave my side again. I've missed ye, lass. So very much."

His lips took hers in a searing kiss and she was lost. Lost to sensation and him. Just him, Aedan, the man she would make a future and life with for all time. This man pulling her hard against him, taking the kiss to searing heights would be the father of her children and she couldn't wait to get started. She would have Gwen cut out the implant stopping conception tomorrow. She couldn't wait to live…with him.

"I love you," she said, breaking the kiss for a moment, laughing as he pulled her against him once more, kissing her hard and deep.

"And I you, and if I don't tell ye that every day, be sure to remind me of my lapse." He smiled and her heart melted.

"I will. I promise."

She kissed him, reveling in all that was him. His moral character, his strength, and Highland heart. A heart that beat only for her. "I'll never leave you again. I promise."

"It pleases me heart to hear such words."

He rolled her over, pinning her beneath him. Abby laughed, and just as quickly sobered as he settled between her legs.

"And it'll please me more to have the pleasure of yer company…again."

"I like the sound of the word pleasure." She leaned in close to his ear, tickling it a little with her tongue. "You're not turning into that dreaded Neanderthal again, are you?"

He growled and she moaned as he slid deep and slow inside her. "One day you'll have to explain to me what exactly that term means, although I'm assuming it's something that resembles an untamed beast of a man."

Abby laughed and nodded. "What's life without a little spice between the sheets?"

He kissed her and she lost track of her thoughts. Instead, she shut her mind on the world, on the future and the past, for within their room, their home, and Highland land, they created magic.

A life of their own.

Epilogue

Abby screamed, cursing her husband who, right at this moment, wasn't beside her, so she could kick him in the face.

"Keep pushing, Abigail. The babe is almost here."

She cringed, wanting to crawl out of her own body, to do anything to get away from the monstrous sized baby she was trying to push out. She didn't need anyone to remind her she was having a baby, she could feel it well enough.

"I see the head!"

Abby glared at Gwen, who along with the clan healer, bent between her legs looking at the little rascal that surely was trying to split her in two. Another contraction tensed her stomach, and she pushed hard, feeling only the slightest reprieve from the pain when she worked with the contractions instead of against them.

"Keep pushing, lass. We're almost there."

"Oh God, it hurts," she screamed, pushing.

"Stop, lass, the head's out."

She panted, trying to halt the need to get this baby out while her body wanted to be rid of it. The baby felt huge, obviously took after his father.

"One more push, lass, and it'll be out. It's almost over," the healer said, nodding energetically.

Tears pooled in her eyes and for the first time in the year and a half she'd been living in medieval Scotland, she wished she was in her own time. A time when there were hospitals, doctors, and an epidural.

One last push and finally, relief poured through her with the announcement the baby was out. A small, gurgling cry sounded and she sobbed, both in relief and gratitude.

She was a mom.

"It's a girl!" Gwen laughed, handing the small little person to her and laying her on her chest. Abby looked down at who she and Aedan had created, and a love, unlike any she'd ever known, assailed her.

There was no doubt she loved Aedan, hadn't thought she could love anyone more with her heart and soul, but she was wrong. As the sweet cherub face scrunched and cried up at her, Abby knew she'd never love another more. She'd die before allowing anything to happen to this little sweetheart.

"Has Aedan returned?" she asked, not taking her gaze from their child.

"I'll go and check," Gwen said, standing and kissing her cheek quickly. "Congratulations, Abigail. She's beautiful."

"Isn't she?" She sniffed, sitting up a little when the clan healer said she was okay to do so. Abby opened the wadding to check her daughter had all ten fingers and toes. Her little face scrunched up in annoyance at being unwrapped and she quickly covered her again lest she become cold.

The sound of shouts from outside, followed by banging doors and yelling downstairs made her start. She lifted her little girl up and kissed her, giving her a little cuddle just as her bedroom door burst open.

Aedan stormed into the room, his face one of worry and

despair.

"I missed it," he said, coming to sit beside her on the bed and kissing her quickly on the temple before gazing lovingly at their daughter. "Are ye well, lass? Is there naught anyone can do for ye?"

"I'm fine, Aedan. I'll be sore for a few weeks, but otherwise, it looks like I survived my first childbirth." She handed the baby over, chuckling a little as her brute of a husband made an awkward attempt at gentleness.

"What shall we call her?" Abby asked, reaching over to touch their little girl's soft cheek.

"It's a girl?"

He sounded surprised and she nodded. "Yes, it is. We'll have a boy next time."

"Just as long as you're healthy, I don't care what we have."

He met her gaze, and her heart thudded hard in her chest. How she loved him so. Over the past year, he'd ensured her transition to Highland life was one of ease and enjoyment. And certain situations had improved since being here. She'd certainly showed them a few new ways to live, hints stolen from the future and put into practice here.

Abby watched him get to know their daughter, her little eyes looking at him, even though she wouldn't be able to focus on anything for some weeks yet. "So," she said, nudging him. "What shall we call her?"

"She's as perfect as a pearl, how do you like Maisie?"

Abby clasped her daughter's little hand, marveling at how small and precious she was. "I love it, and I love you. Thank you for making her with me." Tears fell unheeded and she welcomed the comforting arm Aedan wrapped about her.

"You're everything to me, Abigail. My life has never been more full or happy since the day you landed at my feet. And I promise ye, I will never let harm come to you or Maisie in my lifetime. I promise ye that."

"I know you will."

And Aedan kept his promise. Always.

Author Note

When setting out to write this series and *To Conquer a Scot* in particular, I wanted to use historical events of the past to add adventure, action, and tragedy to the story. The battle between the MacLeod and O'Cain clans was based around the real life disputes between Clan MacLeod and Clan MacDonald. These clans had long disliked the other, and it is true that in a show of peace the laird of Clan Macleod offered his sister to the then laird of Clan MacDonald in a handfasting ceremony. After a year, when the MacLeod sister at the MacDonald stronghold produced no heir, she was sent back to her home, blind in one eye, on a one-eyed horse, with a one-eyed dog and one-eyed servant. The insult infuriated the Laird MacLeod and eventually, war was declared. It was known as the last clan battle in Skye.

About the Author

Tamara is an Australian author who grew up in an old mining town in South Australia, where her love of history was founded. So much so, she made her darling husband travel to the UK for their honeymoon, where she dragged him from one historical monument and castle to another. A mother of three, her two little gentlemen in the making, a future lady (she hopes), and a part-time job keep her busy in the real world, but whenever she gets a moment's peace she loves to write romance novels in an array of genres, including regency, medieval, and time travel. Tamara loves hearing from readers and writers alike. You can contact her through her website, and sign up to follow her blog or newsletter.

www.tamaragill.com

Also by Tamara Gill...

A Stolen Season

Only an Earl Will Do

Only a Duke Will Do

Only a Viscount Will Do

Discover more historical romance from Entangled...

To Love a Scandalous Duke
a *Once Upon a Scandal* novel by Liana De la Rosa

Declan Sinclair is devastated to discover his brother has been murdered, and he's the new Duke of Darington. Clues point to one man, and, he resolves to destroy the culprit. If only the killer's daughter didn't tempt his resolve. Lady Alethea Swinton has cultivated a pristine reputation. But she's willing to court scandal to help handsome Declan uncover the truth behind his brother's death. Until she realizes Declan's revenge will mean her family's ruin.

The Highlander Who Loved Me
a *Highland Hearts* novel by Tara Kingston

Johanna Templeton is on a life-and-death quest. Swept into an intrigue that rivals the tales she pens, she joins forces with a Highland rogue to find the treasure that will save her kidnapped niece. He's as seductive as he is bold...but he may also be the enemy. Connor MacMasters, spy for Queen Victoria, is a man on a mission. Trailing the American novelist who holds the key to the treasure should've been simple, but torn between duty and desire, he wants Johanna in his bed. Loving her would be a fool's game. Blasted shame his heart doesn't agree.

Tangled Hearts
a *Highland Hearts* novel by Heather McCollum

Growing up on a pirate ship, every day was full of adventure for Pandora Wyatt. It was also the perfect place for her to use her magic without persecution. But after her surrogate father is imprisoned in the Tower of London, Pandora leaves the safety of the vessel to rescue him before he's executed. She expects her mission to be difficult, but what she doesn't expect is to have her life saved by the sexiest man she's ever met.

25310220R00176

Printed in Great Britain
by Amazon